The Scoundrel's Lover

(THE NOTORIOUS FLYNNS BOOK 2)

By

Jess Michaels

THE SCOUNDREL'S LOVER
The Notorious Flynns Book 2

Copyright © Jesse Petersen, 2015

ISBN-13: 978-1507591192
ISBN-10: 1507591195

All rights reserved. This book or any portion thereof may not be reproduced or used in any manner whatsoever without the express written permission of the publisher except for the use of brief quotations in a book review.

For more information, contact Jess Michaels
www.AuthorJessMichaels.com
PO Box 814, Cortaro, AZ 85652-0814

To contact the author:
Email: Jess@AuthorJessMichaels.com
Twitter www.twitter.com/JessMichaelsbks
Facebook: www.facebook.com/JessMichaelsBks

Jess Michaels raffles a FREE Kindle or Amazon gift certificate EVERY month to members of her newsletter, so sign up on her website:
http://www.authorjessmichaels.com/join-the-jess-michaels-newsletter/

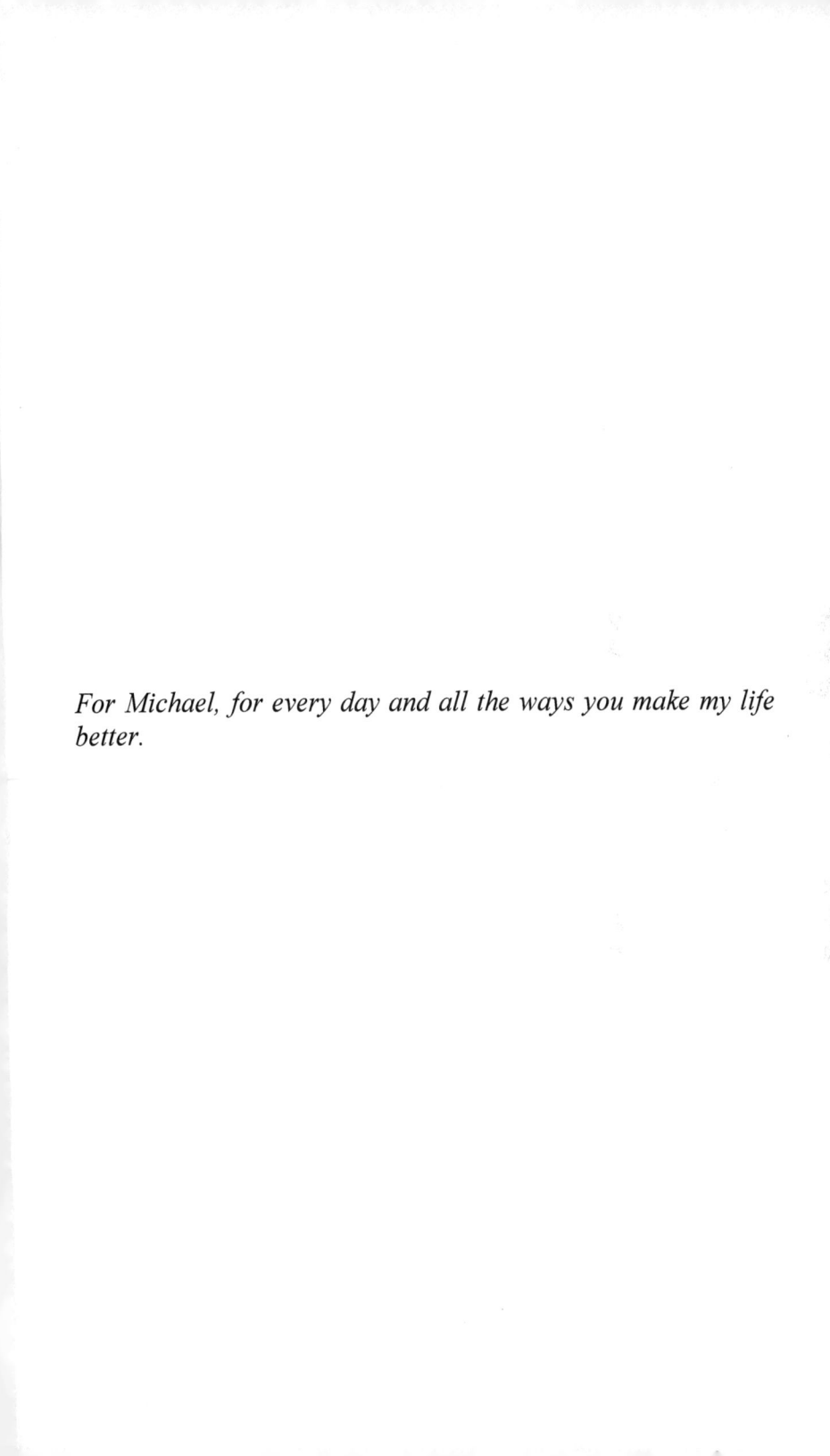

For Michael, for every day and all the ways you make my life better.

CHAPTER ONE

April 1814

The rain slid down the windowpanes like tears down a woman's face, and Annabelle Flynn turned away with a shudder. She didn't want to think about weeping at present. She didn't want to think about heartbreak or failure or humiliation either. Not on the eve of her first Season in the highest of Society. Instead, she smiled at her brother Rafe and his wife of less than a year, Serafina.

It was hard *not* to smile at them, standing across the room, heads close together. Her once-rakish brother's hand rested protectively on the swell of his pregnant wife's belly as they waited for their son or daughter to kick again. They were the picture of domestic bliss and true, passionate love.

Things Annabelle didn't want, nor expect, as she prepared herself to wade into the deep waters of the *ton*.

"Serafina, do you have any advice for tomorrow's ball?" she asked.

Her sister-in-law blushed as she looked up from her belly. But it was her brother who laughed.

"You do not ask me?" he teased as he managed to remove himself from his wife's side. "The duke? Your chaperone?"

Annabelle rolled her eyes. "Your title is only good to gain *entre*, my dear brother. But you've not yet been a duke for a

I

year, so what would you know?"

He staggered back, gripping his chest with both hands as if he had been shot. Annabelle saw Serafina flinch a little at his playful act. Her brother *had* been shot not long ago and his wife still thought of that day, as she had told Annabelle time and again.

"You wound me," he teased. Then he shrugged and walked to the sideboard to fetch a glass of port. "But you are correct. My wife is certainly the better guide for you."

Serafina moved toward Annabelle, taking her hands gently. Annabelle smiled. She had grown deeply fond of Rafe's wife over the months. They had become friends and sisters of the heart as well as marriage. It was a lucky thing, no doubt, as Annabelle had friends who despised the mates of their siblings.

"You and I have gone over the rules and expectations so many times since you announced your interest in a Season— you know them like your own hand," Serafina reassured her. "Be your lovely self beyond those rules and no one could dare do anything but adore you."

Annabelle kept a smile plastered to her face, but inside her heart sank. *Be herself.* Oh no. That was the very last thing she would ever be. The last thing she would show anyone.

Herself was a very dangerous creature indeed. One best kept hidden.

"I do wish you could be there," she sighed.

Serafina touched her belly again. "I show too much, or I would." She smiled at Rafe. "But your brother has been reminded to be on his best behavior. And you have become friends with Miss Georgina Hickson. She won't steer you wrong."

Annabelle nodded. She had met Georgina at one of Serafina's gatherings a few months ago. The daughter of a younger son of the Marquis of Willowbath, Georgina was well versed in everything Society. They had become friends of a sort.

So she would not be alone. Even though it sometimes felt

very much that way.

Annabelle shook off her thoughts when she caught Serafina watching her closely. It would not do to worry her sister-in-law.

"Mother was very sorry she couldn't make it with me tonight," she said as a way to change the subject. "She has not been sleeping well and is overly tired."

Rafe's smile fell at that statement. "Yes, she didn't look well rested the last time we called. What keeps her up?"

Annabelle arched a brow and met his questioning stare head-on. "Would you care to hazard a guess?"

Rafe let out a long breath. "Crispin?"

"Our brother's troubles seem to mount each day. I have never seen him so wild."

Serafina dipped her head, guilt clear on her face. "Since we married, he does seem to struggle."

Rafe turned on his wife and shook his head. "Crispin's decisions are his own. Do not take responsibility for them, my love."

"It's true," Annabelle tried to reassure Serafina as she reached out to squeeze her sister-in-law's hand. "Our brother has been adrift for some time. You and your marriage did not change that."

"Only magnified it," Serafina said softly.

Rafe shrugged. "He will overcome it, he always has."

Annabelle tensed. That was what Rafe had been saying for months, and yet she didn't feel that Crispin was *overcoming* anything.

"How can we help him? What should we do?" Annabelle asked.

"There is nothing we can do. If Crispin wants to wreck himself, all we can do is wait for him to come to his senses."

He paced away, and Annabelle's shoulders rolled forward. She'd had this conversation with Rafe, Serafina and her mother enough times that she knew her brother wouldn't change his thoughts. He had always been so close to Crispin that

Annabelle feared Rafe might be blind to the truth. At least the truth that *she* could see.

Their brother was spiraling out of control, to his detriment, but also potentially to her own. Their family's tenuous inroad into societal acceptance was predicated on Rafe's newfound title, inherited the year before from their rotten cousin.

But Annabelle's chance at a good match and a calm and ordinary future hinged on behavior as well as rank. Both her brothers had endangered her standing before and Crispin might do so again if his antics grew too out of control.

She didn't want to see either of them hurt by his current woes.

Serafina wrapped an arm around her and drew her back to the present. "Will you stay with us tonight?"

Annabelle smiled. It had become a common occurrence for her to sleep at Rafe and Serafina's, chatting half the night and enjoying long mornings at Serafina's side.

"Of course," she said with a smile. "I have heard from Rafe that you are now finished with the nursery."

Serafina's face lit up, and her beauty, which had always been at the highest level, was almost too much to look at. "We have."

"I would love to see it," Annabelle said as she took her sister-in-law's arm and hugged her.

"Come then," Serafina said as she led her from the room with Rafe at their heels. "I am interested in your opinion on the colors."

But as Annabelle smiled and nodded at Serafina's joyful descriptions of her future child's chamber, she couldn't help but have her thoughts wander again. And again they landed on deep and abiding fears that her Season's debut would be nothing but a failure and her future would be destroyed in one broad brushstroke.

Marcus Rivers strode through the open main hallway of the Donville Masquerade with the same certainty to his step that he had always possessed. After all, this was his domain, his livelihood, his trade and his life around him. The fact that his sizeable fortune had been obtained through a very private, very discreet sex and gambling club was really beside the point.

In fact, he hardly saw the debauchery on all sides anymore. The masked attendees, the half-naked women, the men gambling away their lives and futures on how quickly a raindrop would slide down a windowpane...none of it made much difference to Marcus anymore.

It was a means to an end.

As he maneuvered around a table toward the stairway to his office which overlooked the main floor, a lady in a feathered mask and scandalously sheer red gown careened into him, laughing. He caught her elbows to keep her from toppling over and hurting herself, and from her smile, he instantly realized this was her intent. She practically purred as she rubbed her ample breasts against his chest.

"Oh, Mr. Rivers, so quick on your feet and such strong hands," she murmured.

Her crisp accent made him believe that she was likely a woman of the upper crust who came here to alleviate her boredom through fucking or cards or both. And she was certainly soft and supple in his arms. But he set her away firmly.

"I'm glad to be of assistance," he said. "Enjoy your evening."

As he made to move past her, she caught his arm in a surprisingly strong grip. "Wouldn't you like company up in that lonely office of yours, Mr. Rivers?" She batted her eyelashes and wetted her lips, and still his body did not respond.

"I'm afraid not, my lady," he said, inclining his head slightly.

He heard her huff out a breath as he walked away, her anger and frustration made perfectly clear. He didn't so much as spare her a glance over his shoulder as she screeched, "Don't you know who I am?"

He laughed. "No, my lady. And I would suggest you don't announce it here. There is a reason we keep our memberships private."

That silenced her, and he was free to cross the remainder of the distance to the stairway. A guard stood at the bottom, as usual, to keep the revelers and those with complaints out of his personal quarters, including the small bedchamber he kept in the hell itself.

"Good evening," Marcus said as he hesitated at the foot of the stairway. "Carlton, is it?"

The young man standing at his post nodded. "Yes, sir."

"Very good. Abbot will likely be stopping by to deliver the notes in a short while after he makes his rounds. Otherwise, keep all *interested* parties away, will you?"

He motioned his head toward the still-seething lady in red, who he could feel burning a hole in the back of his jacket with her glare.

Carlton nodded. "Of course, sir. As usual, sir." Marcus was about to take a step up to his private quarters when the younger man shook his head. "I dunno how you do it, sir."

Marcus hesitated and shot the man a questioning look. "Do it?"

"Refuse their advances," the other man breathed. "They throw themselves at you nightly—you should hear the reasons they give to get up to your rooms. The things they offer the guards and servants in exchange for a moment of your time. I don't know how you always say no."

Marcus looked the younger man up and down. He had a decade on the boy, likely, but when it came to experience, he could have been in his dotage in comparison.

"Let me give you a piece of advice, young man, that may hold you in great stead when you begin to move up in the world."

Carlton's eyes widened and he nodded with great enthusiasm that almost made Marcus smile. Almost.

"Don't shit where you eat, son," he said, lifting his eyebrows as he made the point. Then he continued up the stairs to let the younger man digest the words. Crass, yes. But oh, so very true.

He pulled a key from the large ring on his belt and unlocked the office. As he stepped inside, he drew a long, deep breath, smelling leather and wood. Smelling success, or at least he had always associated those smells with success.

And success was of paramount importance to him.

He leaned against the door behind him for a moment, then stepped forward to look over the main floor of the club from the wide, clean windows he had installed when he inherited the place ten years before. He could see everything that happened in the main rooms from here. Every debauched sexual encounter, every game of cards, every conversation and assignation.

Here he felt in charge, in power. He liked that feeling.

Which was why he had lived by the words he said to Carlton downstairs. The boy was right. Women threw themselves at him here regularly. Some of them beautiful and soft and so different from the rough, coarse, hard creatures he had grown up with. They could be a temptation indeed, but he never indulged here. When he took his pleasure, it was elsewhere and always without any kind of entanglement being asked for or given.

It was so much better that way. Relationships with others, especially women, were just too complicated.

He was driven from his reverie by the hard rap of knuckles at his door. He turned in surprise as he called out, "Enter."

His business manager, Paul Abbot, stepped into the office and nodded to Marcus. "Rivers."

"Abbot," he replied as he pulled a pocket watch from his vest and snapped it open. "I didn't expect you for at least an hour. You could not have finished your rounds and it's too early for a need to change bills. What is wrong?"

As Marcus shut the watch, Abbot smiled. "I sometimes forget you have the timing of the club down to a science."

"It would be foolish of me to do otherwise." Marcus stepped forward. "There's a problem, I assume."

Abbot's smile fell. "Indeed, I fear there is. The, er, party we talked about last week. He is here tonight."

Marcus pursed his lips. "I see. And he's causing trouble."

"To himself more than anyone, but since you asked me to keep an eye on the situation…"

Marcus needed no other explanation. "Take me to him."

Abbot's eyes went wide, but the surprise at Marcus's reaction vanished in a moment. "Of course. Follow me."

His manager turned and Marcus followed him down the stairs and through the crowded club into one of the private back rooms that couldn't be seen from his office perch. Some of them were for sex and some for gambling.

As Abbot opened the door, Marcus saw that it was a gambling room he had been led to. And slouched over a table, eyes glassy and face shining with sweat as he spoke loudly and almost incoherently to his grinning companions, was Crispin Flynn.

CHAPTER TWO

Marcus pursed his lips into a tight line as he watched Flynn nearly fall off his chair. He leaned over to Abbot.

"How long?"

"Over an hour," Abbot whispered. "He was quite deeply in his cups before arrival."

"And they let him in because he is..." Marcus hesitated. "Well, a friend of mine."

Abbot nodded. "Should I change that policy?"

"No," Marcus said swiftly. "At least here he is safe from being stabbed for his blunt."

"Indeed."

"I'll go in." Marcus took in a deep breath before he walked into the room.

There were six at the table, cards in hand and drinks at their sides, but none was as blasted as Flynn. Five pairs of eyes lifted as he stopped at their table. Crispin's were the only ones that didn't change their bleary focus.

"Gentlemen," Marcus said, his voice low and calm.

Now Flynn jolted his gaze up, and he grinned. "Ah, Rivers, there you are. Come to indulge in a hand or two?"

Marcus cocked his head. "I don't think so this time. Perhaps you gentlemen could clear the room a moment and allow me to speak to Mr. Flynn."

The others shifted, eyes jerking toward each other, toward

their easy mark in Flynn, but before anyone could speak, Crispin staggered to his feet.

"You don't interrupt a man during cards, Rivers. That has to be the first bloody rule in running an establishment such as this." Flynn waved a hand around and nearly toppled himself over backward. "Now sit down and deal in or get the fuck out."

At the door, Abbot jolted, but Marcus lifted a hand to keep his man where he stood. Normally a patron would be kicked out for such behavior, but Flynn wasn't a normal patron.

"Mind your tone," Marcus said without raising his voice.

Flynn looked at him closer, and for a moment Marcus saw a glimpse of the man he did not wish to see. In the depths of Crispin's dark blue eyes there was a deep well of pain. And a challenge to Marcus to keep coming at him. To let him swing. To let him be put out on the street.

Instead, Marcus took a step back. He inclined his head slightly.

"Carry on, gentlemen," he said softly and turned on his heel to exit the chamber. Abbot followed, and as he shut the door behind them, his man gave him a look of shock. Marcus rolled his eyes. "Don't look at me so."

"You *never* allow anyone to speak to you in such a fashion."

He shrugged. "The Flynns and their father did me a favor long ago, one I would not repay by allowing Crispin to be put out in this state."

He frowned. Of course, being left in the room with the jackals all but pulling money directly from his friend's pocket wasn't a much better solution.

"You will do the following, Abbot." He paused as his man grabbed a small notebook and pencil from his jacket pocket. When he was ready, Marcus continued, "You will have two more join the party within. I think Mr. Sweet would be best and pick another who can be trusted to keep his wits about him."

"Williams," Abbot said, jotting down instructions swiftly.

"Flynn has always been a fan of brandy, so fetch a bottle

from my personal collection upstairs and have either Sweet or Williams bring it with them. Have them be certain Flynn is drinking the lion's share."

Now Abbot looked up. "Whatever for?"

"Because once he passes out, Williams and Sweet can take him to one of the private bawdy rooms. I think Lady M was in the Scarlet room not so long ago, wasn't she? If she left some of her bindings, perhaps that would be the perfect place to put him to sleep it off."

Abbot continued to stare and Marcus pointed at his notebook. "Would you like to write it down?"

"I'm not certain what to write, Rivers. Are you truly telling me that you would like two of our men to get Crispin Flynn drunk on your very best and very expensive brandy until he loses consciousness, then to take him to the Scarlet room and tie him down with Lady M's bindings?"

Marcus arched a brow. "Yes. That is exactly what I said."

Abbot opened and shut his mouth several times, but he finally swiftly wrote a few more notes. "And what should we do with him then?"

"I'm going to write a note to his brother," Marcus said with a shrug. "Which *you* will personally deliver. Then he will be the Duke of Hartholm's problem."

Abbot nodded and there was no longer surprise or question on his face, though Marcus was certain the other man felt a great deal of both. But he was trained well enough not to pry. For that, Marcus was glad. He had no intention of explaining to anyone just how big a favor the Flynns had done for him years before.

"While you make your arrangements, I'll pen the letter," Marcus said. "Come to me in half an hour."

Abbot nodded as he scurried off to find Sweet and Williams. With a deep breath, Marcus turned back to his office and the letter he had to write. He could only hope Hartholm would come. If he didn't, that left Marcus in a very uncomfortable position he didn't want to consider.

Annabelle had been curled up on the settee in the darkened sitting room for almost an hour, but was no closer to sleep than she had been when she snuck downstairs to find something to read. Her search of Serafina and Rafe's shelves had been informative, but it hadn't yielded one selection that would help calm her stormy mind.

And so she had simply sat down and allowed her tangled thoughts to wash over her, in the hopes that eventually they would exhaust her. Thus far the plan had proven a very bad one. The worst possible scenarios of her coming out continued to play through her mind, wracking her with worry. Added to that were her concerns about Crispin and her errant mind truly had nowhere to go but further and further into the most dark and deadly fears she possessed.

She was startled from her reverie when there was a sudden knock on the front door. She jumped to her feet and moved to the open parlor door to stare into the dim foyer. All the servants had long ago gone to bed and there was no reason for anyone to be disturbing the household at this hour.

Unless something had happened. She was about to rush to the door herself when Rafe's butler Lathem suddenly appeared at the end of the hall. He was wearing a dressing gown and nightcap, and he had a candle in one hand. She was shocked to see a rather ugly looking bludgeon in the other.

The knocking repeated, and the servant called out, "I'm coming!"

He was cursing under his breath as he rushed past Annabelle's spot hidden in the darkened doorway and didn't seem to realize she was there. He threw open the door to reveal a tall, thin man in a fine coat and hat.

"Can I help you?" Lathem huffed.

The other man bowed. "Paul Abbot here to see the Duke

of Hartholm, sir. I'm sent by Marcus Rivers."

Annabelle stiffened at that name. Rivers was a friend to both her brothers, and he ran an infamous gambling hell. She had met him a few times over the years, but despite only seeing him so little, she could easily conjure an image of him.

He was tall, but that didn't truly express his size accurately. Physically intimidating was a better description, and Annabelle was certain he knew it. There was something about the way the man moved.

He had dark hair and green eyes that seemed to see secrets in every person he laid his gaze upon. She felt…disconcerted when she was around him.

But why would *he* send a man here in the middle of the night?

Her silent question was answered when Abbot continued, "It is about the duke's brother. I have a message."

He held out an envelope, and Lathem stared at it a moment before he took it and stepped back to allow Abbot entry into the foyer.

"I will fetch him," he said, his tone thin and strained. "Please wait here."

Annabelle watched as the other man inclined his head and stepped into what seemed like a military stance. He spread his legs wide, tucking his hands behind him, but he was still stiff and formal as he watched the butler disappear upstairs.

Annabelle shifted slowly. She wanted quite desperately to run into the foyer and demand to be told what the message was about Crispin, but she held back. Revealing herself now would only make her look foolish and when Rafe came downstairs, he would likely send her away rather than have her stay and hear the truth.

So she remained in the shadows, watching and waiting.

Ten minutes passed before Lathem returned. And Rafe was not with him.

Annabelle stiffened as the butler held out a message. "You may return this to Mr. Rivers with His Grace's most sincere thanks."

Abbot shifted. "He will not come?"

Lathem dropped his chin. "He allowed me to relay a portion of his longer message to Mr. Rivers to you. Although the duke loves his brother, he has come to feel that Mr. Flynn must hit the very bottom of the barrel before any help can be rendered that will have a lasting effect. So he cannot come now."

Abbot nodded slowly. "I understand. Tomorrow I hope you will pass along my apologies for my late visit. I'll be certain the letter will be returned to my employer."

Lathem opened the door. "Good evening."

"Good evening," the other man said.

He exited, and Lathem shut the door behind him with a sigh. Mumbling to himself in a sad tone, the butler returned up the long hall.

Annabelle watched it all in shock. Rafe would not go to Crispin? He would let their brother drown in his pain, whatever had caused it, without rendering aid until Crispin "hit the very bottom?"

How could he? Didn't he understand that for Crispin, the very bottom might be death?

She burst from the parlor with a barely stifled cry and threw the front door open. She hurried down the steps and slapped the door to Abbot's carriage just as it began to move.

The driver pulled the horses up short and, after a brief hesitation, the door to the carriage opened to reveal Abbot in the dimness from the street lamps.

"May I help you?" he asked, his eyes wide and filled with surprise at her accosting his rig.

"I am Annabelle Flynn," she panted.

He drew back. "I see."

"I'm Crispin Flynn's sister," she explained further. "Please, why did you come here?"

The man shifted. "You should go back inside, Miss Flynn. My message was meant for the Duke of Hartholm and it has been received and returned. You needn't worry—"

"Balls!" Annabelle burst out as an interruption. Her coarse choice of curse made Abbot jolt and she took advantage of his moment of shock to continue, "I have as much right to know what is happening to Crispin as anyone else. What did Mr. Rivers want from Rafe? Why did he send you here? Were you to fetch the duke?"

Abbot took a breath, but Annabelle saw the truth on his face without him having to say a word. "Mr. Rivers *did* ask you to bring my brother. And he will not come."

Abbot pursed his lips. "And now you know. So I must insist that you back away from the carriage and go back inside. You can take up your thoughts on the subject with the duke tomorrow, I am certain."

Annabelle looked over her shoulder at the townhouse where her brother and sister-in-law slept, cut off from the realities of Crispin's situation and her own. Without hesitation, she stepped up into the carriage and hurled herself into the seat across from Abbot.

"No. I will go with you, Mr. Abbot."

"Absolutely not!" the man cried out. "Remove yourself this instant."

"I shall not." Annabelle folded her arms.

"I will go inside and call for the duke," he threatened, but she could see from the expression on his face that he did not wish to do so.

"If you do, you'll only anger him," Annabelle said. "He might not even believe I did such a thing."

That was a lie, of course. Rafe would certainly believe this man if he claimed Annabelle had stubbornly demanded he take her to one of the most notorious hells in London. Rafe knew her too well.

But *Abbot* didn't know that.

"Please," she said, meeting his eyes. "I understand Rafe's position when it comes to Crispin, but he is my brother too. I cannot imagine that leaving him to ruin is the best course. Mr.

Rivers obviously wanted someone from Crispin's family to come to him, and I am your best bet."

Abbot squeezed his eyes shut with a heavy sigh. "Very well. But Mr. Rivers will not be happy."

"And I will take full blame," she reassured him, almost bouncing with happiness as Abbot shut the carriage door and pounded on the carriage wall so that the driver would move again.

Abbot looked her up and down. "Very reassuring. However, I doubt Mr. Rivers will care. It will be both our heads, Miss Flynn, so I hope you remember that you wanted this when you feel his wrath."

Annabelle stared. "I don't recall him being so terrible when I met him."

Abbot's eyebrow arched high. "You've met Marcus Rivers?"

She nodded. "He and my brothers are friends of a sort. We have not socialized much, but I have been introduced to the man."

She tried not to think of Rivers as she had in the parlor. Right now it was in her best interest to be cool and detached.

Even if that was the last thing she felt.

"I assume you did not encounter Mr. Rivers in the club," Abbot asked.

She drew back a fraction. "Certainly not."

He smiled, a thin expression that didn't reach his eyes. "Then you have never met Mr. Rivers. Not truly."

He settled back against the comfortable carriage seat and they fell into an uncomfortable silence. But Annabelle could not stop her mind from racing to images of dark hair and eyes, dark expressions and rumors of the lion's den she would now be entering.

CHAPTER THREE

The carriage pulled to a stop in front of a rather nondescript building in an area of London that Annabelle knew her mother would not approve of her visiting. She peeked around the curtains for the third time and shivered.

"Without a sign, how do your patrons know where to go?" she asked.

"It is a private club, Miss Flynn, very exclusive. Those who wish to find us have the means to do so." Abbot reached into his jacket and withdrew a simple, gray mask from somewhere within the folds of fabric.

As he handed it to her, Annabelle gave him a questioning look.

"Most of our patrons wear masks in the club, Miss Flynn," Abbot said. "It is not a requirement, but you should comply for your own protection. Since I expected to bring the duke back with me, it may be a bit large, but it will do the trick of protecting your identity. As for what you will see once you enter the club, I can only say that it will certainly be shocking to you. Once again, I encourage you to reconsider coming inside with me."

Annabelle took a breath. The Donville Masquerade was not often discussed in polite company, but due to her brothers' scandalous reputations, she sometimes heard about it. She knew it was a den of debauchery of all kinds. Exactly the kind

17

of place she should not be.

And yet she was here. For Crispin. With that thought ricocheting through her mind, she set her jaw.

"I want to see my brother."

Abbot looked at her for a moment, searching her face, and then he nodded. "Put on the mask and follow me."

She did as she had been told and exited the carriage behind him. The door opened as Abbot approached and a finely liveried servant stood there. He was not wearing a mask and bowed to Abbot.

"Welcome back, sir." He stepped aside to allow them entry.

Annabelle could not deny her curiosity as she stepped inside the foyer. It was a rather plain entryway, with nothing to show that it was anything else but a normal London home. The furniture was simple and the wall colorings the same.

But now that they were off the street, the sounds of faint music tinkled from far in the back of the building. Did they dance here, as if it were no different than Almack's?

Abbot's voice interrupted her thoughts. "Where is Mr. Rivers?"

"I'm not certain, Mr. Abbot," the servant said. "I have heard in his office, but when I was last in the hall he was back in the private room dealing with the, er, *problem*."

Abbot's gaze slipped to Annabelle and his brief expression made her eyes widen. Was *the problem* Crispin? And just how was Rivers dealing with him?

"Follow me," Abbot said, heading down a long, twisting hall. The sounds of the music increased as they moved closer and closer to a large set of double doors, and were now joined with echoes of laughter and the occasional…

Annabelle blushed.

There were *moans* coming from the room.

"Last chance to change your mind," Abbot said, as if he could read her thoughts.

"Open the door," she said, more sharply than she had

intended as she tried to convey a certainty she didn't feel.

He did as she asked and revealed a huge hall, bigger than any she had ever been to in the country or in London. There were tables scattered about the room where men and women gambled together. Gambled and...other activities.

She turned her head with a gasp. People were engaging in very bold deeds! As much as she tried, she couldn't avoid seeing a couple kissing right out in the middle of the room, their tongues tangling and their bodies grinding together.

In another corner a lady was pinned to the wall by her...could Annabelle rightly call him a suitor? Whoever he was, he had a handful of his companion's skirt in his fist and was blatantly revealing her calves and even a flash of thigh to the room at large.

"Stay here a moment, I'll find out where to take you," Abbot said, his tone grim.

Annabelle watched him leave her side with a gasp. He was leaving her here alone! With such things going on around her?

She didn't want to look. But she did, despite herself. Watched the man and woman against the wall as he dropped his head and began to kiss the swollen curves of her breasts, which peeked above her low-cut gown. The woman moaned brazenly and arched her back as if to offer more.

He took it, her skirt ruched higher so that he could place a palm against what Annabelle could plainly see was the woman's bare backside.

Annabelle squeezed her eyes shut so she would see no more. She was a lady, not meant for these kinds of things. She had to remember that.

Or better yet, to forget the low, dark thrill that began between her legs. It had been a long time since she felt that throbbing need. A long time since she allowed her true nature to rear its ugly head.

"Not now," she ground out to herself, willing her nipples to stop hardening, her legs to stop shaking.

Suddenly there was the grip of fingers closing over her

upper arm and her eyes flew open. She found herself staring up into the dark green gaze of Marcus Rivers. Unlike those around her, he wore no mask and his face was alive with emotion in that moment. He looked...angry. *Very* angry. She couldn't help but think of Abbot's words in the carriage that they would both face this man's wrath.

"Come with me," Rivers said.

He didn't wait for her to agree, but merely began to guide her through the crowded hall, past more gaming tables and entangled lovers. Annabelle tried to keep her gaze firmly on the floor below her, but she saw things. She heard things.

And God help her, she felt things, including Rivers' firm grip on her arm, which seemed to send little lightning bolts of awareness through her all the more.

He nodded to a servant as he dragged her up a short flight of stairs. Only at a shut door at the top of the landing did he release her. He fished a key from his jacket pocket and unlocked the door before he opened it and motioned her to enter.

She stepped inside and immediately began to look for her brother. But he was nowhere to be found within the dimly lit office where Rivers had taken her.

The same office where they were now entirely alone. Where he was shutting the door behind him and staring at her.

Her breath caught as she waited for him to do or say something, because she had no idea how to react when he wasn't.

"What are you doing here, Miss Flynn?" he asked at last, his voice rough as it raked over her very senses.

She blinked a few times as she gathered her emotions. Slowly, she folded her arms and glared at him. "I assume your man Abbot told you why when he informed you of my arrival."

Rivers' eyes narrowed. "I haven't spoken to Abbot."

She drew back a fraction. "But—but you came and collected me. You called me Miss Flynn," she said slowly. "How did you know it was me?"

He motioned to the large wall of windows behind her. "I looked down over the club and saw you standing by the door. I recognized you."

Now Annabelle could scarcely breathe. Rivers was watching her so closely, his eyes narrow and unreadable.

"You have only met me twice." Her voice trembled, and she hated herself for it.

He waved a hand as if to dismiss that observation. "*You* are changing the subject. Why are you here, Miss Flynn?"

She observed him for a moment. She'd thought he looked angry before, and that emotion was still there, but here in the dimmer light of his private chamber she saw less harshness to his face. He was really very handsome, though there was nothing soft about him. He was all angles and frowns.

"Miss Flynn," he said.

She shook her head. "You sent for me."

Now his full lips thinned with displeasure. "I most certainly did not. I sent for your brother. I *sent* for the Duke of Hartholm."

She couldn't help how her frown deepened. "Apparently the duke does not think he should come to collect our brother. Your man has a message that explains all, I assume."

"Except how you came to be here."

She sighed. "I cannot agree with Rafe's theory that Crispin should be left to hit the bottom before we save him. The consequences could be far too great and then none of us would forgive ourselves. When I realized my older brother wouldn't come, I couldn't allow that to be the last word. So I threw myself into your carriage with Mr. Abbot."

"And he allowed you to come here?" Now the anger returned to Rivers' voice.

She shook her head. "Not exactly. I'm afraid I may have...*threatened* him a little."

Both Rivers' eyebrows went up and then, to her surprise, he began to laugh. It was a deep, rumbling sound that seemed to wind its way around her, make her think of the intertwined bodies of the shocking lovers downstairs. She gasped at the image and turned away.

"You mock me," she all but panted as she tried to rein in her body's shocking reactions to this utterly unexpected night.

His laughter trailed away. "Never would I do something so foolish. I was only struck by the fact that you surprised me. And that, Miss Flynn, is not easy to do, I assure you."

She glanced out the window bay behind him and shivered at the brief images of all the debauchery going on downstairs.

"I'm sure that is true," she managed to grind out past gritted teeth. "But this is foolish. I want to see my brother, Mr. Rivers. Please, won't you take me to him?"

Marcus had to keep himself from drawing another surreptitious whiff of Annabelle Flynn's jasmine-scented hair and skin. It was almost impossible in the small room, and he hated himself for the lack of control the action indicated.

He wanted this woman. But this was no shock or surprise. He had wanted Annabelle Flynn from the very first moment he laid eyes on her years before. He had been invited to some small fete at her brother Rafe's townhouse, long before the new duke had been elevated in status. The brothers had introduced him to Annabelle, and in that moment he had all but forgotten how to breathe.

She was a vision then and a vision now. An angel clothed in the finest spring green silk that made him want to run his hands up and down her sides, pull her softness against his hardness and find a way to take her in permanently.

He blinked at those errant thoughts. She believed they had only met twice, and that was almost true. Officially he had only shaken her hands that first night and once at a busy gathering the next year. He had also been at her father's funeral, though that obviously hadn't made much of an impression on her.

But he'd seen her plenty of times. A glimpse here, a stolen stare there. He had found reasons to drive past her mother's gate and watch for her. And if she ever knew that, she would likely turn up her nose in disgust.

He was so very far below her.

"You wish to see your brother," he said in answer to the demand she had made what seemed like an eternity ago.

She nodded, her expression icy cold and distant as she readied herself for any challenge he might make to her request. He made none, at least not for a beat. He was too fascinated by how different this detachment she practiced now was from the heated expression he'd seen on her face when he came upon her in the hall not half an hour before.

She had been watching a couple grind against each other, and there was no denying the arousal in her expression and the way her breath caught.

His cock began to come to life, and he turned away to keep that fact from her. "You will not like how you find him."

She huffed out a breath. "If he is alive, that is all that matters to me. Please!"

He spun around at the desperation in her voice. He had felt that way before, he knew the clenching pain of it around the heart. "Very well. Come with me, please."

She blinked, but nodded once, her attitude as formal as his own. He crossed the room, feeling her behind him with every step, and moved down the stairs. As they reentered the hall together, he heard her breath catch and knew she was looking around, seeing what his club was, perhaps equally titillated and disgusted by it.

He ignored his desire to look at her and instead marched across the room and into the maze of side chambers. Moans came from within, echoes of the passions his patrons came there to share. When he reached one of the doors, he stopped and turned to face her.

"I must warn you, he is bound."

She gave a cry and launched toward the door, but he

placed a hand across it to keep her from bursting in. She was not in the right frame of mind yet.

"Why?" she cried out, and her hands fisted at her sides like she wanted to strike him in defense of Crispin. "Why would you do such a thing to him?"

Marcus arched a brow at the fire in her. There, hidden in proper depths, was a flash of the same wildness that her brothers possessed. That Flynn quality that made them all the rage even as it cloaked them in notoriety.

"For his protection," he said softly. "Your brother, I'm afraid, was very deep in his cups, trying to gamble away a small fortune. He was also thrashing about and spoiling for a fight. Tying him to the bed inside was the best method of protecting him from himself. And others."

Her fists relaxed and she tilted her head in question. "Tied to…to a bed? Why would you have a bed in a gambling hall public room?"

"Surely you are not so innocent, Miss Flynn."

Her lips thinned. "I am a lady, *Mr.* Rivers."

He forced himself not to smile so that she would not again believe he was mocking her. "An unconventional one, I think," he said, watching her every caught breath, her dilating pupils, her shaking hands. "I saw you watching when you came in. Taking in the men and women who come here to…play together. Certainly you cannot think that only happens in the main hall."

She swallowed hard, but did not deny his accusation that she had played the voyeur in his hall. "I see."

She took a moment, and he watched her gather herself, calm herself until her emotions were covered and she was once again the collected lady.

"And there just happened to be rope in the room where you tied him?"

He smiled. "Silken rope, Miss Flynn. I assure you it is nothing that will harm him. It was left there by a very special patroness."

"I don't understand."

She said the words, but Marcus was more than aware of the flash of heat in her stare that told him otherwise. There was something more to Miss Annabelle Flynn that he never would have seen if she hadn't come to his lair. And oh, how he was enjoying this. Far more than he should.

"Some of the members here like to be tied, Miss Flynn," he explained. "To lose all control."

Her lips parted slightly and her tongue darted out to wet them. Marcus felt the action deep in his groin, and the responding need was all too powerful.

"I can't believe someone would want that," she whispered.

He leaned in, unable to help himself. "You have no idea."

Marcus could picture her now, spread out on his bed, helpless to his ministrations. Writhing to reach him.

Blinking, he turned back to the door. "Now that you understand, let us go in."

He opened the door, and the man he had put in the room to watch Crispin immediately rose. His eyes widened slightly at the sight of proper Annabelle, despite the protection of her mask.

"You may go, thank you," Marcus said softly.

The man bowed his head and left the room, shutting the door behind himself. It was only then that Marcus looked at Annabelle.

She stood just a few steps inside the chamber, staring across the room at her brother. Crispin had been tied to the bed, but at some point he had obviously stopped thrashing and passed out. He lay limply on the mattress, the extra-long cords of the bindings loose at his wrists.

"Oh, Crispin," she said softly, moving toward him with uncertain steps.

Flynn jerked his head up and let out a low groan of pain, but he didn't open his eyes. Marcus saw Annabelle's face crumple ever so slightly, a flash of emotion she hadn't meant to reveal, if the way she covered it was any indication.

"Crispin," she whispered, but again he made no reply. Her eyes widened, and she let out a cry as she dove toward him, grasping one of his tied hands. "Crispin!" she cried out.

Marcus moved toward her, despite knowing it was foolish to do so, and took a long breath. He was going to touch her. It was going to be heaven and hell at once.

Slowly, he leaned forward and let his hands close gently over her shoulders. "Annabelle," he whispered, finally allowing himself to say her given name. "It's all right. He isn't hurt, just unconscious. He'll sleep it off and probably not even recall any of this tomorrow."

She stiffened beneath his touch and looked at him over her shoulder. He couldn't tell if she was comforted or disgusted by his hands on her, but she met his eyes either way. "How can you say that? I've never seen my brother this way."

He drew her to her feet and turned her toward him, away from her unconscious brother. Then he released her, though he could still feel his warmth in his palms, his fingers, his arms, his entire body. "He drank a great deal, that is all."

She blinked. "How much?"

Marcus squeezed his eyes shut for a brief moment. "He can hold a great deal of liquor, so I can only imagine."

She fisted her hands at her sides and continued to stare at her brother. When she spoke again, her voice cracked. "I couldn't even begin to move him by myself. Even if I could…where to take him? I couldn't thrust this upon my mother, not when she is so heartbroken about him as it is. And Rafe has already refused to help, so I cannot take him there. And home, Crispin's home? Do I dare leave him there alone if he is this out of control?"

Marcus sighed. For no other person in the world would he make the offer on his mind. A fact he refused to consider overly much when he said, "You may leave your brother here."

She blinked up at him. "Here?"

"Yes. He can stay in this room and I'll be sure he is in reasonable shape to return home on his own in the morning. I'll even have one of my men watch over him until he wakes, to ensure he doesn't hurt himself."

"But—but you sent for my brother," she stammered.

He couldn't help but smile slightly. "I did indeed, believing the duke would come and collect him. But you somehow showed up instead and I wouldn't leave the duty to you. It would not be...*right*."

He almost laughed. As if she would believe him. It was obvious he did not live his life in terms of right and wrong. She had seen what went on in the rooms around them. Seen more than a lady of her station and quality should see, that was certain.

But she did not call him on the half-truth. Instead she simply stared at him, and her tone was filled with gratitude when she whispered, "Thank you."

He shook his head. "Why?"

"You are kind when you do not need to be."

Marcus watched her for a moment, a burst of freshness in his jaded world. Then he looked behind her at her brother. He shrugged.

"He is a friend." Once he had said the words, he felt compelled to correct them, because they revealed too much. "And a good customer. But he obviously cannot go on like this."

"No," she agreed, and her eyes swelled with tears she fought valiantly to keep from falling.

She failed, and one streamed down her face. Marcus couldn't help it. He reached out and brushed it away with his thumb, his fingers cresting over her impossibly soft skin and setting him on fire once again.

CHAPTER FOUR

Marcus Rivers touched Annabelle's face, and she found herself looking up and up at him. She should have pulled away from the intimate stroke of his fingers over her flesh, but she could not.

She had seen him before, met him before. He was a friend of her brothers' and one she tried not to think of since he was so disconcerting to her. But now, as she met his dark green gaze full on, she could not deny that she felt *things* when he touched her. Those dark things she didn't want to feel.

But he was so close to her now and he smelled so good. Like...decadent promises and pleasure and *need*. She found herself leaning in, leaning closer, letting his warmth surround her, letting his breath touch her face.

What are you doing?

The voice in her head was so powerful, she almost feared she had said the words out loud as she jerked away from Rivers and his hypnotic, forbidden touch. She spun so her back was to him, hands clenched at her chest and breath coming far too short.

"I should go home," she gasped.

He was quiet for long enough the she nearly turned to face him. But finally he said, "I will escort you."

She squeezed her eyes shut. Considering her feelings, her desires, that was a terrible idea. To be alone with him for close to half an hour? To be shoehorned into a carriage together where it was dark and close when she wanted to feel his fingers on her flesh again?

A very bad idea.

"You needn't trouble yourself," she said, her voice shaking.

His eyes narrowed. "You came here with my man and he is now busy, so there is nothing to it. I will take you back to your brother's home, Miss Flynn. *That* is the end of the discussion."

Annabelle suppressed a very strong urge to turn around and have a wildly inappropriate tantrum, and instead smiled at him when she faced him again. "Fine. I appreciate your concern."

"Wait here a moment, I'll have the carriage brought back and then I'll escort you through the main hall." He cast her one more look before he slipped from the room.

When he had closed the door behind himself, Annabelle let out a long, ragged breath. The man stole all the air in the room when he stood there, looking so intimidating and handsome and…delectable.

"Stop thinking those things," Annabelle ground out to herself through clenched teeth. "Stop. Stop. *Stop.*"

"So sorry."

She froze at the sound of Crispin's voice from the bed behind her. She moved toward him. In the firelight, he looked very young. Very lost. But his eyes were still closed, his mouth a frown even in his inebriated and semi-conscious state.

Marcus said he wouldn't remember this night. She hoped that was true. She wished it were true for herself.

Gently, she smoothed a dark blonde curl away from his forehead. "It will all be better in the morning," she whispered.

But it didn't feel like it would be better. Suddenly all the perfect plans she had been making for her debut, catching a respectable man and living a staid life seemed threatened and not just by her brother's unpredictable behavior.

The door opened, and Marcus Rivers stepped back into the room. He motioned for her, and she leaned down to press a brief kiss to her brother's forehead.

"Will anyone know who I am?" she asked as she slipped from the room.

Rivers motioned for a servant who returned to the chamber to watch over her brother, then shut the door firmly behind them.

"That's why Abbot had you wear a mask. Protection," Rivers explained.

"And my brother? He wore no mask."

Rivers' lips thinned. "He took it off at some point, I suppose. Many forego them, especially the men. They do not feel it as important to protect their identities. They are more allowed to pursue their desires in the open."

Annabelle tried very hard not to stare at the very low cut gown of a lady playing cards with a group of men in the main hall. They were all in varying levels of undress and leering at each other openly.

Her body stirred, and she ignored it. "But their actions...*his* actions...could have an impact on others in their lives."

Rivers maneuvered her into the foyer and down the steps where the carriage she had come in was waiting for them. Back in she went, only this time it wasn't the thin, disapproving Abbot who was her companion, but Rivers. And he looked ever so much more handsome in the dim light.

"I suppose that is true," Rivers said slowly as the carriage began to move. "And I also suppose you mean yourself."

She hesitated and took a moment to remove her mask and set it on the carriage seat next to her. Sharing her fears with this man seemed an intimate exercise indeed. But talking about her plans could only remind her about her decorum. Perhaps it would silence the needs that bubbled up whenever she thought of the Donville Masquerade or its owner's dark eyes.

"I am going out into Society," she explained.

He drew back a fraction. "Were you not out already?"

"Reminding me of my age, are you?" she asked, but there was no heat to the tone. In fact, she smiled as he searched for some way to fix his faux pas.

He saw her face and grinned. "You tease me."

"A little. I am no debutante, no. And I own my years. But I have never been out in London Society, in the company of the Upper Ten Thousand. Now that Rafe is a duke, it opens doors for me."

Rivers observed her closely. "And those are doors you wish to be opened?"

He seemed so incredulous. As if she could never want or perhaps never fit into that world. Was she so obvious? Did he see through her façade and into the darkness she fought so hard to hide?

"Of course I want those doors opened," she snapped, more harshly than she would normally speak. Her defensiveness took her off guard and she softened her tone. "This is the best chance I have to marry well and live a respectable life."

"No one could say you haven't already been living a respectable life," he offered, turning his head to look out the window toward the passing city lights.

She shook her head. "You do not know me, perhaps, but you know my brothers. My reputation is often linked with theirs, so there are many who would no doubt refute your claim. But right now is my chance. Rafe is celebrated as duke, and if I can manage to land a husband before *they* remember what *we* are…"

She trailed off, but Rivers seemed to understand. He nodded slowly. "I see."

"At any rate, I fear Crispin will damage my chances."

He leaned in, and she caught a brief whiff of his scent again. Just as it had in his office an hour ago, it made her body clench desperately.

"But that isn't your only reason to worry," he said.

She met his stare, albeit briefly. "No," she whispered. "I

am terrified he'll hurt himself. Not socially, but physically. Do you think he would?"

Rivers drew away. "Why would you ask me?"

"You said you were my brother's friend and judging from your behavior tonight, I believe that."

"Why?"

"Because you could have simply thrown him into the gutter when he became a difficulty," she said with a shiver at the thought.

Rivers shifted. "As I said, he is a good customer."

Annabelle looked at him when he said it. He appeared very uncomfortable when he was praised for caring for Crispin. Did he think she would take advantage of that fact? Did he believe kindness equaled weakness?

But perhaps in his dangerous world, it did.

She opened her mouth to say more, but Rivers spoke first. "When you snuck from the duke's home, did anyone see you?"

Annabelle blinked at the change of subject. "I—no, I don't think so."

"A footman? A groom? The butler?" Rivers pressed.

She hesitated, and that elicited a frown from Rivers. "Why do you look at me that way?"

He shook his head. "I simply like to know what lion's den I'm entering, Miss Flynn. Because if your oldest brother thinks my man, say, spirited you away to my naughty little club, I can't imagine he will be happy to see me."

Annabelle folded her arms. "I'm certain Rafe went to your club many times before he married."

Rivers laughed, but neither confirmed nor denied her charge. Instead, he said, "What is good for the gander is very rarely allowed for the goose. And you know it. You're too intelligent not to know."

"And what would you know of my intelligence?" Annabelle challenged him, though she had no idea where the impulse came from. "You who have met me all of three times now. Twice I was at a party, not exactly an intellectual high point and tonight I invaded your club demanding to rescue my brother."

Rivers looked her up and down, a lazy perusal that felt infinitely wicked even though he never made so much as a move to touch her. "I hear things," he said.

"Hear things?" Annabelle repeated in confusion, but before they could discuss the subject further, the carriage turned into Rafe's gate and slowed.

"Damn it," Rivers muttered under his breath as he looked out the window.

"What is it?" Annabelle asked.

"I just hate being right sometimes," he sighed.

Before Annabelle could say anything or look out the window herself, the door to the carriage was pulled open and Rafe's face appeared there. His very dark, very angry face.

"Good evening, Annabelle, Rivers," he said, obviously through clenched teeth. "Why don't you two join me in my study? It appears we have much to discuss."

Marcus followed behind Annabelle and Rafe, watching the way her hips twitched beneath her gown. How he had come to be in this situation, he really couldn't say. One moment he was minding his business, trying to do the right thing, the next he had been descended upon by a woman who seemed determined to drive him mad with her presence.

This was why he avoided emotional entanglements.

Rafe opened his study door and ushered them all inside. He said nothing as he crossed the room and poured himself a brandy. He glared at Marcus, then poured him one too.

As he crossed the room to hand him the drink, Rafe said, "An hour ago, a servant came to my chamber, interrupted my slumber and nearly woke my wife. Apparently he had seen something he was loathe to share and had been hemming and hawing about it ever since. Do you want to know what he saw?"

To Marcus's surprise, Annabelle rolled her eyes in response.

Rafe continued, "He saw *you*, dear Annabelle, sneaking into a carriage and disappearing in the middle of the night. And now here you are. Do either of you want to explain what the hell is going on?"

Marcus might have said something in an attempt to mitigate Rafe's anger toward Annabelle, but she gave him no chance. With no thought for consequences, Annabelle hurtled forward and stood toe to toe with her brother.

"Mr. Rivers sent his man to you tonight, asking for your help when it came to Crispin, and you refused him," she said, her body all but vibrating with the accusation.

To Marcus's surprise, Rafe turned his head, his cheeks darkening not with anger, but with shame and pain.

"You don't understand," he said softly.

Annabelle glared at him. "No, *you* don't understand because you didn't go there. I did, Raphael. I saw him there, and he is not well."

Rafe scrubbed a hand through his hair. There was no denying the struggle he seemed to be having when it came to Crispin. And although Marcus generally stayed far, far away from these kinds of domestic issues, he couldn't help but feel sorry for the duke. He had seen the brothers together, many times. He knew how much they cared for each other.

"Annabelle, I have spoken to him numerous times over the past six months. He has refused my help and my counsel over and over again," Rafe explained. "Until he is ready to take it, chasing him all over London and extracting him from his consequences will not urge him to change."

Annabelle's face twisted with pain so powerful that Marcus felt it in his gut. Her brown eyes sparkled with tears, but she all but vibrated with anger.

"You cannot abandon him. Mr. Rivers might be kind

enough to offer him sanctuary, but others will take advantage of him. He could be killed, Rafe."

Rafe shot Marcus a look, but then refocused on his sister. "You think I don't know that? You think it doesn't turn my stomach and keep me up at night during what should be the happiest year of my life?"

His raised voice and pained expression stopped Annabelle. She stared at him, their faces mirroring images of worry and fear.

"Please don't abandon him," she whispered.

"I'm not abandoning him," Rafe said, his voice rising again. "Goddamn it, Annabelle!"

She fisted a hand at her side and opened her mouth to speak again, but Rafe lifted a finger to silence her. "We are not having this conversation in the middle of the night. Go to your chamber and we'll discuss it in the morning when you are less overwrought."

"I'm not overwrought," she protested.

"Annabelle," he said, his tone low now, but perhaps more laced with emotion.

Her lips thinned, pressing together until they were nearly white with the pressure. She spun around, putting her back to her brother, and marched over to Marcus.

He straightened up as she reached him, uncertain as to what she would do after this emotional night. But she merely looked up at him, her face beautiful even though she was pale.

"Thank you again, Mr. Rivers, for your kindness tonight. I shall not soon forget it. Good night."

She didn't look at Rafe as she exited the room, slamming the door behind herself as a final statement on her brother's refusal to hear her. Rafe shook his head.

"God save me from intelligent women. I am swimming in them and they are as frustrating as they are fascinating."

Marcus smothered a smile, because he knew the duke was angry at him and wouldn't appreciate it, and waited for Rafe to turn his attention to him. His friend did so almost immediately.

"Would *you* care to explain this?"

Marcus shrugged. "What your sister said is essentially the truth. She overheard your refusal to come fetch Crispin and hurtled herself into my carriage with Abbot. After some threats, I haven't gotten the whole story from him—"

Rafe sighed. "I'm certain she threatened him, though."

"As am I," Marcus laughed. "Your sister is a singular lady."

Rafe's eyebrows lifted. "Yes, she is that."

Marcus erased the smile from his face. The way Rafe was looking at him, he could see the duke didn't approve of Marcus and his sister being alone. And why would he?

"Well, I thank you for sending Abbot to me about Crispin," Rafe said as he sank into the settee. "I hope you do not judge me as harshly as Annabelle does about my response."

Slowly, Marcus joined Rafe in taking a seat. It was an odd thing, to be having this little chat in the middle of the night. Oh, he'd been to Rafe's townhouse before, of course, but not since his friend had become duke. He hadn't expected to be invited after that.

Not that he had been.

"I understand, as perhaps Annabelle does not, that life is infinitely complicated," Marcus said. "Crispin has no interest in being saved at the moment."

"Do you think he will at some point?" Rafe asked, his tone hollow and empty.

Marcus thought of Crispin, spoiling for a fight, drunk to oblivion. "I hope so."

"As do I." He shook his head. "But I fear if Annabelle inserts herself into the situation as she did tonight that she will only be dragged down by Crispin's riptide."

"She mentioned she is utilizing your new connections to find a suitable husband," Marcus said, he hoped mildly. "I admit, I have a hard time picturing her being interested in some titled fop."

"Careful, I'm one of those now," Rafe said, but his bright

grin told Marcus he had not offended.

"No, you are not," he laughed.

Rafe shook his head. "My sister is...she may not fully realize what she wants. Or perhaps she simply hopes to deny it. Either way, I would not put her off from her plans. She will either find a man who strikes her fancy or she'll realize a good many of those with titles aren't fit to shine her riding boot."

"You don't want her to marry a man of rank?" Marcus asked, surprised.

Rafe shrugged. "I want her to be happy."

Marcus pushed to his feet. This topic suddenly felt far too personal. He didn't want to know about Annabelle's plans or Rafe's concerns about them. It brought him too close and he didn't want to be close. Especially since he would likely never see Annabelle Flynn again, unless it was in one of those desperate passing moments.

He really had to stop going to her mother's gate. It was pathetic.

"Once again, I apologize for my man allowing Annabelle access to the club. I will speak to him about it."

Rafe shook his head as he joined Marcus on his feet. "Don't be too harsh on Abbot, he's a good man. And Annabelle can be an unstoppable force."

Marcus just barely kept himself from the laughing agreement that inappropriately leapt to his lips. He didn't know Annabelle. At least, he shouldn't know. He couldn't know.

"And thank you, for your kindness to her and to my brother," Rafe continued, "Crispin is safe?"

"For the night," Marcus said with a nod. "Would you like me to keep you apprised as to when your brother is at the masquerade?"

Rafe hesitated, and then he sighed. "Yes. I do not know if I will come and I certainly don't expect you to watch over him or keep him from harm, but I want to know if it isn't too much trouble."

Marcus shrugged. "We both know I owe you and your

brother quite a bit. It is no trouble to me to keep Crispin out of harm's way when I can. Or to let you know of his movements in the walls of my club."

Marcus set his drink down and held out a hand. Rafe shook it without hesitation and followed Marcus as he left the study and reentered the foyer.

"Good night, Your Grace," Marcus said with a slight bow.

Rafe shook his head. "God, man—Rafe or Flynn as usual. 'His Grace' is for the fops and in public. Good night and thank you, once more."

Rafe clapped him on the shoulder, and Marcus smiled before he walked down the steps to the still-waiting carriage. But as the driver maneuvered them back toward the club, he couldn't help thinking of Annabelle and the shocking desires the lady stoked in him.

Ones he could never, ever let her or anyone else see.

CHAPTER FIVE

It turned out that the balls of the Upper Ten Thousand were just as boring as the fetes put on by those without title. Annabelle stood in the corner of the huge ballroom, watered down drink in hand, watching as couples spun by in each other's arms.

In each other's arms, but decidedly unconnected. She had never seen so many stiff, formal, dreary faces. Some of the couples did not even look at each other and seemed gloriously happy when the music ended.

She couldn't help but think of Marcus's Donville Masquerade. There the opposite was true. Couples in that wicked hall couldn't even wait for privacy to touch each other and did such passionate things together without a care for propriety or who watched.

"Annabelle?"

She jolted as Georgina Hickson joined her, completely oblivious to Annabelle's wicked thoughts. Georgina was the daughter of a younger son, so she had no title, but she had been raised to catch a titled gentleman. Although Georgina was younger than Annabelle, they had become friends of a sort and the other woman was trying to help Annabelle figure out how to land her own marquis or earl.

"That very odd look on your face will not attract the bees to honey, my dear," Georgina said with the falsely bright expression that seemed to always grace her cheeks. "Smile now and try to look enamored with it all."

Not for the first time, Annabelle wished desperately that Serafina could have come out for the ball. Although she too had been raised as a lady in every sense, there was nothing false or put on about her. They certainly would have had more fun.

But Annabelle *did* appreciate Georgina's attention and help, so she did as her friend demanded and plastered a fake smile on her face.

"You have had some success tonight," Annabelle said, through her grinning teeth. "Didn't Lord Poppington dance with you?"

Georgina nodded. "The earl was very attentive, yes."

"But, er, isn't he a bit *old* for you?" Annabelle asked as she caught a glimpse of the ancient man in the crowd.

Georgina blinked. "Whatever does that matter? He's an *earl*, Annabelle!"

Annabelle shivered. That attitude was so mercenary and yet it was exactly how she was meant to feel if she wanted this exercise to be a success. A title at any cost.

"And what of you?" her friend asked.

"I've received a plethora of side glances," Annabelle sighed, putting her misgivings aside. "But not many brave enough to approach a Notorious Flynn to dance. So my dance card is still only occupied by my brother's name."

She looked across the room and found him there, talking with one of his new, titled friends, Lord Aldridge. Rafe was very handsome in his evening clothes and looked every inch the duke. And yet those around him still occasionally scrunched their noses up and whispered behind their fans.

And why wouldn't they? After all, this was the man who had, not three years ago, won the old family home of Lord Sternbridge in a scandalous game of cards, and then gleefully had every single room inside painted purple before he returned it—not to Sternbridge, but to his wife. The man who had raced horses through Hyde Park with their brother and damn near killed the future king.

It seemed this would be more difficult than she had hoped.

Gossip had destroyed the future of far loftier girls than her. And she hadn't even begun to consider Crispin. In fact, she'd been trying not to consider him at all since two days before and her journey out to the Donville Masquerade. All she knew was that Crispin had not communicated with her since that night. Rafe had taken Marcus's opinion that her brother would likely not even remember she had been there with him.

"You are not smiling," Georgina hissed.

Annabelle jolted. Her tangled thoughts betrayed her again. She shrugged. "I'm only considering my circumstances, I fear. And I am worried about my brother."

Georgina's glance circled the room until it settled on Rafe. "He seems fine."

"No, my other brother, Crispin."

Georgina's lips thinned and she swung her look back on Annabelle. "Oh yes. *Him*. Annabelle, may I ask you a question?"

Annabelle slowly nodded, uncertain if she truly wanted to be asked her friend's question.

"Do you want respectability?"

Annabelle drew back. "How can you ask me that? Of course I do! That is why I'm here in this stuffy hall, standing in the corner like a ninny, waiting for some titled gentleman to decide I'm worthy."

When she said the words out loud, they made her flinch. Certainly they didn't sound like the foundation to a long and happy relationship. But they didn't seem to faze Georgina at all. She nodded, approval bright on her round face.

"I didn't mean to offend, my dear," she reassured Annabelle. "I only ask because of course everyone knows of your family's reputation and you must know you are fighting an uphill battle when it comes to acceptance."

Annabelle wrinkled her nose. "Thank you?"

Georgina laughed. "An uphill battle, but one you can win, I think. You are very pretty and very rich, both of which will certainly catch a man's eye, especially if you act with nothing but decorum."

Something deep inside Annabelle, that same something that had been titillated at the masquerade and intrigued by Marcus Rivers, began to scream. She somehow continued to smile and nod at her friend's words.

"May I offer a small bit of advice, though?"

Annabelle drew in a long breath. "Of course. I am happy to hear any advice you may have for me on this subject. I truly appreciate your greater experience in this matter."

Georgina initially blushed at the compliment, but immediately she was back to a very businesslike demeanor. "Annabelle, you must not think of your brother. Either brother, really. You must worry only about yourself."

Annabelle shifted. Clearly Georgina didn't have the kind of family connections she did. The idea that she could forget Crispin or Rafe was ludicrous. She adored them both, no matter how wild or humiliating their actions. No matter how damaging.

She might have said that, defended them, but suddenly Georgina's attention shifted to something behind her.

"Oh my," Georgina whispered, her eyes lighting up. "I see Lord Claybrook coming this way, and he is looking right at you."

"Lord Claybrook?" Annabelle repeated, panic gripping her as she tried to remember to whom her friend referred.

"He's an earl," Georgina whispered swiftly. "His annual income is above ten thousand. Forty years of age, but he looks thirty."

Annabelle nodded with a look of gratitude just as Lord Claybrook reached them, with their hostess Lady Warren in tow.

"Good evening," Annabelle murmured, casting her eyes downward as she had been told was proper, at least by

Georgina.

"Good evening," Lady Warren responded. "Miss Hickson, Miss Flynn, I would like to introduce you to the Earl of Claybrook."

Both Georgina and Annabelle curtseyed low at the same time, but while Georgina kept her eyes downcast, Annabelle couldn't help but steal a glance at Claybrook.

He was handsome in his own way, tall and lean with a pronounced nose and angular features. His hands looked very soft and he was perfectly manicured and primped. Yet he didn't seem to be a dandy.

Not that she had much room to be choosy, considering her lack of partners throughout the evening.

"Ladies," he said, his voice deep and low.

"My lord," they responded in kind.

Lady Warren's eyebrows knitted together as she searched across the ballroom. "Excuse me, I must attend to an issue."

Once she had gone, Claybrook smiled. It was a nice smile, after all, and Annabelle found herself returning it with ease.

"I hope you will forgive my forwardness, ladies," he said. "I had been waiting for an opportunity to be introduced to you by the Duke of Hartholm, but I have never quite caught him to make the inquiry. I hope my use of Lady Warren is acceptable."

Georgina elbowed Annabelle lightly when she didn't answer for a moment, and she was forced to do so.

"Of course, my lord," she said. "That is most agreeable. I'm very pleased you approached us, though I'm certain my brother would have been more than happy to make the introduction."

She shot a side glance toward Georgina, who smiled with encouragement, right before she leaned in and said, "It was a very great pleasure to meet you, my lord. However, I see my mother motioning to me and I'm afraid I must go to her. I'm sure you will find Miss Flynn a very happy companion."

Claybrook nodded. "I'm certain I will. Good evening,

Miss Hickson."

Georgina gave a very proper incline of her head, but the moment she was behind Claybrook's back, out of his line of sight, she shot Annabelle a look filled with meaning that only served to ratchet Annabelle's nervousness all the higher.

She took a deep breath. "How do you find the party, my lord?" she asked, although she certainly couldn't say she cared greatly about the answer. But it was small talk—and the *ton* adored their small talk.

"It is very lovely," he answered. "A bit crowded, though."

She looked around. Every corner did seem packed with people. "It is that," she agreed.

"Perhaps you would like to take a turn with me around the room?" he suggested.

Annabelle glanced down at her hands, clenched before her. She had rather hoped Claybrook would ask her to dance, but it seemed that was not to be. Still, a walk around the room couldn't be sneezed at. At least they would be seen together.

"Certainly."

He held out an elbow and she slipped her hand into the crook of it. She was surprised at the wiry strength of his arm and the certain way he led her out to walk the large room.

"I have not seen you in Society before, I don't think."

Annabelle pursed her lips. He was touching on a very delicate subject. One she had been training herself to deal with.

"My family is a bit unconventional," she said, the words tasting as false as they likely sounded.

But Claybrook gifted her with a very kind smile. "Indeed, they are. And yet, is that the worst thing in the world?"

Annabelle swallowed hard. The earl seemed sincere in that comment that all but dismissed the Flynn reputation. Was this possibly a man who could overlook her name and actually see *her*? It was hard to tell at this early stage. But his answer gave her a slender reed of hope.

One that continued as they strolled around the room. She knew eyes were on her, but she managed to talk with

Claybrook about everything from the weather to the current state of the newspapers. And though she had to fight not to talk too much or be too bright or show her true self, when they found themselves near the punch bowl a half an hour later, she had to admit it had been a very good conversation, at least in terms of husband-catching.

Claybrook gave her a nod. "Thank you again for this time, Miss Flynn. I certainly hope I shall see you again soon."

She smiled at his compliment and nodded. "I would very much like that, Lord Claybrook."

He bowed and said his good nights before he walked away, leaving her to watch him. And she did watch, unable to keep herself from judging his form as he walked away.

When her gaze settled on his slim, flat backside, she turned her face and her cheeks flamed. Great God, what was she doing? Looking at him like that? So intimately and improperly?

Except she had, and her stomach churned a little. Claybrook was very nice thus far, yes. And he was titled and completely respectable. But there was no spark there. When she examined him, even inappropriately, she couldn't say that there was a desire that grew in her.

Unlike when she looked at Marcus Rivers.

Spinning around to face the refreshment table, Annabelle gritted her teeth. What was she doing thinking about *that man*? Hadn't she spent two whole days purging all thoughts of the club owner from her mind? How dare he intrude upon this place?

This place, where she belonged.

Except it didn't really feel like that. And she feared it never would.

"Rafe didn't want to come in with you?"

Annabelle jumped at the words called out to her from the parlor and poked her head into the dim room to find her mother curled up on a settee, reading by candlelight.

"Rafe wanted to get home to Serafina," she said as she entered the room and pressed a kiss to her mother's forehead. "I didn't know you would still be up."

A smile was her response. "I will likely always wait up for you, it is an old habit."

"It must have been a dreadful one when my brothers still spent their nights here," Annabelle teased.

When her mother didn't return her smile, Annabelle took a seat next to her.

"What is it?" Annabelle asked.

Her mother shifted. "Nothing at all. Tell me, how was your night? A coming out. I'm sorry I couldn't attend, but your brother's title gives you far more influence in those circles than I could, I think."

"I would still like you to come with us one night," Annabelle assured her. "If only to see the finery. And my night was...well, it was a debut, I suppose."

Her mother frowned. "It did not go as planned?"

Annabelle stared at the fire for a moment. "I was not asked to dance by anyone besides Rafe, I'm afraid. I was watched by a few men. And a handful spoke to me when I was in the company of other ladies. But only one man approached me in any way that could indicate interest."

"Only one? What ninnies."

Annabelle laughed. "There were a great many of those, yes. But it was the Earl of Claybrook who came to talk to me especially."

"He didn't ask you to dance?" her mother pressed.

Annabelle shifted. When said like that, it sounded a bit like a set down. "No," she said slowly. "He didn't. But we took a long turn about the room and talked. Perhaps next time he will ask me to dance."

Her mother pushed to her feet and walked across the

room. She poured herself a glass of sherry before she looked back at Annabelle. "I do not like the sound of that."

"It was fine. We all knew it wouldn't be easy. Our family has shunned such society for so many years and there are the antics of my brothers and even our father to contend with."

They exchanged a sad and knowing smile. Being a Flynn woman was not always easy. Not for either of them. But their trials and worries over their male relations had brought them together. Annabelle saw her mother as a friend and confidante.

She forced a smile. "Of course Rafe's title and the money in my dowry will help."

Instead of showing relief, her mother's face fell further. "That sounds like a man will settle for you, despite misgivings."

Annabelle flinched. "Perhaps that is the best we can hope for. You needn't worry, though. I would only ever pick a man I had some liking for on some level."

She thought again of Claybrook, but also of Marcus Rivers. Two different men there could not be. So why did each cross her mind at this moment? She was obviously overly tired.

"Still, I do not want you to find someone who cannot see your fine qualities—your humor, your wit, your intelligence, your talent, your beauty."

Annabelle blushed at the recitation of her supposedly finer qualities. It was likely good her mother could not read her sometimes very dark and dangerous thoughts or she might not think so highly of her.

"We cannot all have a love match," she said softly.

Her mother frowned. There was a moment of reflective silence again and then she cleared her throat. "Do you think Crispin's recent behavior will come back to haunt you?"

Annabelle leaned in. There were lines of worry around her mother's eyes and she could see now that she had been crying.

"What has happened?" she whispered.

Her mother dipped her chin. "I am too obvious, I see."

"Mama!"

"Crispin came here tonight, a few hours ago. He did not look well."

Annabelle gripped her fists at her sides. Neither she nor Rafe had told their mother about the strange night that Crispin had spent at the Donville Masquerade. It would only worry her and that did no good.

"Was he in his cups?" Annabelle whispered.

"I think he'd had a drink," her mother admitted. "But he wasn't drunk. Yet there was a hollowness in his eyes, a wildness to his behavior that concerned me greatly. I asked him to stay here with me, but he refused."

"Did he say where he was going?" Annabelle asked, thinking again of the Donville Masquerade. Of Marcus Rivers.

She blinked and tried to maintain focus on her mother's answer. "He said something about a card game, a masquerade?"

Annabelle let out her breath in relief. If her brother had gone back to Rivers' club, there was a very good chance he would look out for Crispin. She didn't understand why he would do so, but he did. And there was more to that than Rivers' mere explanation that Crispin was a good patron.

But would the other man know when her brother had truly reached his limit? Would he keep an eye on him at all times, no matter what? Would he refuse him if that was what Crispin needed or intervene at the right moment?

Those questions haunted Annabelle.

"Rafe seems to think our brother requires the rope to hang himself, I fear," she whispered.

Her mother squeezed her eyes shut, and the pain was plain on her face. "I hate to think that will be the solution, but he may be correct. Crispin changed after Rafe inherited his dukedom. It is as if he was lost, and I don't know why it affected him so powerfully. It is almost as if there was more to it, though he won't confide in me."

Annabelle nodded. "Or anyone."

"And that is the material point that Rafe's attitude

addresses. If Crispin doesn't want to be reached, I don't know what else we can do. He is of sound mind and body and far into his maturity."

Annabelle snorted at that comment. Crispin was not acting like a man "far into his maturity" at all. "I'm surprised you are willing to take Rafe's side."

"What else could I do? It isn't as if I could follow him to the club every night, watching over him like a hen." Her mother sighed. "Now it is late and I think we both will feel better about these situations once we rest."

Annabelle nodded, but as her mother rose and kissed her on the cheek, leaving her alone in the parlor, her mind had begun to spin a plan. One that could certainly get her into more trouble, but might also save her…and her brother.

CHAPTER SIX

Although he made his money in the wee hours of the night, Marcus always preferred his club during the day. In the quiet hours before patrons began to trickle in for passion and profit, the rooms seemed huge, the silence never-ending. He could lose himself in mindless accounting or reading over reports and forget, if only for a moment, that he didn't deserve any of the riches that he had made off the backs of the prosperous and titled.

He let his eyes flicker up and out the large windows of his office. Down below, the tables were empty and the room echoed whenever the servants spoke as they readied for another night of randy entertainment.

Normally, he would feel pleasure in that fact, but lately he had begun to be troubled by the desperate element that drove some of his membership, his patrons. Crispin Flynn had been back at the Donville Masquerade the night before and while he had been less out of control, Marcus couldn't help but think of Annabelle while he watched his troubled friend.

Annabelle and her bewitching dark eyes, her soft skin, her sad expression when she spoke of the brother she loved and was losing thanks to whatever darkness drove him. Annabelle, who Marcus longed to touch, to kiss, to possess on a deeply physical level.

There was a light knock on the door, and Marcus jerked as

he was brought back to reality. "What is it?" he barked out, his tone sharp as he moved to accommodate an increasing erection thanks to his inappropriate thoughts.

Abbot opened the door and stepped inside. His face was long and drawn down, and Marcus frowned at the sight of him.

"Please don't tell me you are still brooding over our discussion about you allowing Annabelle Flynn into my carriage?"

Normally Abbot wasn't one to pout, but they had exchanged some rather strong words after Annabelle's unexpected entry into Marcus's lair.

Abbot shook his head. "Of course not."

"Then why is your face drawn into such a sullen frown?" Marcus pressed, getting up now that his body no longer betrayed him.

"Because she is *back*," Abbot said.

Marcus froze. He could not have understood that sentence correctly. Abbot couldn't mean Annabelle had returned to the club—it was not possible. The lady had fulfilled whatever duty she had to chase her brother; it was clear they would never see each other again. In fact, Marcus had been counting on that to clear his mind of these troubling thoughts of her.

"*She* who?" he asked, hating how his voice was now cracked and broken.

"*She* the bloody queen. Who do you think?"

Marcus scrubbed a hand over his face. "Are you telling me that Annabelle Flynn is here, in my club, at..." He paused to look at the clock. "...at two in the afternoon?"

"Precisely. She beat on the door until poor Vale had no choice but to answer and then refused to leave until she saw you. She and her maid are in the foyer as we speak." Abbot tilted his head. "I would like to point out that this time it is not my fault."

Marcus pursed his lips. "The woman is a menace."

"Indeed."

He paced to the window again. From here he couldn't see

the trouble waiting just outside the main double doors. But he could picture her perfectly, down to her full, pink lips perfectly made for sin.

"Send her in," he managed to growl out. "But make sure her maid stays behind."

"Why?" Abbot asked, his eyes widening.

Marcus gave a half-smile. "If she insists on seeing a wolf, I would like to remind her that she is a sheep. Perhaps *that* will stop her from coming here."

Abbot nodded and left the room, but as soon as he was gone, Marcus all but collapsed back into the chair. He might bluster a good game, but his heart had already begun to pound erratically in his chest at the mere idea that Annabelle was in such close proximity. She shouldn't be. And he hoped he could frighten her off.

And yet he *wanted* her here. With him. In his office. With no one else around to ruin the atmosphere.

He heard them on the stair and got back to his feet. The door opened and Abbot motioned her inside. "May I get you anything else?" he asked.

Marcus stared at Annabelle and didn't look away as he said, "No."

The door shut and he drank the look of her in. Her green and yellow striped day dress only accentuated the slender lines of her body. It was expensive—but of course it would be—and fitted to perfection. It fastened in the front. How long would it take to remove it?

"Why are you here?" he asked, his voice rough.

She had been watching him intently, but his question seemed to break the spell between them because she finally blinked. "I-I—" she stammered.

With a curse beneath her breath that he was surprised a lady knew, she hurried past him and stood at his window where he had brooded not a few moments ago. Her back was to him, but he saw her taking a few long breaths, as if to calm herself. Were her nerves because of whatever she'd come here to say or because of him?

"It is different here in the day," she mused, almost as if to herself.

He held his gaze on her back, stunned that she had just voiced exactly his musings before she stepped into his club for the second time.

"Yes," he said, his voice still stiff and formal. "And I must ask again, why are you here?"

She faced him, and he saw the determination on her face and the light of strength in her eyes. He couldn't deny how much he admired them both, even before she explained herself.

"I have been pondering Crispin a great deal," she began.

"Have you?"

"Yes. I believe he may have been here again last night," she explained.

Marcus's eyes widened. "Please do not tell me you snuck into my club again last night."

Her brow knitted. "I have never snuck into your club at all, sir!"

He let out his breath in frustration. "You know what I mean. Did you come here last night, Annabelle?"

"No! I was at a ball last night. I surmised this was where Crispin might have gone from clues he gave my mother." She broke her gaze from his at last. "I did *consider* coming here—"

"Miss Flynn—"

"—but I did not do it," she finished. "I know my sneaking out frightened Rafe, and I would not do that to my mother, at least not without a good deal of planning ahead of time so there would be no chance she might find out. She was in enough of a state as it was, thanks to Crispin. I am the closest thing to a respectable child as she has. I couldn't create worry over me."

She sucked in a breath as she finished that statement. Her face was flush with emotion and her eyes lit up with even more.

"Will you sit down?" he offered, wanting in some strange way to calm her.

She seemed to ponder the merits of accepting his offer for a moment as she looked around his austere office. "Your guests, your members, they do not...they do not take their fun *here*, do they?"

Marcus lifted his brows. "No. This is my private office. There is no entertaining done here."

Of course, through a door just behind her was a bedroom where he could easily change that. But he shoved the thought aside to gather with the other inappropriate things this woman brought out in him.

She touched one of the wooden chairs across from his desk, gliding her fingers across the surface before she slowly sank into its seat. She sighed as if she had been holding back exhaustion. "You must think me quite hysterical," she said without looking up at him.

He came around the desk and perched on the edge in front of her. He looked down at her, watching how the light hit her face. "No," he said softly. "You are worried about your brother. I admire your loyalty to him. Though I certainly did not expect you to invade my club before opening."

She glanced up at him. "I did not invade—" When he met her gaze, she stopped. "Fine, I suppose invasion is not such a bad comparison. I only wished to talk to you in private, before there would be...be distractions."

"You mean my patrons," he said, thinking of what he'd caught her staring at just a few nights before.

She nodded, a blush darkening her cheeks.

"You are here now. Talk to me," he urged softly, even though he knew he should order her to go home and probably tell the Duke of Hartholm what she had been doing on her own.

But he didn't.

She shook her head. "I don't know you, I realize that. And you owe me nothing, not even the kindness you have shown toward me so far. I realize I sound like a frantic woman, silly to the core, but my brother means the world to me. I don't know what has driven Crispin to this wild behavior now, but I do know he is swiftly passing to the point of being out of control. And I fear for him, Mr. Rivers."

She looked up at him, luminous brown eyes locked on his and creating a lush prison where he feared he could be locked up forever and not complain.

"Rafe thinks he knows best, and I cannot argue with the logic of his response. However, he is busy with his new role as duke, his marriage and the baby he has on the way so soon. Perhaps if he wasn't, he might see things differently."

"You mean he might pursue your brother as you wish to do," Marcus said softly.

She nodded, her face lighting up as if she were happy he understood what she meant on some small level. "Yes. That is it exactly. Rafe might see that we could lose Crispin if we don't act. And I can't lose him."

Marcus pressed his lips together. This was building to something, that was clear. Annabelle hadn't just come here to vent her feelings to a highly inappropriate stranger. Her intelligent, bright face told him there was more to her visit.

"And what do you want to do?" he asked.

She stood up suddenly and moved forward a fraction. With him seated on the edge of his desk, they were almost the same height, and now her face was too close to his. He could smell her intoxicating scent, heady jasmine that he wanted to get his fill of.

"I do not think it would be fair to ask you to watch over him," she said, seemingly oblivious to what her closeness did to him. Though her voice was more breathless when she continued, "But I would like to—to do that. Myself."

He leaned away. "I beg your pardon?"

"I want to come here and watch over my brother," she repeated. "With your permission, of course."

Marcus stood up, and now they were even closer. He was going mad from her scent and could hardly see anything but her. "You cannot mean that."

"But I do. I would not be in your way, I assure you. I'll

wear a mask at all times. I could even pay a membership fee if you would like."

"Damn it, it isn't about the money, Annabelle!"

She blinked at his sudden outburst and stiffened. "What is it?"

"Your safety, both physical and mental," he snapped. "You are an innocent—you cannot possibly understand."

"I saw things, you know," she said, that fierce blush returning to her skin. "My brothers had a few books that I found, I read, and they were quite descriptive. If you are talking about the acts I saw here at your club, I'm certain in time the shock would wear off and I would hardly notice them anymore."

Marcus shook his head. He had seen her increased breath when she watched the couple grind against each other the first night she came here. He'd seen how focused she was on the intimacies they shared. In some way, she was titillated by the acts, by the voyeurism. And oh, how he liked that idea. On a deep, visceral level, he had loved watching it. He had wanted to awaken those dark and hidden desires even more.

Which was exactly why he couldn't allow her tempting offer.

"I would not ask for you to take responsibility for me," she insisted.

"But I would *be* responsible," he said. "At any rate, you are now out in Society. How would you ever pull off such a feat?"

She stared at him a moment, and then she began to laugh. It was a warm sound that seemed to fill the cold room with light and color. It touched his ears and curled through his blood, settling low in his groin.

"What is so funny, Miss Flynn?"

"You forget who I grew up with," she said, her laughter fading to a bright smile. "I will have responsibilities to attend to, yes, but nothing could be simpler than dodging a chaperone, whether it is my mother or my brother. I can tell one that I'm with the other and trust me, my family doesn't verify these things. I could be spending the night with a friend or sneak out my damned window if it comes to that. Mr. Rivers, you have no idea of the depth of my ability to be a Flynn in every way that works in my advantage."

Marcus smothered a smile. It was hard not to be impressed with the woman who stood before him. She was confident and bright, as well as beautiful. But the idea that she would come here, that she would be here with him in his den of inequity…it was as dangerous as it was tempting.

"Your brothers' books may not fully prepare you for what you find in these walls," Marcus said and found himself inching forward until her skirts brushed his thigh. "What you saw the first night you came here is only the beginning."

To his shock, Annabelle's pupils dilated at that statement and her pink tongue shot out to wet her lips. Staring up at him with an expression of both innocence and desire, she was suddenly no longer a temptation he could resist.

He cupped her chin, tilting her face toward his even more. He waited for her to step back, or to wallop him with a punch he was certain one or both of her brothers had taught her to throw over the years. But she did neither—she just looked up at him, trembling in anticipation.

Whatever small shred of civility he had left floated away on the harsh exhalation of her breath, and he lowered his mouth and claimed her lips just as he had been dreaming of doing since the first moment he laid eyes on her so many years ago.

CHAPTER SEVEN

Annabelle had been kissed before, but those caresses paled in comparison to Marcus's...*possession* of her. His mouth slanted over hers, demanding entry that she had no choice but to give. His tongue swept past her lips, massaging and tasting, teasing and tempting and without meaning to she moaned deep in her throat.

That low sound only drove him on. His arms came around her, dragging her against him, and she was helpless to resist the animal desires he stoked in her. She lifted to her tiptoes to get closer to him.

He tasted so good, like fresh mint with a hint of smoky whisky. She could easily drown in those flavors, lose herself entirely as she let her tongue tangle with his.

Her response seemed to stoke him further. He let out his own groan, and then his hands slid down her sides. He cupped her backside through her gown and tugged her against him even harder. She felt the rigid length of his erection against her belly.

Her mind flashed to images of the first night she'd come to Marcus's club. To the tangled man and woman, how they ground together in a sensual rhythm. How the man had cupped the woman's bare bottom.

She wanted to do those things. She wanted to surrender her body to this man and have him teach her about the dark desires that sometimes all but overtook her in her bed and made her fingers work wildly over her sex. She wanted to be *his*.

The thoughts made her jolt in shock, and she pressed her hands to his chest and shoved.

"No," she said, but the word had no heat behind it.

Despite that fact, he immediately released her and retook his seat on the edge of his desk. He said nothing as she backed away from him, but watched her with such intensity that she had no choice but to turn away just so that she could remember how to breathe.

"I'm sorry, Mr. Rivers. I'm certain you must think very low of me," she whispered.

"Why would I think any less of you, Annabelle?" he asked, his voice soft and seductive over her shoulder. She couldn't help but turn and found his expression utterly unreadable. "I believe it was I who kissed you."

She swallowed. That was most definitely true. She might have wanted to kiss him, in that dark place she needed to destroy, but she never would have been so bold as to actually instigate the caress.

"But I—I responded," she said, shaking her head as she relived that response in every nerve ending of her shaking body.

"Yes, you did that. But again, I couldn't judge you. In fact, I very much enjoyed it."

Heat filled her cheeks, and Annabelle fought hard to remember her goals. Her desires. Respectability would not be found with a notorious club owner who awakened the worst longings in her.

"Still, I can't," she whispered. "So I shouldn't have so eagerly allowed this transgression."

"You can't, Annabelle, or you won't?"

Annabelle clenched her hands. His question was at the core of her current situation. Yes, she could give in to what her body seemed to want more and more. She *could* march over to

Marcus's desk and continue what they'd started.

But she wouldn't, because she knew once she surrendered to that part of herself, that very Flynn element that haunted her every thought and action, there would be no going back. And for a woman like herself, there would very likely be ruin and pain.

"Either can't or won't, the result is the same," she said. "I am not like them. I can't be. Or won't be. You can take your pick if it pleases you."

He didn't look pleased as he stared at her, holding her as if he had pinned her to her spot. She had no idea of his thoughts, and she found she wished she did. Rivers was…fascinating.

He got up and moved around to sit properly at his desk. The barrier between them made it somehow easier to breathe, and she allowed herself to ease back toward him as she awaited his response.

"Your brother is a regular visitor here on Tuesdays and Thursdays," he said, his tone brusque and professional again. "He comes at other times during the week, but those are the times I can almost guarantee he will be here. He comes around ten most nights."

She blinked. "Are you saying you will allow me access to the club to watch over him?"

He hesitated, and she could see this was truly a struggle for him. Whether it was because he didn't want to the trouble of her coming here or because he felt she would be in danger or he simply was upset that she had pulled away from his kiss, she didn't know.

After a moment, he said, "Yes, you may come on those nights. And I will attempt to inform you of other times Crispin comes to the Masquerade."

Her heart leapt and she stepped closer. He watched her as she did so, and her body reacted accordingly. She ignored the tingling response.

"Tomorrow is Thursday," she stated.

He nodded. "Yes. If you come, be sure to bring a mask

and put it on before you leave your carriage. Make sure your maid has one as well, if you insist on bringing her as you did today. She will be taken to the servant area."

Annabelle worried her lip. "Will Deirdre be safe there?"

"You think the debauchery here continues below stairs?" Marcus asked, brow arched.

"It would be foolish to assume it didn't. I may have no choice but to bring my maid and I would never want to put her in danger."

Marcus smiled slightly at that answer. "The servant quarters do sometimes get wild, but those who want to partake in the same kind of fun as their mistresses and masters must go to a different area. It is policed as carefully as upstairs is. No one comes to my club and is forced to do anything they don't wish to do. So your Deirdre will be very safe, I assure you. Your only worry will be her wagging tongue."

Annabelle shook her head. "She would not betray me, I'm certain. But I'll be sure we both have masks. Are there any other instructions I should know about?"

"At the door, they will require a name, to check it against our membership roster," Marcus said.

Annabelle froze. She hadn't thought about that fact, but of course it would be true. Part of how Marcus made his money was through the memberships and he couldn't allow just anyone off the street inside, both for financial and safety concerns.

"I would obviously prefer not to be on your books," she whispered. "Though I could give you the fee if you tell me what it is."

"Three hundred pounds per annum for a basic membership," he said softly. "Five hundred for the inclusion of the use of private rooms. A lifetime membership can be purchased for five thousand pounds."

She blinked. "That is more than many people's income entirely."

He smiled, but there was little pleasure to the expression.

"People are willing to pay for pleasure and privacy, Annabelle."

"I can get you three hundred pounds," she began, but he held up a hand to stop her.

"I wouldn't ask you for a fee," he said. "But I do have a request since you are not officially on our books."

Annabelle nearly sagged in relief. She had the money, of course, but to remove that much for her pin account would likely raise the eyebrows of the solicitor. He would report the activity to her mother and probably to Rafe.

And she couldn't imagine either one would be happy to know what she'd spent her funds on.

"What is it, Marcus—" She broke off abruptly and brought her hand up to her mouth. Had she just called him by his given name? "I'm sorry, Mr. Rivers."

His eyes lit up and she saw his desire as plainly as could be. "Now I have *two* requests."

She squeezed her eyes shut. That hypnotic, seductive tone of his couldn't bode well. "What are they?"

"First, that you will call me Marcus, at least when we are alone."

Her lips parted. The intimacy of his first name was almost as great as the intimacy of the kiss they'd shared. And she'd already made it clear that she couldn't ever repeat the kiss.

But what could she do, deny him this simple request and jeopardize the boon he was allowing her? That seemed very foolish.

"Very well, Marcus," she whispered, hating herself for how much it moved her to say his name aloud again. "What is your second demand?"

"Request," he corrected her. "And the second one is that when you come to the foyer, give my man the name Jasmine. I'll be sure that is on the list of allowed guests and it will protect your identity. It will also signal to my staff that you are to be brought directly to me."

"Do you mind if I ask you why you chose the name

Jasmine?"

He held her gaze steadily. "Because you smell of it."

She stood captive to both that simple statement and to the very complicated look on his face. This man wanted her. He wanted her very much. But she had been in a room with him before and not seen it, so why now?

Unless she just hadn't wanted to see before. After all, his intensity had always troubled her, making her think about him for days after any encounter between them.

"You say your staff will bring me to you—why is that?" she asked, this time her voice no more than a dry croak.

He leaned back in his chair. "So that I may protect you, Annabelle."

"Why?" she whispered, uncertain she was ready to hear the answer, but desperate to do so anyway.

"Because I want to," he said through clenched teeth. "Now, no more questions. Go home, Miss Flynn, and I will see you tomorrow evening."

He tilted his head and his focus returned to the ledger on his desk. She watched him for a moment despite his dismissal of her and couldn't help but shiver at the sensual curve of his lips and the angled perfection of his jaw and cheeks. He was dashedly handsome, damn him.

And he was right. It was far past time to go before she made more of an idiot of herself than she already had.

The carriage turned onto the street away from the private, sheltered drive of the Donville Masquerade before Annabelle's maid folded her arms and stared at her across the distance. She shifted with discomfort. Deirdre did not look pleased.

"Miss Annabelle, do you know what kind of place that is that we just left?" her maid began, the light tones of her Irish accent strengthened by high emotion.

Annabelle almost laughed as she thought of her first night at Marcus's club and all she had seen. "Yes."

Her maid's blue eyes widened further at her one-word, certain answer. "I don't understand."

Annabelle brought a hand up to cover her face. Deirdre had been her maid for well near a decade now, and Annabelle knew she could trust her. Certainly Deirdre had never whispered to anyone about the family's eccentricities and Annabelle could well imagine her maid had been asked about them below stairs from the spying servants of others.

"You know Crispin is struggling," Annabelle whispered.

Her maid blushed slightly and nodded. "Yes, Miss."

"He comes to that place, to the hells, to gamble and…" She shook her head. "And God knows what else. I have gotten the owner of that particular club, Mr. Rivers, to agree to let me come and watch over my brother from a distance."

Her maid drew back. "You cannot mean to bring yourself to that place at night, when there are people there doing…doing things unfit for a lady's eyes and presence!"

Annabelle, looked out the window. "I have done so once already," she mused softly.

Deirdre made a strangled sound in her throat and Annabelle frowned. This was the reaction of her maid—she could only imagine that the response of those in her new circles within the *ton* would be worse. After all, they didn't give a damn about her and were predisposed to view her in the worst light.

"I know I have no place to tell you what to do," Deirdre said. "But I cannot be comfortable with this idea of you coming to that place with only me as chaperone. Can you not speak to your mother or the duke?"

Annabelle jerked her gaze away from the scene outside and back to her maid. "No! Please, Deirdre, you and I have been together for many years. You know me and you know my struggles thanks to the reputation of my family. You must know I would never endanger myself, especially now when I have a chance of finding respectability."

"But you might not have a choice in a place such as the Donville Masquerade," Deirdre reasoned, her hands clenching and unclenching in her lap. "If your family knew—"

"I'm begging you not to involve them," Annabelle interrupted, reaching across the carriage to lay a hand over Deirdre's clasped ones.

Deirdre's foot tapped nervously. "But Miss…"

"I understand your hesitations completely, and I appreciate your worry on my behalf more than you could ever know," Annabelle said. "But I won't be alone. Mr. Rivers is a friend to both my brothers and he has agreed to look out for me while I am within the walls of his club."

Deirdre blinked. "Mr. Rivers," she repeated incredulously. "And you trust this man, despite his involvement in such a shocking place?"

That question brought Annabelle's explanations and pleading to a screeching halt. Did she trust Marcus Rivers? She hardly knew the man, and he had already severely breached decorum by kissing her so passionately. Those were very good reasons to be wary of him, and yet she didn't feel that way. She felt…safe when she was with him.

Safe, and other things.

"Yes," she said, bending her head just in case her unexpected desire for the man was too obvious on her face. "Yes, I trust him."

Deirdre folded her arms. "I wouldn't be so bold as to go against what you are requesting, but I want you to know I don't like it."

Annabelle nodded. "I understand entirely, Deirdre, and I appreciate your agreement to keep what I am doing between us."

They rode for a while in silence, but Annabelle couldn't help but reflect over and over again on Marcus Rivers. Deirdre might not like this arrangement she had made, but Annabelle couldn't help but fear that *she* might like it all too much.

CHAPTER EIGHT

Abbot paced across Marcus's office floor, his normally calm face bright with angry color and his movements jerky and erratic.

"I cannot believe you would make such a foolish bargain with Annabelle Flynn, Rivers!" Abbot repeated for what felt like the tenth time since they had begun this highly unpleasant discussion not half an hour before. "And then you didn't even inform me?"

Marcus arched a brow. "I believe that was what I was doing when we started talking this evening."

"That is the point—*this evening*. You could have told me yesterday or this morning or this afternoon. But you waited until the club opened to spill this little secret of yours."

"And what would have come out of telling you an hour ago or ten hours ago?" Marcus asked, keeping his tone mild as he watched Abbot pace and grouse.

"I could have had time to prepare!"

"She is a woman, Paul," Marcus said softly, shifting to his friend's first name. "Not an invading army."

But even as he dismissed her, Marcus could admit, at least to himself, that *he* had been preparing for Annabelle's return since her departure the previous day. It was all he could think about. That and the passionate kiss they had shared. He had always wanted her, but now he knew she wanted him in return.

That was an almost irresistible draw.

"An invading army is almost exactly what she is!" Abbot insisted. "Great God, man, you cannot pretend you don't see the risks in what you've arranged. The woman is an innocent, she is not even a paying member in your club and she is here to *spy* on someone who *is* a paying member."

"You are being dramatic," Marcus said, though he knew full well that Abbot was anything but that.

"What if someone found out her identity and purpose? And that you had sanctioned it?" Abbot threw up his hands. "The trust you have built with your patrons would be shattered, Rivers."

Marcus pursed his lips. Abbot was entirely correct, of course. The arrangement he'd made with Annabelle was outrageous and dangerous, in more ways than one. And yet he had no intention of going back on it.

"How would anyone ever find out?" he pressed.

Abbot opened and shut his mouth as he sputtered, "Too many ways to count. Not the least of which is that someone could recognize Miss Flynn."

"She is very driven to protect her identity and reputation, I assure you," Marcus said, swallowing past the suddenly bad taste in his mouth when he thought of how she had shoved herself away from him the previous afternoon.

The kiss they'd shared had haunted him ever since. Even now, his body began to react to the mere memory of holding Annabelle against him, her slender frame trembling as she returned his kiss with a fire worthy of a goddess.

Abbot sighed and drew Marcus from his thoughts. "I do not feel, in good conscience, that I could watch out for her. Not with everything else I must do."

"I'm not asking you to do so."

Abbot stared at him. "But—but *someone* must do so. You certainly cannot let her roam the rooms alone, not with the activities your patrons openly engage in."

"I'll protect her." Marcus said it quietly, because he knew

the power of those words. And the impact.

He was not disappointed. Abbot's mouth dropped open. "You."

"Yes."

"Even though you are running the club, trying to keep up with the books, dealing with the rowdy and randy, *you* will take time from your schedule and watch out for this woman."

"I think that's what I just said," Marcus drawled.

Abbot stared at him for what seemed like an eternity, and then he folded his arms. "You like her."

Marcus pushed back from his desk, his chair legs screeching across the wooden floor. "Don't be ridiculous."

"It makes perfect sense," Abbot mused, ignoring Marcus's denial. "I can think of no other reason why you wouldn't kick her out the very first night she forced herself in. Why you would make this foolish bargain with her to allow to her spy on Crispin Flynn."

Marcus clenched his fists at his sides. He had always been very careful to hide his emotions, even from those he was closest to. But now Paul Abbot seemed to see through him as if nothing but a sheer veil covered his soul.

"Are you finished?" he asked.

Abbot shrugged. "Yes."

"Good." He slapped a hand down on his desk. "I don't have to explain myself to you. I can well manage my business, as I have for nearly a decade. Just make sure that 'Jasmine' is sent upstairs to me the moment she arrives, and then you can happily not worry yourself about her. Do I make myself clear?"

Abbot stared at him a moment, but Marcus could tell his old friend wasn't particularly moved by his sudden sharpness. In fact, he seemed to be smothering a smile that was as irksome as his interference. "You make yourself clearer than you would probably like, *sir*. And if that is all, I have a few things to do before the crush arrives."

"That is all," Marcus said through clenched teeth.

Paul gave a cheeky salute and left, leaving Marcus alone

in his office at last. He turned to the window and stared out at the rapidly filling main room of the club.

Paul was one of the few people he let anywhere close to him in his life. That was the only reason Abbot could see his true motives so clearly. But he had to be certain no one else would ever guess what he held in his heart.

Especially not Annabelle Flynn.

Annabelle waited for her turn to give her name at the entrance to the club. At her side, she could hear Deirdre's increased breath, a sure sign that her maid continued to disapprove of her decisions. But she couldn't worry about that at present. She had to focus on her goals.

Marcus.

No, that wasn't right. Marcus Rivers was a distraction. Her goal was Crispin and doing everything she could to help him.

"Focus," she muttered to herself.

"I beg your pardon?" the liveried servant asked as she stepped up.

"A—" she began, then cut herself off. She couldn't allow herself to be so flustered that she forgot herself. "Jasmine."

The servant's eyebrows lifted ever so slightly, and then he bowed. "Of course, Miss. You are expected. Your servant may go with Carter, and if you wait a moment, I will find someone to escort you to your destination."

Annabelle nodded and then turned her attention to Deirdre.

"I don't like leaving you, Miss...Jasmine," her maid whispered.

Annabelle caught her hand and squeezed gently. "But you will, and I'll be fine. I promise you. If you have any trouble, please have them send for me. But Mr. Rivers said no one shall bother you."

Deirdre frowned deeper, but then nodded. "Very well. Be careful."

Her maid turned and followed another servant from the room. Once Annabelle was alone, she expected some weight would come off her shoulders, but instead, anxiety began to build in her chest as she awaited her fate.

To her surprise, when the door to the main hall opened a few moments later, it was Mr. Abbot who appeared. He looked her up and down from the door, and Annabelle tensed as her hand drifted up to touch her mask.

This time, she had chosen the mask that would protect her identity. Instead of the plain gray from before, she had gone with an elaborate design of bright blue with peacock feathers and paste jewels around the eyes. She had been quite pleased with the effect until Deirdre had questioned if she was "dressing for someone."

It was ridiculous notion. Annabelle was dressing for no one—she just knew that the ladies here all wore pretty masks. She would fit in more by doing the same rather than going with something austere.

"Good evening," Abbot said as he strode up to her.

"Hello again, Mr. Abbot," she managed to squeak out.

"We've been expecting you." He motioned her toward the main hall door. "Although I must say that fact was a surprise to me when Mr. Rivers informed me of it earlier this evening."

Annabelle heard the strain in the other man's tone and glanced at him from the corner of her eye. He didn't look particularly happy to have her here.

"I'm sorry if I am causing you trouble," she said softly.

He turned partially toward her as he hesitated at the door. "Don't mistake me. I understand your drive to the fullest and I admire your dedication to your family. But you must equally understand that Rivers is taking a risk to the reputation of this club by allowing you to come here as you are. I hope you'll be mindful of it."

Annabelle stared at him a moment, reading the true care

he had for Marcus on his face. "I will do my very best not to damage Mr. Rivers or what he has built."

"Excellent." Abbot smiled and then opened the door, leading her into the club once more.

Over the last twenty-four hours, Annabelle had focused on any technique she thought might help her remain unmoved in the face of the debauchery she would encounter in that room, but as soon as the door opened, she realized it was all for naught. She was bombarded once again by the smells of incense, the moans of those already exploring passion and the sights of bare breasts, seeking hands and wet tongues.

Her heart fluttered and her feet faltered as she fell behind Abbot, trailing behind him through the hall. Her gaze darted to a table where a woman was splayed out, dress up around her stomach and two men leaning over her. One had his hand between her legs and was stroking just like Annabelle did to herself on the darkest nights in her bed.

The other had his member out and the woman sucked it greedily.

"Oh God," Annabelle moaned beneath her breath, turning her face even though she knew that erotic image would stay with her for a long time to come. It would be fodder for her dreams and fantasies, no doubt.

She forced herself to look straight ahead for the rest of the winding route through the club. She forced herself *not* to look at the gamblers and lovers and those who were preparing to do one thing or another. If her brother were here, she would wait until she was with Marcus to find him, rather than look and find what she didn't want...couldn't want...to see.

At the bottom of the stairway, a servant stood, just as he had the last time she came here when the club was open. And just as last time, the man's eyes went wide as Abbot took her past him.

Abbot acknowledged the man with a brief nod, but said nothing as he guided Annabelle up the staircase and back into the plain office Marcus had above the club.

As Annabelle stepped inside, she stopped and looked around, bracing herself for the overwhelming presence of her host. But the room was empty.

She turned to Abbot with a wrinkled brow. As if he recognized the unspoken question, Abbot smiled. "He will be here shortly. He knows you have arrived."

To her surprise, the other man then turned on his heel and left the room with nothing further to say. Annabelle gaped at the door as it shut her in, alone in Rivers' office.

"I certainly do not understand the society Rivers keeps any more than I understand the *ton*," she muttered as she paced away from the door across the room, tugging off her mask as she did so and setting it aside on a small table beside the door.

Before she had been distracted, but now she took in more details of Marcus's lair. The furniture and other accouterments were simple, yes, but they were clearly very fine and expensive, reflecting the wealth that Marcus had built here. She fiddled with the clock on the mantel, which read nine forty-five, before she walked across the room again.

She found herself stopping at the door at the back of the office. The one she had noticed on her first visit here.

"What is he hiding?" she murmured.

Immediately her errant mind turned to one of the French fairytales she'd read as a girl. One particularly gruesome one was about Bluebeard, the man who hid his dead wives in a chamber. She laughed, though her stomach fluttered as she grasped the knob.

She was surprised when it actually turned and the door opened to reveal not a chamber of horrors like in the story she feared, but a bedroom. A bedroom with a huge bed as its centerpiece. A bed with crisp linen sheets that looked so inviting. Would Marcus lay her across those sheets if she asked? And do more than merely kiss her?

She gasped as she yanked the door shut. Spinning around, she leaned against it. The chamber of horrors from the Bluebeard story would not have disturbed her so much as that errant fantasy of Marcus claiming her. Especially since the second seemed so much more in reach than the first.

She rushed across the chamber to the wide swath of windows and stared down, but what she saw gave her no more solace than the chamber had. There were the writhing bodies that made her want what she should not desire. The things that made her body tingle in a way that could only be relieved by touching herself.

She spun from that and found herself facing Marcus's desk. She braced herself on the wooden surface, drawing long, panting breaths to calm herself.

"Stop, just stop," she pleaded out loud. "You cannot give in to this."

Tears stung her eyes as she stared unseeing at the papers scattered across Marcus's desk. But slowly she began to focus. Her mind stopped thinking about his bedchamber or the lovers downstairs and began to truly see what was before her.

There were a few ledgers with figures scratched messily in the proper—and sometimes improper—boxes. There were a few letters that seemed to contain membership fees for the club, but she couldn't see where they were recorded on the ledger.

"What a mess," she murmured as she reached into her pelisse and withdrew her spectacles. She balanced them on her nose and slowly sank into the chair behind the desk as she sorted through the piles, trying to find some organization for what was there to be done.

All her life, she had taken an interest in contracts, budgets and ledgers. Studying them had always come naturally, and her parents had never discouraged her inclination. Hell, she'd even gone over contracts for her father and her brothers, including Rafe's inherited marital contract just the year before. As always, reading and working on things such as this soothed her, brought her away from tangled emotions and unwanted thoughts and planted her firmly on the ground. Soon, she lost track of everything except for what was before her and what she could do with that information.

Lost, that was, until the door to the chamber slammed. She jumped and jerked her face up to find Marcus standing beside the door, staring at her.

"What the hell do you think you're doing?" he snapped.

She blinked and reached up to snatch her spectacles off. She shoved them in her forgotten pelisse and jumped to her feet. "I was just looking at—"

"My personal papers," he interrupted, taking a long step toward her.

As always, he was impossible to read. His tone was angry, but she couldn't tell from his expression if that was a mild feeling or a rage. He hid himself just too damned well. But she blushed regardless.

"Yes, I'm so very sorry I didn't mean to pry."

"And yet you were."

She wrung her hands before her. If he wanted to, he could kick her out of his club this very moment and she wouldn't be able to watch out for Crispin. Or see Marcus again.

But of course the first was far more important to her than the second.

"Mr. Rivers," she began, and his frown deepened. "Marcus," she corrected herself as she thought of what she had agreed to the previous day. "I was waiting for you, and I admit I was distracted by the papers on your desk. I have a bit of a head of such things and it is sometimes hard for me to resist the temptation to reorganize."

"A head for business?" he asked, and the anger in his voice had begun to bleed away, replaced by shock at her words. Of course, she was accustomed to that. Men were always shocked—and often annoyed or even disgusted—by her ability to read sums and contracts as well or better than they were.

She blushed. "I-I shouldn't have said anything."

He moved closer again, and suddenly she was very happy for the desk that separated them. He was too close and she could already feel the radiating heat of his body curling around her and making her weak.

He tilted his head to read the ledger upside down. "Did you reenter my sums?"

She bit her lip. "I did, I'm sorry. I only thought it would be clearer if they were put this way. It is a terrible habit and I cannot apologize enough. We don't have to discuss it anymore, and I promise you I won't ever do it again."

"No," he insisted, his dark green eyes snaring her and holding steady. "I am interested in this. How is it that a lady of your caliber has a head for business?"

Annabelle blinked. A lady of her caliber. In the *ton*, she was a lady of no caliber at all, yet Marcus spoke of her like she was a direct descendent of the king.

"I—well, you know my brothers," she began slowly. "So you must have ascertained that our family was not exactly…typical."

He grinned suddenly, and her heart stuttered. She had never seen him smile like that before and it made his stern face suddenly bright and so utterly, ridiculously handsome that she could hardly find breath.

"Typical is not a word I would use," he drawled.

She dipped her head so that his appearance wouldn't distract her further. "Well, I may be even less so than Rafe and Crispin. You see, I was always exposed to the same education as they were. My father thought it could be very important for me to be clever in every way. So even when the boys went away to school, he insisted my tutors give me a mirrored education to theirs. Much to the chagrin of the teachers. Some quit in protest to such a shocking thought."

"But your father was not deterred," Marcus said.

She swallowed back the pain that met her at the mention of her father. Thoughts of him were still difficult, even after all these years. Living hard and wild was his way, but he had been kind and loving to her every day of her life. Sometimes she ached for the hole his death had left behind.

"No," she said, barely allowing the word to carry. She shook her head, hoping Marcus couldn't see her emotional state. "But I am not here to look at your books or tell you stories of my childhood. I'm here for Crispin. Is *he* here?"

She was trying to focus, but it was almost impossible when Marcus was watching her so closely. When his hooded stare made her think only about his mouth covering hers with hunger and purpose.

"No."

She blinked at the one syllable answer that ripped her from her fantasies. "I beg your pardon?"

"Your brother isn't here."

Panic rose in her chest at that answer. "Oh, but I thought you said Crispin came every Tuesday and Thursday at ten."

He shrugged. "Usually that is true, but it is only just ten now. He is often a bit later, so if you would like to wait, my men have been given instructions to come fetch us when and if he arrives."

"And what will we do in the meantime?"

She shouldn't have asked the question. She completely understood its double meaning, and from the way Marcus's eyes lit up, he knew it too. Slowly he came around the desk, edging into her space, making her knees wobble as he leaned in just a touch too close. She wanted to let her eyes flutter shut, she wanted to lift her mouth to him and have that kiss she had been thinking about for over a day.

"What do you *want* to do, Annabelle?" he whispered.

She couldn't help it. She groaned, just a little, but enough to humiliate herself. Her cheeks flamed, but she couldn't bring herself to pull away from his captivating, powerful gaze.

He smiled again. "Perhaps you would like to tell me more about my books."

The spell was broken with his unexpected suggestion. She flushed. "Are you teasing me, sir?"

He shook his head swiftly. "Of course not, Annabelle. I am very impressed by the abilities you described and by the alterations I could see from the other side of the desk. I would very much like your opinion on my management of the club if you would be willing to provide it."

She stared at him. He looked utterly serious. A part of her thrilled that he would respect her mind and ask for her assistance. Normally it was only her family who did that, everyone else was appalled by her intelligence and capability.

But part of her was also disappointed. When he stalked around the desk at her, she certainly hadn't thought he would ask her to help him with his accounting. She had expected him to kiss her or offer her even more decadent wickedness in his bed behind the door across the room.

She shivered at the thought and promptly shoved it aside where it would no longer trouble her.

"Very well," she agreed as she motioned to the desk. He pulled out the chair for her and she retook her place there, with him looming over her, a massive, handsome distraction. "Let me show you where I feel you can better organize."

CHAPTER NINE

Marcus leaned over Annabelle's shoulder, doing his level best not to be utterly distracted by the jasmine scent of her hair. The only reason he could maintain control was because the things she was saying were so damn fascinating.

He had spent years quietly watching this woman, intrigued by her beauty and poise, picturing her body beneath his and her smile turned on him like a light.

Now he found he was just as intrigued by her intelligence as by anything else. Annabelle not only understood the basic tenants of running a business, but her thoughts on how to reorganize his books were not to be ignored. She had even caught a few mistakes he or Abbot had made in accounting.

"I should hire you," he said with a laugh.

Her head jerked up and she slowly turned to look at him from the corner of her eye. "I—what did you say?"

"You are right you have a head for business," he explained. "I could use your acumen."

She shifted, and for a moment he was able to see the smooth curve of the tops of her breasts through the gap in her gown. His body tensed and all the desire he had been trying to tamp down rushed back to the surface and made him hard.

"I-I would be happy to look over these things when I come here," she said softly. "If you need me."

Marcus leaned in, smelling her hair deeply. "You should

not talk to me about what I need, Annabelle. Not when I can still taste you on my lips."

She gasped at the highly inappropriate comment and pushed to her feet. As she spun toward him, she staggered into his arms. He caught her there, drawing her against him so he could feel every inch of her soft, supple body. How many ways could he have her, claim her? Here in his office, downstairs in the playrooms, out in the damn street if it pleased them? He was overcome by the desire for her and he cupped her face to draw her closer.

He felt her breath on his mouth, the flutter of her body as she molded to him even closer. He was about to claim her lips when there was a sharp rap on the door behind them.

Annabelle let out a little cry and wrestled from his arms so suddenly that she nearly deposited herself in the floor next to his desk. She covered her pink cheeks with her shaking hands, refusing to meet his gaze.

With a scowl, he turned toward the door. "What?" he barked out.

The door opened slowly and the guard from the bottom of the stairs slowly poked his head inside, his face pale as if he expected punishment.

"I'm sorry to interrupt, sir, but Mr. Flynn has arrived."

Marcus squeezed his eyes shut. It was too easy to get caught up in his ever-mounting desire for Annabelle and forget she hadn't come here for him, for whatever heat was developing between them. She was here for her brother and he could see, as he turned toward her, that she would not be deterred from her mission to save a man Marcus feared did not want to be saved.

Annabelle repositioned her mask and tried to keep up with Marcus's long strides as he led her across the main hall of the club. Around her, the passions and pleasures continued, but his purposeful stride didn't seem to indicate he had any interest in them.

She couldn't understand why. The moans and flashes of flesh from the corner of her eye made her own body edgy and wet. But earlier he had seemed to have great interest in her, so it couldn't be that he was a monk. It was all infinitely confusing and arousing in ways she did not wish to be aroused.

He produced a key from his pocket and swiftly unlocked a narrow door next to the hall. Without saying a word, he clasped her hand and drew her into a dark passageway, then closed and locked the door behind him.

In the dark, her other senses were obliterated, and she stopped breathing as she fought to control the panic that suddenly rose up in her chest.

"What are you—" she began, but he spun around and lifted two rough fingers to her lips. She had a very sudden and powerful urge to lick those fingers.

"Shhh," he said, his voice low. "Let your eyes adjust and I'll show you."

She pulled away from his distracting hand and squeezed her eyes shut. After a slow count to ten, she opened them again and found that the hall wasn't so dim anymore. There were small slivers of light all along its length, though she couldn't understand their source. They weren't candles or lamps.

"Ready?" Marcus asked, still whispering.

"Yes, I suppose," she said, hesitant when she still didn't understand in the slightest *what* they were doing here. He could do almost anything to her.

Which should have been far less pleasing a notion than it was.

He caught her hand once more, his rough fingers stroking over hers, and drew her down the hall. After a few steps, he stopped and gently slid a small portion of the wall away. A column of bright light cascaded into the hall, and she gasped.

It was a peephole, leading into one of the chambers on the

other side of the hall. That explained the small lights. There were half a dozen of the peepholes lining the wall, and even when they were closed a small portion of the light from the room they revealed came around the opening.

"Mar—"

He held a finger to his lips to signal her to be silent and merely motioned toward the room. She gritted her teeth and stepped up to look inside.

There was a large table in the room, and at it sat five men…and her brother. Crispin faced the place where she stood, but seemed oblivious to her presence as he laughed and dealt out a round of cards to his companions.

It was rare to see him unguarded and…well, sober anymore. She drank in the sight of his still-bright face and the smile that could make anyone forgive him anything if he used it to his advantage. She lifted a hand to cover her lips, afraid she would call out to him if only to see him put those clear eyes turned on her for a moment.

But her joy faded as he lifted a tumbler of scotch at his side and made a salute to the others before he downed it in one swig.

With a sigh, she turned away. Marcus stared at her a moment, then quietly slid the spying mechanism closed. They were silent in the dark for a while as she gathered herself. Then she turned toward his shape in the darkness.

"Do you have these spying holes to ensure your patrons are not cheating?" she asked.

She heard his low chuckle, and even though she couldn't see his handsome face, the dark sound hit her in the gut and then wound lower, lower, until her sex began to tingle. She scowled.

"Am I amusing?"

He stopped laughing, but there was still the sound of a smile in his voice as he said, "No, not at all. But I'm not certain you want to know the answer to your question."

"I would not have asked it if I didn't," she said, peevish in the face of his teasing.

He hesitated. "Very well. No, my dear, not to prevent cheating. We let our patrons work out those details, and most are quite honest when it comes to their cards."

"Then why?" she asked, trying to think of some reason beyond her suggestion.

He caught her hand and drew her to the next peephole in the hall. When he slid it open, she leaned forward and her eyes went wide.

In this chamber, she could see a large bed against the opposite wall, and on it were the tangled bodies of a man and woman. They were both completely naked and the man was lying between the woman's legs, licking her most private of areas with great gusto. She arched with every slurping lick, crying out in pure ecstasy.

Annabelle spun away, and Marcus closed the little door. She leaned against the opposite wall, wishing she could read his expression in the dark.

"There are some who get a thrill out of watching others," he explained. "And being watched."

"You mean they *know* there may be people in the hallway observing them?" she asked, utterly shocked at the notion.

He nodded. "There are many private rooms in the club which do not have these devices, so those who come to these rooms are well aware they may be watched."

"Why not just do their business in the main hall?" she asked, her mind bombarding her with so many sensual images that she could hardly think straight.

"There is something more erotic about being 'caught' rather than being blatant."

She covered her hot face with her hands, trying to control her breathing and failing miserably at the act.

"I think, Miss Flynn, that you very much like watching," he said.

She took a step away in shock. "How dare you?" she whispered.

He reached out, and his fingers dragged her hand down slowly. "How dare I? I have watched you observe those in the main hall when you come through. And I heard your breath catch—not just in shock, but in desire—when I opened the window to this room. In fact, I think if I opened it again, you would not be able to help yourself but to look at what that couple will do next."

"You go too far," she whispered, but she couldn't put any heat into her words. She couldn't even deny he was correct.

"I know I do," he said, his voice now rough. "But I cannot seem to help myself."

He slid the little window open a second time, and the light hit Annabelle's face like a slap. She tried to turn away from it, to prove to Marcus that he was wrong about her. But the moans of the woman in the room had now turned to moans from both the participants and she found herself turning toward the scene, edging closer until she could see the couple again.

They had shifted on the bed so that now the lady was straddling her lover's face. While he continued to lick her, she leaned over him, sucking his member deep into her throat. Annabelle caught her breath. She had seen such things in naughty books over the years, but never in person. Now she stared, mouth agape, unable to look away even though she was now proving Marcus right in the most humiliating way possible.

The couple continued to writhe together until the lady suddenly threw her head back and began to cry out, not in pain, but in pleasure. Her body quaked, grinding down over her lover until she collapsed against his body weakly.

He sat up and gently shifted their position until he was behind her. His hard cock pressed to her entrance, and he grunted as he shoved forward, entering her slickness without any hesitation.

Annabelle gripped her fists at her sides, trying not to feel the tingling pressure that worked its way through her body as she watched the couple join in erotic bliss. But when Marcus stepped behind her and his arms came around her, she nearly collapsed on the floor in a puddle of needy desire.

He said nothing, just pushed her hair aside and began to suckle her neck as they watched the couple before them. The man was taking the woman with great passion now, driving into her as she screamed out pleasure with every thrust.

Marcus's hands covered her breasts, and Annabelle leaned back into him with a shuddering sigh. His fingers were like magic as he plucked her nipples through the thin fabric, jolting her with every magnificent stroke.

Inside the room, the man on the bed let out a shout and withdrew, spurting his seed across his lady's back before he flipped her over, collapsed against her, and they kissed deeply.

Marcus reached forward and slid the window shut, putting them in darkness again. But he didn't withdraw from her. Instead he turned her until her back pressed against the wall and leaned in, cupping her backside and lifting her into an erection that was far more impressive than the one possessed by the man she'd just watch claim his lover.

She gasped, and Marcus caught the sound with his lips, kissing her deeply, tasting her like she was a fine wine and he was dying of thirst. She wrapped her arms around his shoulders, holding tightly as he ground against her.

His lips moved from hers, sliding across her jaw and her neck. She tilted her head for greater access as she whispered, "Marcus."

He froze, and in the darkness she heard his breath hitch. Then, unexpectedly, he set her back on her feet and took a long step away.

"Marcus?" she whispered, watching his shadow in the dimness. "Did I—did I do something wrong?"

"No." He sounded like he was clenching his teeth. "Not at all, Annabelle. I only fear that if I don't stop I'm going to do something that cannot be undone. And that you would likely regret."

She blinked. He meant he would take her. *Claim* her. And

while there was a wild moment where she considered hurtling herself at him to force him to do just that, a tiny voice in her head told her that if she allowed it, her future would be over. No respectable man would want to marry her if she had surrendered herself to a scoundrel in the hallway of a sex club. And even though she could hide the truth for a while, she had read enough to know that she wouldn't be able to pretend she was untouched on her wedding night.

"Marcus," she whispered.

He held up a shadowy hand. "You should go, Annabelle. Leave now. I'll be certain to keep a close eye on Crispin and protect him if he needs me to do so. But if you stay even a moment longer, I can't guarantee I would be able to make the same promise to protect you. So *go*."

His voice lifted on the last word, the strain obvious. Annabelle turned and all but ran down the hall away from him. Away from the desire it seemed neither of them could control. Away from the heat in his voice that told her he was in danger of losing himself. And away from the need that made her body ache and her heart throb only for this man who could never be what she needed.

CHAPTER TEN

Another Society party was in full swing, and once again Annabelle stood on the sidelines, watching the others dance and laugh. Georgina spun by in the arms of an earl or a viscount or some such rot, grinning as if she had won a bet in the club.

Annabelle turned and clenched her fist. Ladies did not bet in clubs. Ladies did not *go* to clubs. Ladies did not watch other people make love to each other in clubs while wicked club owners did magnificent things with their big, strong hands.

"Stop," she said out loud, in the hopes she could clear her mind of the thoughts that had been tormenting her for two days, since she last saw Marcus.

"Miss Flynn, are you quite well?"

She froze at the voice behind her. The voice that had apparently heard her talking to herself. She slowly turned to face the man and gasped when she realized it was the Earl of Claybrook who had approached her.

She forced a smile. "My lord, I did not see you there."

He tilted his head and his kind eyes flickered over her. "I would say not. You seemed quite engrossed in your thoughts."

Annabelle let out a nervous laugh that was just a touch too loud. If only he knew.

"Yes, my thoughts," she said with a shake of her head. "But what can we do—we cannot control them, can we?"

He wrinkled his brow now, concern clear on his face. "I suppose not. But perhaps I can distract you from them."

Annabelle smiled, even though it felt very false. "That would be very kind of you."

"Perhaps a walk would do you good."

She frowned. No one had asked her to dance yet. And as Georgina had pointed out not an hour before, the longer that denial went on, the less likely it was that anyone would do so. Which meant her Season would be an abysmal failure.

But they'd had formulated a plan for this. One Annabelle abhorred, but she put it into motion regardless with a pretty pout. "Oh, I did so hope to dance this evening. I do *adore* dancing."

She saw Claybrook's gaze shift to the dance floor ever so slightly, and the expression on his face told her he was reluctant to be the first to grant her a little acceptance. He seemed to battle internally for a moment, but then he offered her his arm.

"I could not deny you this greatest wish, of course," he said.

She almost sagged in relief as they entered the dance floor. The spinning couples stared as they began to join in the steps, and Annabelle wished her cheeks didn't darken with a blush. She hated for them to see that weakness.

"Your dark thoughts, would you care to share them?" Claybrook asked. "Perhaps I could be of assistance."

Annabelle faltered in her steps. The man did not know what he was asking, that was for certain. If he did, he would likely shove her from his arms with cries of "Jezebel!" on his very proper lips.

"I only had an unexpected encounter with a person," she explained slowly. "Nothing for you to trouble yourself with, my lord."

He shook his head. "It must have been very unpleasant."

"Far less than it should have been," she whispered, once again mobbed by thoughts of Marcus and his hands and mouth.

"I beg your pardon?" Claybrook asked.

She cursed herself for these thoughts and smiled. "I will survive, I assure you."

"I-I recognize this must be difficult for you," he said. "But you are holding yourself with nothing but dignity. It will get easier, I'm sure."

She jerked her face toward his at the unexpected words. He really was quite handsome, despite being nearly fifteen years her senior. He wasn't Marcus, of course, with his strong jaw and big hands and casual certainty in all he did and said.

But Marcus was something she could never, ever have.

"Thank you," she whispered.

"Would you mind very much if I requested your brother's permission to call on you in the near future?" Claybrook asked.

Her breath stuck in her throat. A call! That was exactly what she had come to Society to gain, the attention of a very proper man like this one. And he was certainly not the worst of the bunch.

She nodded. "I would like that. I hope you will."

The music ended and Claybrook released her with a proper bow that distanced them again. "Thank you, Miss Flynn. And a very good evening to you."

She curtseyed and took a path back to Georgina, who was now waiting for her on the edge of the dance floor with a wide grin on her face. But even though she smiled back to her friend, inside there was a part of her that was screaming. After all, she had what she wanted—the attention of a proper gentleman.

And yet the only thing she could think of was the most improper man she had ever met.

Marcus stared at the ledger before him, but he couldn't concentrate on the numbers. Not when Annabelle's swirling handwriting filled the margins of the document. Not when he swore he could still smell her on the papers, on his jacket, on his skin. For two days, he had thought of nothing else but seeing her, talking to her, having her. And while he could give himself some relief with his own hand, that was temporary at best and within half an hour of finding release the tormenting thoughts always returned.

It was a sickness. That was the only way he could describe his obsession.

There was a light knock on the door, and he breathed a sigh of relief at the interruption.

"Yes?"

The door opened to reveal Vale. Since the older servant very rarely visited him in his office during open hours and especially so late on a very busy Saturday night, there was no doubt something had happened.

"What is it?" he asked. "Is everything well?"

"Yes, sir. I believe so. But you have a visitor." The butler frowned. "Miss Jasmine has returned."

"Jasmine," Marcus repeated in disbelief.

He'd honestly thought he'd frightened Annabelle away permanently with his ardor in the viewing hallway. It would have been better if that were true. And yet his entire spirit lifted at the knowledge she was so unexpectedly there.

"Should I allow her entry or send her away since we did not expect her?"

"Have her brought to me," Marcus said, unable to keep the thrill from his tone. "I will see her."

Vale nodded and stepped from the room. Once he was gone, Marcus jumped to his feet. Why would she come here tonight? Crispin was not in attendance, he had heard nothing of his friend being in trouble…why would she be here, especially after his behavior two nights before?

He didn't have a chance to ponder further, for at that moment Vale reappeared, only this time with a masked Annabelle at his side.

"Sir," he said, motioning her inside.

She hesitated at the entryway, her dark brown eyes flitting across the chamber and finally settling on Marcus to reveal questions, desire and torment that somehow matched his own.

"You may go, Vale," he said softly, and the servant seemed eager to do so, leaving Annabelle in the doorway without another word.

She stepped past the threshold and reached behind her, dragging the door shut slowly and then leaning back against the barrier. She did not speak, even as she lifted her hands to remove the same pretty peacock mask she had worn here two nights before.

"Annabelle," he said after clearing his throat. "Why are you here?"

She shook her head rather than answer and paced into the chamber, past him to the window that looked out over his debauched empire. Her fists clenched against the wide sill and her breath left her lungs in a shuddering sigh.

"Annabelle," he repeated.

She stared down at the writhing crowd below, tears bright in her eyes, ready to fall down her pink cheeks. Marcus stared, uncertain of what had upset her so much but desperate to help her.

"What is wrong?" he asked. "Is it Crispin?"

She shook her head, and finally she spoke. "My brother, no. No. Is he here?"

"Not tonight. I would have sent word to you if he had come." He moved forward, hesitating to touch her because it seemed whenever he did so, he lost all sense of control. "Annabelle, tell me what is wrong."

"I don't want to want these things," she whispered, a desperate confession she seemed to make to herself more than to him. "I don't want to feel these things. I'm trying to be better, I'm trying to be proper and yet I can't stop...wanting *this*."

His eyes went wide as her trembling hand lifted ever so slightly to point at the scene below. "These dark thoughts torment me when I am here," she continued, "but also in my bed at home. I can't stop them, Marcus. I can't even keep them from intruding upon my normal day."

He drew back, suddenly understanding. "Are you talking about *desire*?"

She swallowed a sob. "Yes." She spun on him suddenly. "How do you control it, Marcus? Surrounded as you are by all these…things…these people surrendering to their most base needs. I've heard them whisper below that I am the first woman you've taken to your office in years. And when we walked through the hall two nights ago, you hardly looked at those engaging in such wicked acts. Somehow you are able to control your lust. How do you do it?"

Marcus could hardly breathe. Annabelle was staring up at him, eyes wide and misty, hands shaking with what he now realized was need she couldn't control. Knowing her body was on the edge, knowing she was likely wet with desire…those things made his body hard and hot.

"I don't know if I'm the best person with whom to discuss control, Annabelle," he ground out. "Because when it comes to you, it is nearly impossible for me to exercise it."

Her wild stare cleared for a moment, comprehension dawning on her face. "Wh-what?"

"You heard me," he growled. "I want you, Annabelle, I have wanted you for years. And whenever I am within arm's reach of you, I ache to snatch you against me and claim you in every way my wicked mind can conjure."

Her breath shortened, her tongue darted out to wet her lips, and Marcus almost groaned with the fire she stoked in him. At some point that inferno would explode and he feared he would destroy them both with it.

Which was why her being here was such a terrible, terrible mistake. One he had no intention of rectifying.

"But you don't claim me," she whispered and to his surprise, she moved closer in the face of his finally voiced need. "Even when you kiss me, you don't overpower when you could so easily do so. Tell me how so I that I won't want to…want to…"

She trailed off with a hitch of breath and a reddening of her cheeks.

Marcus squeezed his eyes shut. What he *should* tell her was that she should run away and never come back. That she should forget their arrangement, forget they had kissed, that the only way to end the spiraling heat between them was to never see each other again.

And yet he didn't. Instead, he took the one small step that separated them and caught her elbow. Slowly, he dragged her against him until her breasts were flat against his chest, until his cock pushed against her belly, until he could feel her breath on his face.

"What if the solution to our problem is not to resist or control ourselves at all? What if the only way to save ourselves is to give in?"

She gave a strangled moan and pulled from his embrace. "You do not know the temptation you are creating, Marcus. But I can't give in."

"Why?" he asked, knowing the answer, but needing to hear it.

"Because I'm in the midst of trying to catch a husband," she said softly, her gaze flitting away from him as if she were embarrassed by the admission.

"What we did here would be no impediment. I would certainly not march into a ballroom and declare that you were mine. You would not be mine, no matter what we did." He said the words and his chest ached.

Her lips pursed. "Perhaps you are right that any man courting me might not know what I did alone with you before we wed. But after…" She cleared her throat, and her cheeks flamed with bright red color. "I have been led to believe that a man would know if his bride was not a virgin. I could not commit a fraud against a man I call husband. It would be a terrible way to start a lifelong union."

He couldn't control the shock that jolted through him. He had plenty of experience with women of rank and privilege. They filled his hall every night, exuberantly giving in to their every sexual whim. Many did not come here to explore with their husbands, but behind those same spouse's backs. They didn't give a damn about their vows.

And here Annabelle was, not having made any yet, and she honored them regardless.

"Is the state of your virginity your only resistance to what I propose?" he asked.

She swallowed hard, her eyes bright with desire. "Yes. I know it makes me sound like a wanton, but yes."

"It doesn't make you sound like a wanton," he assured her. "It makes you sound alive, Annabelle."

She frowned, and he could see she wasn't certain of what he said. Her foray into the highest Society made her question herself, and he hated it.

"But I can give you what you need," he continued, voice shaking. "I can get what *I* need, without penetrating you. And no matter how much I want to do that—" He somehow stifled a moan. "—I vow to you that I will not, Annabelle. I can give you pleasure, you can give me the same, and I won't spoil you for whatever man is lucky enough to make you his bride. Will that satisfy you?"

CHAPTER ELEVEN

Annabelle blinked. She couldn't believe she was having this conversation with Marcus. Or more to the point, that a man like Marcus, who could obviously have any woman he desired, would offer her something like this. Could he truly mean he would give her pleasure, allow her to purge her darkest desires without ruining her for someone else?

It was thrilling, but deep inside she felt a tug of unpleasant disappointment she refused to analyze or acknowledge.

"Annabelle," he pressed, his voice barely carrying in the quiet room. "I'm afraid you must agree or disagree to my proposal. I wish I could read your mind, but I cannot."

"I'm sorry. I think I understand what you mean," she whispered. "I've read books, I've seen things here that look pleasurable without fully claiming. If you would be willing to leave my virginity intact, then I would…I would very much want what you offer."

The moment the words were spoken, Marcus moved on her. He pinned her so her back was to the glass, pressed against the cool surface and kissed her with such wild abandon that she was almost afraid. Here was a man always in control who couldn't stop himself when he was with her.

But he had made a promise, and she had the feeling he honored his vows. She relaxed in his arms, giving in to the kiss she had dreamed of since the last time they touched. She felt his manhood against her stomach and arched against it, smiling when the movement elicited a moan from him that disappeared into her mouth.

They kissed for what seemed like an eternity until finally he drew back and said, "Come with me."

"Why?" she asked, uncertain if her shaking legs would allow for movement.

He smiled. "Because anyone who looked up from the hall could see you pressed against the glass. And I don't want an audience the first time I make you come."

She blushed as she looked over her shoulder. For the first time, the debauchery below didn't interest her as much as the man across from her. She took the hand he reached out to her and let him take her across the room toward the chamber she had spied upon just a few days before.

"Why do you have a bedchamber here?" she asked, uncertain if she wanted to know the answer, since it likely included passionate encounters with ladies who gave him everything he desired without limit.

His eyebrows lifted as his hand hesitated on the handle to the chamber door. "And how do you know I have a bedchamber attached to my office?"

She blushed but refused to lie. "I, er, did some spying the first time I was left here alone."

"And you went into my chamber?" he asked.

She nodded. "And saw your bed and wanted..." He opened the door to reveal the very bed she spoke of. "I wanted what we're about to do," she admitted at last.

"I can fulfill that fantasy," he promised, drawing her in, closing and locking the door and then pulling her into his arms for another deep, probing kiss.

She felt him turn her toward the bed, then his fingers found the fastenings on the back of her gown. He wasn't clumsy as he unhooked her, even though he couldn't see what he was doing. His fingers were warm as they brushed along her spine through her thin chemise, but she shivered from the stroke of them regardless.

He drew her gown down, and Annabelle turned her face as he tugged the dress off her arms to hang at her hips.

"I have imagined you like this a hundred times," he mused.

Her breath caught. That was the second time he had spoken of desiring her for far longer than the short time she had been coming to his club. Could that be true? Could this man have wanted her for that long?

It was a thrilling idea. But oh, so very dangerous.

"Just like this?" she managed to squeak out before she hooked her fingers into the folds of the gown and let it fall at her feet. She kicked it away. "Or like this?"

"That," he admitted, staring at her from head to toe. Her flimsy chemise did very little to cover her. The fabric allowed the dusky tips of her breasts to be outlined against the silk and the chemise was so short that if she turned around he would have seen the swell of her bottom without her having to bend over even a touch.

No man had ever seen her like this, though she had examined herself in this state in the mirror so many times. She had watched as she touched herself, fascinated by how her body changed when she found pleasure.

Would it be different when she received that pleasure not from her own fingers, but from this man? Would she ever be the same, even if he left her hymen intact and no one would be the wiser?

"I have also pictured you in less," he whispered, breaking into the thoughts he couldn't read and moving toward her. He dragged his fingers down the apex of her body until his hands fisted the bottom edge of her chemise. Never breaking eye contact with her, he lifted the silk up and over her head and tossed it aside with the rest of her gown.

She was naked now. With a man. With *this* man. Slowly, she moved her hands to cover herself, but he caught them to push them away.

"Don't," he murmured, his green gaze intense and imprisoning. "I want to look at you. Worship you."

She could hardly breathe now as he burned a brand into her with the heat of his stare. She shook at the intimacy of it, the way she couldn't move or think or do anything except stand before him and allow him whatever he desired.

"Please," she whispered, her voice broken. "I want to look at you too."

His gaze jerked up. "I'm not nearly so beautiful as you are," he warned her.

She reached out and slid a hand down his chest. She felt the muscles ripple beneath his clothes, and her fingers trembled. "I cannot believe that is true, Marcus."

She saw the strain on his face, the mask of desire he was just keeping under the surface so that he wouldn't overwhelm her with it. He stepped back and unbuttoned his jacket. After he'd tossed it aside, he went to work on the rest, but he took his time unbuttoning buttons and unhooking hooks. It seemed to take forever, but finally he tugged his crisp white shirt over his head and let her see his chest.

She held back a gasp of pleasure as she stared. "You are a liar," she managed to squeak out as she held out her hand to press her fingers to his flesh.

"How so?" he asked, tone strained.

"*You* are beautiful. Like a god."

She drank him in, examining him in the firelight. He was thickly muscled, with broad, defined shoulders. She moved closer, circling him to look at his back, also cut with muscle. But something else too. As she began to turn to come back to face him, she saw the slashing mark of a scar that started in the middle of his back and curled around his side, disappearing under his arm.

"Marcus," she whispered.

He caught her hand and brought her back to face him. His expression was tight and drawn. "No."

"But—"

"No," he repeated. "Just touch me, Annabelle. Touch me."

She wanted to ask more, but she could see what the results would be. If she pried, he would push her away for good and this would be over before it began.

She couldn't risk that. She simply had to accept that their relationship would be one of passion only, not shared secrets. With a shuddering sigh, she set her questions about the scar aside and leaned forward, dragging first her fingertips across his bare chest and then her lips.

"Mmmm."

His hand came down to tangle in her hair. "What?"

"I wondered how you would taste," she said between licking kisses. "Delicious."

He cupped her chin and tilted it up, his green eyes glittering in the dark. Then he crushed his mouth to hers and shoved her the rest of the way back until she tumbled into his bed.

She yelped as he bracketed his hands over her, imprisoning her in a cage of his hot, hard body. He crushed his mouth to her throat and sucked hard until pleasure merged with the slightest of pains and her back arched.

"Very nice," he purred, moving lower to trace her collarbone with his tongue, lower until his mouth crested over the swell of her breast.

Annabelle cried out when he closed his hot lips around her right nipple, and her hands came down to clench in his thick, crisp hair. He smiled against her flesh, but didn't let up in his relentless and pleasurable assault. He swirled the tip of his tongue around the nipple, he sucked hard on it until it tingled and the answering reverberations spread throughout her entire being. And just when she thought she would lose all reason, he abandoned her right breast and turned her attention to her left, repeating each and every act until she panted with desire and lifted into him helplessly.

"And now I'm going to find out how *you* taste," he said, lifting his head to look at her.

She gasped, her mind shifting wildly to the images from two nights ago, when she had watched the man and woman through the peephole downstairs. The man had been feasting on the woman's most private parts.

"You—you can't mean—" she began.

He chuckled, his eyes lit up with dark and dangerous desire and slid down her body, kissing her stomach, her thigh. Finally, he pushed her legs open wide, draping one over his shoulder and settled between them, looking at her sex.

"Don't you want to know how it feels?" he asked, his tone teasing and taunting. "Because I know that watching this act made you wet and ready. Just as you are now."

"Please," she said, clenching the coverlet in her hands.

He smiled up at her. "Please what? Please do this or please stop?"

"Do it," she cried out, her voice cracking. "Please!"

The teasing left his face and he looked back at her wet body. Slowly, he peeled the outer lips of her sex back and gently stroked just the tip of his finger over her. She jolted at the intimate contact.

She was being touched *there*. By this man. It was as if every dark fantasy, every wicked impulse, had come to this. She should have hated herself, but she didn't. She only arched her hips, trying to drive him closer, trying to make him do what she wanted but couldn't express with words.

He didn't deny her. His mouth came down, settling over her sex. First it was merely a tender, close-mouthed brush of his lips. Still, she lit on fire. His breath was like sin and his lips impossibly soft against the sensitive flesh. But almost immediately the tenderness of that kiss changed. He darted out the tip of his tongue and sliced it across her entrance not once, but twice, three times.

"Marcus," she whimpered.

It was shocking how much sensation he could coax from her body with such a slow, easy seduction. Oh, she had felt pleasure before, from her own hand. But not like this. Never like this.

This was explosive. Powerful. Inescapable.

And she loved each and every moment.

He held her thighs apart and delved deeper, tasting her folds, piercing her entrance and finally swirling his tongue around and around the sensitive nub of her clitoris.

She arched as the sudden wave of her orgasm hit her with a power she'd never experienced before. As he suckled the tender collection of nerves, wave after wave of pleasure hit her, building higher and higher, never ending, until she lost all control and her cries echoed in the room around them. And he licked on, forcing more from her, taking every drop of her passion until she collapsed, limp and languid on his pillows.

He stroked a few more times with his tongue and then grinned as he moved up her body. He bracketed her in with his big arms and stared down at her, examining her face in the firelight.

"That was quite something, Miss Annabelle Flynn," he said.

She could hardly catch her breath. He was so outrageously handsome with his lips slick from her juices and his eyes still bright with the passion they had shared.

And she wanted oh so much more.

"It was indeed," she murmured, the wicked woman she normally kept leashed inside of her loosened for the moment. She caught his chin and drew him down. "But I don't think we're finished yet."

She caught his mouth with hers, tasting the earthy flavor of her sex still on his lips. She was surprised at how arousing it was to taste herself there. He moaned against her, relaxing his body so that he fully covered her. His weight was heaven, as was the insistent pressure of his cock against her thigh through his trousers.

"Undress," she whispered as she pulled away. She pressed a kiss to his bare neck.

He pulled back, his green eyes wide. "Annabelle—"

"You would not deny me, would you?" she asked. "Deny me the ability to please you as you have pleased me?"

He stared at her. "I would want that more than anything, but perhaps you aren't ready to—"

She lifted a hand to cover his mouth. "Marcus, if this *thing* we share is truly meant to purge all my wicked urges, all your desires, then we can't hold back. Please, let me do this. Let me feel this."

She could see him struggling with some faint gentlemanly urge to protect her from what she wanted but didn't fully understand. But the wickedness in him prevailed at last and he pushed away from her to get to his feet. He toed off his boots and then his hands hesitated at the fastenings of his trousers.

She sat up and smiled at him. "Marcus, I trust you."

"You shouldn't," he growled. "My God, you don't know the things I want to do to you."

She laughed even though his words moved her beyond measure. "Take off your clothes and then we can negotiate."

He stripped out of his trousers, revealing toned thighs and calves and the hard, long length of his cock. She drew back a fraction. He was huge, perfectly in proportion with the rest of his body. She couldn't help but think of her tight sex. Was it even possible he could fit inside of her?

Not that it mattered since he wouldn't. He had promised her. She had vowed the same.

"Have you changed your mind?" he asked, a wry smile tilting her lips as she stared at him.

"Not at all," she reassured him, licking her lips. "But I would very much like to…to touch you."

He stepped to the edge of the bed, finally within reach. "As you said, Annabelle, I would not deny you. I couldn't even if I wanted to."

"Good." She extended her hand and gently stroked the entire length of him with the back of her fingers. To her surprise, his flesh was soft, stretched tight over the hardness beneath. She moved to sit on her knees and stroked him again, marveling at the feel of him.

He gritted his teeth, his air exiting his lungs in great gulps as he watched her. "You do test a man," he grunted.

She smiled and wrapped her fist around him. "I don't intend to test you, Marcus. Only please you."

She stroked him, watching his face as she did so. She wanted to read his reactions, to see if her instincts led her true or if she needed to change. The veins in his neck bulged and he dropped his head back with a long moan as she stroked over and over.

It was heady to give him such pleasure, to watch this man, so much more experienced than she was, begin to shake as she worked her hand over him. And yet, it wasn't quite enough. She thought once more about the man and woman in the room two nights before. He had tasted her, and now Marcus had done the same.

But the lady had tasted her man as well. Leaning forward, Annabelle darted out her tongue and gently stroked it over the very tip of his member.

He jolted at the contact and jerked his face down to look at her.

"Annabelle," he breathed, both a warning and a plea.

She smiled up at him and then covered him fully with her mouth. She took as much as she could, pressing her tongue to the underside of his cock before she gently sucked him.

He swayed slightly, and suddenly his hand came up to rest on her head, though she wasn't certain if that was for encouragement or to keep from falling over in a heap. Either way, she kept him in her mouth and looked up at him.

"Woman, you may kill me," he muttered, almost more to himself than to her. "Move, Annabelle, move over me like you saw those people doing while we watched."

She nodded slightly and did as he asked, sliding him almost all the way out of her mouth and then taking him as far as she could again. To balance herself, she gripped the base of his shaft and stroked there too, letting the wetness from her mouth lubricate her actions.

Although she had only ever seen the act in a few books and then in the chamber here in the club, she found she truly liked performing it. There was something immensely powerful about knowing that *her* actions were what made Marcus grunt above her, his hips flexing and his muscles straining. Powerful and highly erotic. Her own sex, so recently satisfied by his tongue, grew even wetter as she worked. She ached for him to touch her again.

But she set that aside, instead focusing on him. She increased the movements of her mouth bit by bit, taking him deeper, sucking as he entered and exited, and finally he moaned low in his throat. To her surprise, he jerked himself from her mouth just before he cried out an incoherent sound of pleasure and his thick, white essence shot from the head of him.

She stared up at him, captivated by the look of pleasure on his face, the one that made him look younger and more innocent. He panted as he collapsed forward, supporting himself on the edge of the bed.

She leaned toward him, pressing her forehead to the back of his head, and they rested that way for a while until both their breathing returned to normal.

"That was wonderful," she whispered after what seemed like an eternity had passed.

He lifted his head, forcing her to move. His face was mere inches from hers and he smiled. "I would have to agree. I didn't expect you to be so proficient, Miss Flynn."

She shrugged, though the compliment made her blush. "I-I told you, I've read things and now I've seen things. And all I had to do was pay attention to your reactions to see what you liked."

He nodded slowly. "That best lovers always do."

He leaned in and kissed her, this time gently. She longed to melt into the kiss, to continue what they had started but he pulled away before she could do so.

"It is late, Annabelle," he said softly. "And you should go home before someone discovers you missing."

She pursed her lips. "Will I—will I be allowed to return?"

He tilted his head. "For your brother or for this?"

She slid off the bed and straightened up, trying to have as much strength as she could when she was utterly naked. "Either. Both."

"I already told you that you could come here to observe Crispin," he said. "This new arrangement changes nothing about the original. And if you still feel those dark and wicked urges you tell me you want to purge in my bed, then I welcome the chance to have another taste."

Annabelle shivered from head to toe at the way the word *taste* rolled from his tongue. He was teasing her, although it didn't seem like he was doing it unkindly.

"I do want more," she admitted. "Both received and given."

His smile faded a fraction and darkness lit up in his green stare. "Then I cannot wait until next time we are together. But for now, get your dress and we will do our best to fix you."

But as Annabelle stooped to get the gown she had discarded not so long ago, she couldn't help but wonder if she would ever be "fixed". After all, the desire she felt in her heart, in her body for Marcus didn't seem diminished in the slightest by this encounter.

Already she was dreaming of the next one. And wishing she could have more than just his intimate kiss.

CHAPTER TWELVE

Marcus shifted with discomfort and straightened his cravat for what seemed like the tenth time since he had been left alone in the parlor of the Duke of Hartholm. His friend...or was it former friend? Either way, Rafe had called for him two days after Marcus's encounter with Annabelle, demanding he come to Rafe's home.

And now Marcus waited for the arrival of the duke and wondered why the hell he had been summoned here. Of course, one reason came to mind.

Annabelle. Rafe knew about Annabelle. And if that were true, this conversation could easily end with calls for a duel at dawn over her honor. Marcus would deserve no less. After all, he was taking advantage of a lady, wasn't he? Turning her desires against her in order to fulfill a fantasy he'd had for years?

Only it hadn't felt like he was manipulating her when she sucked his cock into her throat and gave him pleasure unlike any he'd known...perhaps in his entire life.

The door opened and Rafe stepped inside. The sight of the duke shoved all inappropriate thoughts of Annabelle aside, but Marcus remained cautious as he approached him.

"Your Grace," he said, holding out a hand.

Rafe took it without hesitation, shaking it with enthusiasm. "We're in my home, Rivers—as I told you before, please call me Flynn."

Marcus wrinkled his brow. "It still seems highly inappropriate for me to do so."

"It is," Rafe admitted. "But any time I can have a moment where I pretend I am not duke, I'll take it. And when I'm with friends, I remain as I ever was, I assure you."

Marcus watched Rafe move to the side bar and pour two drinks. Was it possible for a man to become titled and remain the same? He couldn't imagine that was true. All those with titles Marcus knew held themselves a little apart, reveling in the fame and fortune most hadn't earned but had stumbled into due to a twist of fate in birth family and order.

And yet, as Rafe turned with a grin and held out a glass of scotch, his friend truly looked the same as he had a year ago, long before his inheritance.

"How is the club?" Rafe asked, motioning to the chairs before the fire.

Marcus took one and sipped the scotch before he spoke. "Very well, same as ever. Your membership remains, you know."

Rafe grinned. "I find I'm not tempted by such things now that I am wed."

Marcus lifted a brow. He had heard rumors of the beauty of Rafe's bride, Serafina, though he had never seen the lady in person. Everyone knew the tale of how the two had been forced to wed when Rafe inherited the dukedom and how they had been viciously attacked just weeks after that marriage.

He'd also heard that Rafe was completely in love with his wife.

"So it is true that you are happy in your choices…or what was thrust upon you without choice," Marcus offered, his tone free of judgment.

To his surprise, Rafe's face lit up. "Entirely so. There is no happier moment for me than the moment when Serafina was brought to me. The circumstances are not ideal, but the woman is…more than so. I adore her, Marcus. I love her with all that I am. And I realize you are shifting in discomfort now because you cannot believe I would wax poetic about a lady, but I am a changed man. Changed by love."

Marcus examined him closely. "Yes, I can see that. And if you are happy, then I am happy for you." He raised his glass. "To the duchess."

"To the *beautiful* duchess," Rafe agreed.

Their glasses clinked together and they each took another sip of the fine liquor. It was only after he had swallowed that Rafe's joyful expression fell a fraction.

"As pleasant as these topics are, I do not think we can pretend I invited you here for such conversation. You must know what troubles me."

Marcus pressed his lips together. "I may have a notion, yes."

His mind filled with images of Annabelle, spread out on his bed at the club. Annabelle arching beneath him. Annabelle peering over his books with her spectacles perched on her nose.

"I want to talk to you about Crispin."

Marcus blinked. "Er, yes, of course, Crispin."

Rafe's eyebrows lifted. "You seem surprised. Is there something else we should be discussing?"

Marcus shook his head. "No, of course your brother must be on your mind. I only thought you had made it perfectly plain that you refused to intervene until your brother asked for help. If you sense surprise, that is the only reason why."

Rafe nodded, accepting Marcus's lie. Marcus exhaled a long breath. His mind was truly addled if he could not control his expressions.

"I do stand by my assertion that Crispin must desire our help before any offer will make a difference," Rafe said, setting his scotch aside. There was no mistaking the troubled expression on his face. "But I do worry about him, regardless, and have been thinking about the situation since you last called on me. Crispin goes to the club a few times a week, doesn't he?"

Marcus nodded. "Twice a week, Tuesday and Thursday. And occasionally at other times."

"So he keeps our old schedule," Rafe mused. "And is he always out of control?"

Marcus pursed his lips. "Not always. I would say half the time he is his old self. He drinks, but it doesn't make him reckless, he gambles, but he doesn't lose too much, and he indulges in the ladies, though not as often as he once did."

"And the other half of the time?" Rafe asked, his tone suddenly soft.

Marcus shifted. "You know it isn't in my nature to share personal details of those who come into my club. It goes against the very spirit of the Donville Masquerade. But you and I have a history, Your Grace."

"Flynn," Rafe reminded him.

Marcus inclined his head. "Flynn. So I will tell you that when your brother loses control, he loses it spectacularly. He throws away hundreds, even thousands of pounds on cards and makes outrageous side bets. He drinks until he loses consciousness. Worse, there is no pleasure in these actions for him. I see his face and he is…"

"Lost," Rafe supplied.

Marcus nodded. "That is the best way to put it. But I can assure you further that he is looked after, at least in my establishment."

"By you?" Rafe pressed.

Marcus flashed again to Annabelle. "By myself and others. I will continue to report his actions to you if you would like."

"That gives me more relief that I could possibly express, especially since I know this situation has caused you trouble. Between Crispin and Annabelle—"

"Annabelle?" Marcus interrupted.

Rafe shook his head. "Well, yes, her little stunt climbing into your man's carriage and insisting to be taken to your club. You were graceful about the situation, but you could not have been pleased by her antics."

Marcus fought the urge to laugh rather inappropriately. "I actually find your sister rather fascinating."

"That is certainly one way to describe her," Rafe said with a sigh as he downed his drink in one swig.

Marcus arched a brow, suddenly driven not just to defend Annabelle, but also to take this opportunity to know more about her. "You would describe her another way?"

Rafe pushed to his feet and moved to the mantel, where he stood, leaning against the it and looking into the fire. "She is willful and wild. Not exactly unexpected considering her last name. But she is also…very smart."

"An interesting combination indeed," Marcus said, hoping he sounded mild.

"She spent her life getting into trouble and then wrangling to avoid it." Rafe shook her head. "I think my brother and I have not made it easy. The older I get, the more I realize how much she lost over the years because of us."

"Such as?" Marcus pressed.

"Friends. Standing. Perhaps even a proposal or two." Rafe scrubbed a hand over his face. "But now she has insisted upon her Season in the Upper Ten Thousand and she seems determined to wed a gentleman before the year is out."

Marcus flinched despite himself. This was only a reminder of what he already knew, what Annabelle herself had told him. She had never hidden her ambitions.

"Why is she so resolute in her decision?"

Rafe flopped himself back into his chair. "Who knows? Fear that Crispin or I will destroy her only chance? Desperation for acceptance and security in her future?"

"It sounds very boring for a woman such as her," Marcus said.

Rafe stared at him, and Marcus bit his tongue. Damn him for letting words slip that revealed too much. But Rafe only shrugged.

"Yes, I agree. I think she could do better than some fop

who would judge her for being her own lovely, funny, intelligent self. But she will not be deterred. And I'm certain it will work out as she hopes. She seems to have an interest in an earl, Claybrook. I've determined nothing unsavory about the man, so I see no need to discourage the suit."

Marcus said nothing, but his stomach churned at the words his friends had said. They felt like a knife to his gut, even though he was fully aware of Annabelle's activities and desires for her future.

Rafe shook his head. "Great God, from your expression I see I must be boring you. I apologize and I thank you sincerely for talking to me."

Marcus stood, ready to be dismissed. "I'm always happy to oblige, Flynn."

Rafe got to his feet as well and slapped Marcus's arm good-naturedly. "And now you must stay for supper."

Marcus blinked. "I beg your pardon?"

"Unless you have another engagement," Rafe said, tilting his head.

"It isn't that," Marcus admitted. "Only that…you are a duke."

"And?"

"And married," Marcus continued, waiting for Flynn to see the myriad of issues that should keep a man like him from the table.

Instead, Rafe laughed. "And?"

"You don't want me in your dining room," Marcus said quietly, wishing that the sting of having to say those words was not so very high.

Rafe's brow wrinkled. "I asked you, didn't I? Come, the family will begin to arrive soon and I assure you, you will be most welcomed by us all."

"The family?" Marcus repeated, trying not to let his mind wander to inappropriate places yet again.

"My mother," Rafe explained. "And Annabelle, of course."

Marcus clenched a fist at his side. To see her here, in her natural environment, to be reminded just how far out of reach she truly was...

He wasn't sure he could take that.

"Flynn, I—"

Rafe cut him off by lifting his hand. "Rivers, I insist. You *will* join us tonight. I'll hear no further argument about it. Now if you will wait here a moment, Serafina should be almost ready and I'll fetch her. I know she's thrilled at the idea of meeting you."

His friend didn't wait for an answer, but all but bounded out of the room. Marcus paced to the fire where Rafe had once stood. He felt as troubled as the duke had looked then, though for very different reasons.

Put him in the underground and no other man in the world could be more at peace with himself. But here in the parlor of the titled, even a titled friend, and he felt very much out of place. Add Annabelle to the mix and Marcus wasn't entirely certain that tonight wouldn't be an exercise in humiliation and destruction.

And yet the thought of seeing her made him feel utterly alive.

Annabelle linked arms with her mother as they strolled through the parlor behind Rafe's butler Lathem.

"I'm so glad we're spending the evening with Serafina and Rafael," her mother said with a happy sigh. "Though I do wish Crispin would come. We have not had a family gathering in months."

Annabelle frowned. "He was invited, Mama, I'm certain of it. Perhaps he was simply engaged elsewhere."

Her mother darted a look at her. "You needn't try to protect me. I lived with your father, if you recall. I recognize that my son is struggling."

Annabelle squeezed her eyes shut. She hated to see her mother so troubled by Crispin's actions. Perhaps she could talk to Rafe about him again tonight, convince her eldest brother to help her in her schemes to watch over and perhaps even help Crispin.

At least she could try.

"Mrs. Flynn and Miss Annabelle," Lathem said as he opened the parlor door and let them inside.

Annabelle forced a smile on her face as she entered the room, but it fell almost instantly, replaced by what she was certain was a look of utter horror. For standing across the room, talking to Serafina and Rafe, was Marcus Rivers.

Her Marcus Rivers.

"Mama, Annabelle," Serafina said, crossing the room with her arms outstretched. She embraced first Annabelle's mother and then Annabelle. "I'm so happy you're here. I would like to introduce you to our guest, Mr. Marcus Rivers."

Annabelle continued to stare, struck almost dumb as she watched her mother walk toward Marcus, hand outstretched.

"You know, I think we have met before, Mr. Rivers," she said.

His eyebrows lifted in surprise. "We have, Mrs. Flynn, though it must be four years back."

She nodded. "At my husband's funeral gathering."

Annabelle's eyes went wide. Yes, Marcus *had* been there. She had all but forgotten that in the layers of her grief from that day, but now it rushed back. He had murmured his apologies at her loss just like the others, but then…

She jerked up her face to look at him. He had squeezed her arm in a simple, yet completely inappropriate, gesture of comfort.

"Your husband was the best of men," Marcus said, his tone low and reverent.

"He was that. And now I am so happy to see you again under much brighter circumstances. Have you met my daughter, Annabelle?"

Her mother turned slightly toward her and Annabelle realized she would be forced to move toward him now. To talk to him politely and try to pretend that she hadn't felt his mouth on her, that he hadn't glided his hands over every inch of her body, that just the thought of him made her ache.

"We have met," Annabelle forced herself to say as she held out a trembling hand. "Mr. Rivers. How nice to see you again."

His rough fingers closed over hers and he shook her hand quite properly, but she saw the look in his eyes. The dark, swirling desire for her that did not fade even in a room full of her family. Her body gave an answering twitch that made her jerk her hand away suddenly.

"It—it's very nice to see you again," she said.

He smiled. "Your brother insisted upon my joining your party tonight. I hope you do not think I am intruding."

It was her mother who answered. "Goodness no," she insisted. "I am always happy to see a friend of this family, no matter how long it has been."

Marcus looked at her, his surprise at her utter welcome clear on his face. In that unguarded flash of a moment, Annabelle could see just how uncomfortable he was in being here. And the sight of that vulnerability on the face of a man who was always perfect in control was rather…

Enticing.

Rafe move across the room and slipped his hand around his wife's waist. "That is what *I* told him, Mama."

"He did indeed," Marcus said with a laugh. "And I'm pleased to be here."

Annabelle shifted as they all continued chatting, as if it were normal that her…well, what was he? Her lover? Not exactly, but it was the closest term to the truth. How could they all stand and talk to her lover as if this were normal?

She felt like her own voice was too loud when she said, "Mama, you should see what Serafina has done to the nursery."

She knew the effect that comment would have. Despite the inappropriateness of her suggestion with a guest in the house, her mother's face lit up. "I would like to see it."

Serafina grasped her mother-in-law's hands with a bright smile before she glanced at Marcus in apology. "Would you mind very much if we snuck away?"

Marcus shook his head. "Of course not."

The two women scurried toward the door, Serafina calling out, "We will be back shortly."

Rafe laughed as they left. "Mama is over the moon about her first grandchild."

"As she should be," Marcus said with a gentle smile unlike anything Annabelle had ever seen.

Rafe opened his mouth as if to reply, but Annabelle rushed to fill the space in the conversation. "Rafe, would you mind getting me a drink, I am parched."

"Certainly," her brother said slowly. "What would you like?"

She smiled. "Some of Serafina's special madeira."

Her brother flashed a grin. It was well known that he specially ordered the drink for his wife because it was her favorite. "I'm afraid I have none in this parlor. She hoards it away, I think," he said with a laugh.

Annabelle tilted her head. "Would you mind very much fetching a bottle? I have been dreaming of it since the last time I came here and shared a glass with her."

Rafe pinched his lips together. "I'll get your drink, Annabelle. But if you wanted to talk to Mr. Rivers alone, you could have asked. I would suggest apologizing to him again for sneaking into his carriage."

He shook his head as he left the chamber. Annabelle glared after him, cheeks flaming.

But she was brought swiftly back to reality when Marcus touched her arm. "Are you planning to apologize?"

She pivoted to find him smiling at her, eyes dancing. "No, of course not," she said. "But we only have a few moments before he returns."

"But what a person can do in a few minutes," he drawled, but made no move to touch her. Still, his implication made her shiver despite herself and it took all her willpower to focus on what she needed to say.

"Why are you here?"

His smile faltered. "As I said, your brother invited me."

"To supper?"

He shrugged. "That was not the initial reason for my visit, no. He called me here earlier."

Her eyes went wide and she gripped her hands at her sides. "Does he know?"

Marcus arched a brow as he drawled, "About us?"

She nodded, tossing a glance over her shoulder to make sure Rafe hadn't rushed in his retrieval of the wine. "Yes."

He folded his arms. "Do you think your brother would invite me to supper if he knew I made you shake, quiver and scream out my name in bed?"

"Marcus!" she burst out, eyes wide at his description and body trembling and tingling despite the deep inappropriateness of this entire situation.

He gave her a slow smile, and her sex clenched as betraying wetness gathered there. Damn him for making her so weak.

"He has guessed nothing," he reassured her. "As far as he knows, the last time we spoke was the first night you barged into my club."

She let out a breath of relief, even though her body could find none. "Then why did he call you here?"

"Crispin," he said with a shrug. "You are not the only one concerned about him."

She leaned in. "Oh, Marcus, does that mean he will help our brother?"

He stared at her for a beat, his expression unreadable. "His feelings about your brother's fall remain the same, Annabelle. He waits for Crispin to ask for help."

She turned away, all desire crushed in that moment of utter disappointment. "How can he be so callous?"

Marcus's fingers closed around her upper arm and he slowly turned her back toward him. "He isn't being callous," he reassured her. "Rafe is obviously deeply troubled about Crispin, he asked for a great many details about his activities. And he was pleased that I was watching out for him. He isn't immune to Crispin's difficulties, Annabelle. He simply has a different tactic in addressing them."

The sleeve on her gown was short, and as he moved his thumb in a gentle stroke, he touched her bare skin. She shuddered, her eyes fluttering shut of their own accord. What he could do to her.

"Marcus," she whispered, but before anything else could be said, Rafe walked back through the door, madeira in hand. Marcus released her instantly and Annabelle backed away, working to measure her breath.

"Did I give you enough time to batter Mr. Rivers with apologies and questions?" Rafe asked as he grabbed a glass and poured her the drink she hadn't even truly wanted.

"Yes," she murmured.

"Excellent, because I heard Mama and Serafina coming down the stairs as I came back to the parlor and I am famished. So drink up, sister, and let's eat."

CHAPTER THIRTEEN

Marcus leaned back in his chair, unable to stop himself from laughing at the very amusing story Lady Hartholm had been telling. To his surprise and despite all his misgivings, he had been having a smashing time all night. Mrs. Flynn was nothing but kind and welcoming, Rafe was his old self, Serafina was lovely...and then there was Annabelle.

Wonderful, fiery, magnificent Annabelle, who he wanted so much that it physically hurt him to look at her sometimes.

Mrs. Flynn wiped tears of mirth from her eyes and smiled at him. He could see Annabelle in her face, in her eyes, in the way she tilted her head. Perhaps that made him like the older woman even more than he normally would have. He couldn't help but return her smile.

"So how is it that you and my son are acquainted, Mr. Rivers?" she asked.

Marcus felt his expression falter, and he slid his gaze toward Rafe. There was really no appropriate way to explain this, especially not to ladies. And he found he didn't want Annabelle's mother to think less of him, as she surely would if she knew the truth.

Hell, *Annabelle* might think less of him if she knew the truth.

Rafe leaned back in his chair, all calm and certainty as he flashed a big grin toward his mother. "Ah, Mama, I am not certain you want to know the answer to that question."

She shook her head, but there seemed to be no upset on her face, nor even surprise. "And here I thought I had asked it."

Rafe shrugged. "You know our wicked ways, Mama."

Now Mrs. Flynn's smile vanished and Marcus flinched as he waited for her to turn a judgmental gaze on him. Instead, she merely ran her finger along the tablecloth reflexively.

"I suppose by *our* that you mean he is a friend of yours and Crispin's?"

It was amazing to Marcus to watch the mood of the table shift with the mere mention of Crispin's name. Serafina reached out to take her husband's hand, Mrs. Flynn's shoulders slumped and Annabelle went stiff as a board as she stared at her plate like it was the most interesting thing in the world.

He cleared his throat. "I do know your younger son, Mrs. Flynn," he admitted. "He is as fine a man as your oldest."

She lifted her gaze, snagging his. He saw her pain, her struggle, and it nearly took his breath away. He had been raised most of his life without anyone to love him, to give a damn whether he lived or died. That had changed thanks to…well, thanks to the sons and husband of this very woman.

His painful past meant he appreciated love even more. This family cared for its own. Annabelle was not alone in that.

"Thank you, Mr. Rivers," Mrs. Flynn said softly.

With a screech of her chair, Annabelle leapt to her feet. The entire table turned toward her, eyes wide, including his own.

"Mr. Rivers, would you like a tour of the gardens?" she asked, hands opening and shutting at her sides.

He blinked, taken aback by this strange request.

"In the dark?" Rafe asked, tilting his head to look more closely at his sister.

Marcus held back a groan. If Annabelle kept requesting, no *demanding*, time alone with him, the true nature of their arrangement was going to become crystal clear. And yet, the idea that she wanted to be with him was almost irresistible.

"There is a moon," Annabelle insisted through clenched teeth.

"Annabelle, we were about to retire to the parlor for port and wine," Serafina said, watching her sister-in-law just as closely as the duke was currently doing.

"We would only take but a moment."

"If you did not stray too far, I couldn't see the harm," Mrs. Flynn surprised him by saying. "You have been a bit high strung tonight, Annabelle—perhaps the night air will do you good."

With her mother's blessing, Marcus rose to his feet and offered Annabelle his arm. She took it, sending a brief glance over her shoulder before she motioned toward an adjoining door to a parlor with an exit to the terrace. He felt three pairs of eyes on them with every step that took them away from the party.

But when he left the house and closed the veranda door behind them, he knew they were once more alone. And the things he wanted to do to this woman were wildly inappropriate.

She didn't seem to sense his desire, but pulled from his arm and paced away to the edge of the terrace.

"Marcus," she began.

"If you are going to scold me for speaking so openly to your mother or for being here, then please don't." He shrugged. "This is not a night that will likely be repeated."

She looked at him, surprise on her face. "I was not going to scold you at all," she said, her tone suddenly gentle. "Your presence here has actually been good for my mother. Mama is obviously very hurt by Crispin's actions of late and tonight is the first time I've seen her smile so brightly and engage with another person so completely."

He drew back. "If that is true, then I am pleased for any part I have to play in her happiness. I truly like your mother." He couldn't help it. He edged closer. "But is she the *only* one who enjoyed my company tonight?"

Annabelle sucked in a harsh breath, and he saw the answer on her face before she whispered, "You know she is not. You know that I have been unable to focus on anything other than you since the moment I walked in the door and found you with my brother and his wife."

"I like that answer," he murmured, cupping her chin and tilting it up. He leaned in, loving that the shadows of the trees just along the terrace provided them with protection from those inside.

He took the opportunity and pressed his lips to hers. Immediately she let out a desperate little moan and opened to him. He took what she offered, delving his tongue deep inside her mouth, sucking and tasting and teasing her until her hands came up to grip his forearms and her breath was short and heavy.

He wanted to back her into the corner and lift her skirts. He wanted to violate their agreement and claim her until she arched against him and moaned his name. He wanted to do wicked things to her, the fact that her family was feet away be damned.

But instead, he gently set her aside and paced away, hoping the raging length of his erection would subside if he could no longer smell the tempting waft of jasmine, taste her breath, feel her soft body mold to his.

When he dared to look at her, she had also put her back to him. Her hand was gripped against the top of the wall, her shoulders lifting and falling with every harsh breath.

"What are we doing, Marcus?" she whispered. "Why can't I control myself whenever I see you?"

He reached out, but forced himself to lower his hand and not touch her. "Whatever it is, we both suffer the same affliction," he said.

She turned, her beautiful face pale and luminous in the moonlight. It was like she was made of porcelain, impossibly fine but breakable. He didn't want to be the one to shatter her and her dreams.

And yet he still took a step toward her and whispered, "Will you come back to the club?"

Her gaze darted to his and held there. "Tuesday," she affirmed, her voice trembling.

"Good," he said, hoping his immense relief wasn't reflected in his voice. Her coming meant more to him than it should. He cleared his throat. "Now take me back inside and I'll excuse myself."

She sucked in a breath. "Marcus?"

He shrugged. "Being near you is too difficult, and your brother is no fool. He'll see a connection if we allow him to observe us for too long."

She bit her lip gently and nodded. "I suppose you're correct."

"And I *should* go back anyway. As you know from examining my books, there is always work to be done at the masquerade."

She smiled. "Always. Come with me, then."

She turned and began to make her way back to the parlor door, but before she could open it and bring them back to propriety and reality, he took a step toward her.

"Annabelle."

She stopped and faced him. "Yes?"

"I like your family."

Her face brightened at the comment, magnifying her beauty until it was almost too much to look at. "I'm glad, Marcus."

"But I don't believe, even in my wildest fantasies, that I belong here. Or that I belong with you." He pursed his lips "It's important we both realize that as we move forward in our…our arrangement."

Her smile faded at those blunt words, and for a moment Marcus was certain he saw a flash of disappointment cross her face. But then it was gone and he must have imagined it, because Annabelle had plans and they didn't include him. What he'd said to her was as much for himself as for her.

"Come," she said, opening the door.

He followed her inside, but deep in the pit of his stomach, he had a keen sense that he had lost something. Even though it was something he'd never truly had.

Annabelle stared at her reflection in the mirror, focusing on her hollow expression, her empty eyes. She shook her head.

"Miss?"

She jumped at Deirdre's voice and looked over to find her maid waiting for her to unclench her hands so that she could remove the gown she had been unbuttoning while Annabelle lost herself in thought.

"I'm sorry," she said, opening her hands and helping Deirdre remove the dress.

Her servant shook out the fabric and carefully folded it, placing it on a chair where it would be taken to be washed.

"You are very quiet," her maid observed without looking at Annabelle.

Annabelle squeezed her eyes shut. Was she so obvious? She'd been trying so hard to remain unmoved since Marcus left her brother's house hours ago. Trying to remain normal, as if it were an everyday occurrence for her secret lover to come to call.

"I'm sorry, I seem to be woolgathering, Deirdre," she murmured.

Deirdre motioned to Annabelle's chemise and she tugged it over her head, then bent to roll her stockings away. Deirdre handed over her nightgown before she took the clothing Annabelle had removed and folded them to be added to the laundry.

"I know Mr. Rivers was at the gathering at your brother's home tonight," her maid offered after enough time had passed that Annabelle was already beginning to return to her reverie.

Annabelle jolted at the accusation and carefully smoothed her nightgown with both hands before she replied. "Oh do you? Who told you that?"

"My sister is your sister-in-law's maid," Deirdre said with a slight smile. "And we talk below stairs. You know that."

"What was said about Mr. Rivers?"

Deirdre shrugged. "That he was an unforeseen guest at the dinner table. Some of the servants teased a little about Lord Hartholm's past, but Lathem always shuts that down, no matter how good natured the words are."

"Good old Lathem." Annabelle smiled. "But no one judged Marcus…Mr. Rivers?"

Deirdre's eyebrows lifted. "You mean was his reputation discussed?"

Annabelle nodded.

"No. Eluded to, but never discussed. However, everyone knows what he is, Miss. Who he is. I'm a little afraid for you, for your reputation."

"Were they talking about me?" Annabelle burst out, taking a step toward Deirdre.

"No, no of course not! No one knows what you're doing or where you're going," her maid reassured her.

Annabelle almost sagged in relief, reaching out to support herself on her bed. "Thank God."

"But you still risk yourself by going to that club. You wear a mask, yes, but what if your carriage were recognized? Or a gown was familiar? Or your voice?"

Annabelle covered her eyes with her hand for a moment. "I know. These are all things I have considered, Deirdre, but what am I to do? My brother needs *someone* looking out for him."

"Is that—is that all you're doing? Because I wonder if—" Deirdre blushed and then turned away suddenly, cutting off her words.

"What?" Annabelle asked.

Her maid shook her head, fiddling with the clothing

stacked on the chair. "I shouldn't."

"Please," Annabelle said, trying to keep her tone calm. "Please tell me what is on your mind."

Deirdre turned to look at her. Her face was pale and her voice trembled as she said, "It isn't my place, I know, but I see things and I hear things and I know you, Miss, after all these years. I wonder if you might *like* Mr. Rivers too much."

Annabelle tensed. Her maid was out of line to bring this up and she would have been in her rights to reprimand her. It would certainly close the subject if she did. However, over the years Deirdre had become much more than a mere servant to her. She was a friend. One who had seen her through many a difficulty with kindness.

Deirdre was also the only person in her life who knew even a fraction of the truth about her current activities. She had no other confidante and no other person who would listen to her without judging. Certainly she couldn't tell Georgina, of all people, about her obsession with Marcus.

And if she said something to her mother or Serafina? Well, that was like directly reporting to Rafe, himself. Her brother wouldn't understand. He would likely be enraged at both her and Marcus.

"Have I gone too far?" Deirdre asked, voice trembling.

Annabelle reached out to cover her maid's hand gently. "No, of course not. I'm only pondering your accusation. And I must admit that you are…right. I may like Mr. Rivers too much, it is true."

Deirdre's eyes went wide at the admission, and heat flooded Annabelle's face.

"You needn't look so shocked," she said with a forced laugh. "He is handsome as can be, but also very intelligent and…*interesting*."

"But he isn't the kind of man you have claimed you wish to affiliate yourself with. Marry." Her maid shook her head. "Unless you've changed your mind."

Annabelle swallowed. Since her night with Marcus, she'd

had an increasingly difficult time focusing on her goals. And yet she couldn't change them. She'd come so far.

"No, I haven't changed my mind," she said softly. "I know the risks when it comes to spending time with Mr. Rivers. And I know the lines I cannot cross. And I *will not* cross them. Not when I'm finally so close to respectability."

Deirdre's face suddenly grew sad. "But Miss Annabelle, you are respectable. No one could look at you and think otherwise."

Annabelle barked out a laugh. "But they do. They do and I'm certain you know it thanks to the very talk below stairs we discussed earlier."

"There is a difference between a few snotty maids who need to be put in their place and Society at large," Deirdre huffed.

"Oh, you dear. If you put someone in their place, then I adore you for it." Annabelle let out a long, heavy sigh. "But there is no difference. What is said below stairs is fed from above. Because of my family and their antics, my chances at a staid, respectable future have been materially damaged."

She shifted. That was what she'd told herself for so long: that it was Crispin and Rafe and even her father who had altered her future with their ways. As much as she loved them all, she sometimes felt resentment for their lack of thought.

But now she had to wonder...was *she* just as much to blame?

"After all," she mused out loud. "Perhaps those around me can see my true self. My dark heart and the desires it makes me feel."

Desires that had been powerfully awakened in Marcus's bed. Desires that were stronger now rather than weaker.

"There is nothing dark about your heart," Deirdre protested, her face a mask of horror at the suggestion.

Annabelle smiled at her maid's defense, but her thoughts did not change. She knew what she was capable of. What she desired in the dark of night in her chamber, when her fingers found her sex and she shamefully gave herself release. Or worse, when she allowed Marcus to touch her and her body surrendered to everything it could not, should not have.

"I *can* control myself," she said. "I *will* do so. Because if I do not take the chance laid out for me right now, I fear it will not repeat itself. And then my future will be—"

She cut herself off as errant thoughts of Marcus clouded her mind. Marcus touching her, kissing her, pleasing her...Marcus in her parlor as he had been in her brother's parlor tonight. Of them laughing together, of making love completely, without the barriers she had erected in their arrangement.

"It cannot be," she whispered. "I can't let it distract me."

But as she smiled at her maid, hoping to reassure Deirdre further before she surrendered to her bed, she knew she was already distracted. By Crispin, by her own desires, by Marcus.

And if she wasn't careful, she could lose everything she was trying to build.

CHAPTER FOURTEEN

It had been months since Marcus had last sat on his horse outside of Mrs. Flynn's gate, watching the house, waiting for a glimpse of Annabelle.

The first time he'd done it was after their initial meeting years ago. Mr. Flynn had still lived then and there had been nothing more joyful than their chaotic family, talking at once and welcoming all comers.

And yet Marcus had known he didn't belong there that night. Just as he'd known he didn't belong just twelve hours before in the same hall with the same family. He had stood to the side all those years ago, holding his drink, watching the merriment, happy to be there even if he wasn't truly a part of it all.

Until Annabelle Flynn entered the room.

She was twenty-one then, her face fuller than it was now, her eyes a bit brighter and less jaded. She had burst into the room like sunshine through a dark veil, and suddenly he couldn't think or breathe or move.

Rafe had introduced them, and he'd known she felt none of the same lightning bolt that had struck him. She'd smiled, of course, politely nodded. He thought he'd seen her take a second glance at him a short while later before she slipped away with a group of friends, but that couldn't have been correct.

He hadn't meant to ride his horse back to her father's home the next day. He hadn't meant to sit and watch through the gate at the courtyard to catch a glimpse of her as she boarded her carriage with her mother and her maid at her side. But he had. That day and other days.

Including this one.

The gate was open today, allowing him an unobstructed view of the courtyard. The courtyard where a carriage was parked. A carriage which belonged to a very rich and very titled-looking man who had strolled up to the door not half an hour before and gone inside, obviously welcomed and invited.

Marcus gripped the reins of his horse tighter. *This* was what Annabelle wanted. What she deserved. He couldn't be peevish or foolish about it. He'd never thought she would be his, no matter how sweetly she surrendered.

He stared for a moment longer at the stranger's carriage, then turned his horse and rode off. He needed to talk to someone about this drive, this desire, this woman.

And he knew the perfect person, the only person, who he could truly confide in.

Annabelle sat on the edge of the settee, hands folded in her lap, false smile plastered on her face, ankles crossed perfectly and stared at Lord Claybrook. He had arrived not half an hour before for a planned tea with her brother, Serafina and her mother.

Thus far they had chatted amiably about the weather, the roads, Society in general and Claybrook's horses. No one could say that the gathering had not been perfectly pleasant. But she also couldn't help but compare it to the one she'd recently shared with her family and Marcus.

Sitting with Claybrook was agreeable enough, yes, but he didn't make her mother laugh. He didn't melt into her family like he was born to be a Flynn. He didn't make her body tingle.

Not that she wanted him to do the last. That sort of thing was exactly what she was supposed to be avoiding.

"Miss Flynn, would you care to take a walk in the garden?" Claybrook asked.

Annabelle jolted, yanked from her reverie with the unexpected question. She shot her mother and brother a look, and Claybrook followed her stare.

"With your family's permission, of course," he said.

Her mother smiled, but it was faint. "I see no objection."

"Excellent," Claybrook said as he rose to his feet and offered Annabelle an arm.

She got up and took it with a smile for her mother and her now-frowning brother, then allowed Claybrook to take her from the room. It was only as they walked through the hall together that she realized she'd never actually *agreed* to this little excursion. Claybrook had been satisfied with her mother's permission if not her own.

She pushed that thought away as they exited the house into her mother's beautiful garden. Breathing in a long waft of the fragrant, flowered air, she immediately began to relax.

"A pretty little garden, isn't it?" Claybrook said as they moved down the pathway.

Annabelle shot him a look from the corner of her eye. Was he being dismissive? It was hard to tell.

"My mother oversees all gardening herself," she explained. "This garden is her fourth child."

"Fourth?" Claybrook asked.

"Well, yes. There is Raphael, Crispin and me."

"Ah, yes. Your other brother." Claybrook looked at her briefly.

She frowned. Did he truly forget she had a second brother? It wasn't as if Crispin were dead or gone away. Although both those things were fears that often troubled her.

"Yes. He does not come into Society," she said, somehow wanting to explain Crispin to his man who was…well, wooing her was the phrase, wasn't it? Though she didn't feel particularly wooed when Claybrook was with her. Although he held her arm, he never made an attempt for anything more. And they had never discussed anything deeper than the color of her gown.

But perhaps this topic would change all that.

Claybrook shifted as if uncomfortable. "No, he doesn't make the rounds in the *ton*. But then, he isn't a duke like your brother and he isn't a lovely lady such as yourself."

Once again, Annabelle frowned. Claybrook was definitely being dismissive this time. "He is a wonderful person, though," she insisted. "Perhaps someday you will meet him."

For the briefest of moments, there was an unguarded expression on her companion's face. A look of disgust at the very idea of Crispin Flynn. But then it was gone, and Claybrook was benign again, devoid of any extreme emotion.

"Of course. Perhaps at your mother's home or your brother's one day." He released her arm and stepped into the little circle of roses and lilies that made up the center of her mother's garden. "My, isn't this pretty."

Annabelle pursed her lips together. So that was the end of the discussion regarding her brother, it seemed. And although she was somewhat relieved by the end of the exchange, she was also irritated.

This man didn't know anything about her family, only rumor. Worse, he didn't seem to *want* to know her family. Or at least not any part of it that wasn't perfect. Which meant he wouldn't want to know *her* if she proved not to be.

But perhaps that was unfair. After all, he had approached her, regardless of her disadvantages in Society. He had danced with her, after only a bit of hesitation. And he was here, coming to call, his carriage with its seal parked right in her drive where anyone could see.

And yet she still felt second class with Claybrook. Like all of this was *despite* who she was, not because of it. Like he was granting her a boon by his very existence in her life.

"You look too serious," Claybrook said, motioning to the bench in the middle of her mother's flowers. "Come, let us rest a moment."

She pursed her lips but followed him, and they took their places on the bench. She noted that he was careful not to let their legs touch, despite how close they had to sit thanks to the size of the seat.

She watched him. He seemed perfectly content in this moment, smiling broadly and apparently unaware of her discomfort.

Yet, she had to be fair. As much as he avoided any knowledge about her life, she knew almost as little about his. He was titled and respectable, which had been all that mattered to her up until now. Wasn't that just as dismissive and mercenary as anything Claybrook did? If she wanted him to open up, perhaps she had to express more interest first.

"You know, Lord Claybrook, you have met much of my family now, but I realize I know very little about yours," she said.

"What?" Claybrook grunted, straightening up a bit. He examined her for a very brief moment and shrugged. "We have one of the finest pedigrees in England, of course. Titled for thirteen generations."

Annabelle tried to smile. "Oh no, you misunderstand me. I meant your *family*." When Claybrook's face remained blank, she continued, "Do you have brothers or sisters?"

"Ah," he said, the confusion clearing from his face. "I have two brothers and two sisters. The sisters are older, both married very well. My youngest brother married into the house of the Duke of Westenfield."

His chest puffed out as he said that, as if somehow his brother's marriage made him...*better*.

"I see," she said. "And is your mother still alive?"

He shook his head. "No, she's been in the ground since even before my father."

"I'm sorry," Annabelle said, reaching for his hand

reflexively.

He looked at her fingers covering his and then pulled his hand away slowly. "It is nothing, I assure you."

She frowned. In most cases she would assume his dismissal meant he wasn't ready to share his grief, but in Claybrook's case the fact truly didn't seem to trouble him.

"Are you close to your siblings?"

He shrugged. "As close as is warranted. We see each other at the holidays sometimes."

She waited for him to elaborate, but he seemed to have no desire to do so. In fact, he got to his feet and moved to examine a rose a bit closer. "Do you like hunting, Miss Flynn?"

She jolted at the closing of the prior subject. "I do not often go, but I have no objection."

He smiled. "Excellent. I have the best hunting bitches in seven counties."

She nodded as he launched into a long monologue about his dogs. After a few moments, she let her mind drift. This man was courting her, yes, and he seemed nothing but decent. But she knew nothing about him, he nothing about her, and that seemed to be just fine with him.

So as she looked at him, looked at the future he presented, she couldn't help but feel that it was the most unsatisfactory conversation she had ever had with a person. And as her mind wandered, it of course landed firmly on Marcus. A place that was dangerous to go, and yet she couldn't seem to steer her ship away from the rocks of his shore.

Marcus stood in the parlor and couldn't help but smile. It was the same as it had ever been, bright...too bright...and decorated with wildly disparate items of furniture. Looking at the room was like a visual experience of a clanging bell. Yet it was anything but unpleasant.

The door behind him opened, and through it burst a tiny, colorfully dressed woman who perfectly matched her wild parlor.

"Marcus!" she said, rushing toward him.

"Calliope!" he said as he entered his embrace. "You look wonderful."

They parted and she waved him at the settee. "Sit, sit. If I'd known you were coming, I would have had some of those biscuits you love."

Marcus laughed as he settled into his seat. He watched her as she buzzed about with his tea. He had known this woman for half his life. She and her husband had been his saviors. And she was the closest thing to a mother he had.

She handed over his tea and took a seat across from him. "Love, you get more handsome every time I see you. Such a gentleman."

Marcus looked down at himself. His fine clothes were what she meant. "I'm still a wolf under it all."

"Nothing wrong with a wolf, love."

He frowned. "Not when a sheep is required."

Her eyebrows lifted slightly. "Who wants you to be a sheep?"

He set his tea aside and leaned forward, his elbows draped over his knees. He was not one for confidences, but right now he needed council. And Calliope would give it without judgment, but also without sugar coating whatever truth he needed to hear.

"I suppose I am not being asked to be a sheep," he clarified. "Only wondering if I could be. Knowing I couldn't."

"Is this about a woman?" she pressed, sipping her tea even as her gaze stayed focused on his face.

He hesitated and then nodded. "Yes."

Her smile was his reward. "Wonderful. You really have reached an age where you should stop flitting about, caring only for that club you and your father loved so much."

Marcus couldn't help but smile too. His "father", her late

husband Oliver, who had owned the Donville Masquerade when it was nothing more than a rundown set of rooms where gentlemen came to box and game. How much things had changed.

"Do you remember the Flynns?" he asked.

Calliope's face softened. "'course, I do. They brought you to us, didn't they?"

Marcus turned his face. "Yes," he whispered, trying to block out thoughts of his life before Calliope and Ollie. "They have a daughter."

Calliope laughed. "Well, that seems the perfect match, doesn't it? A woman raised by wolves, why would *she* ever want a sheep?"

"Because she was raised by wolves," he sighed, scrubbing a hand over his face. "You must have heard that Raphael Flynn took on this dukedom last year and married a lady of the highest quality."

Calliope nodded. "Everyone knows that. Though it's hard to picture that hellion as a proper duke. Not when I remember him almost setting the curtains on fire in one of those clubs as some kind of bet."

Marcus stifled a chuckle. "His father made him pay for the damage out of his own pocket. I believe he might have had to sweep floors."

Calliope grinned along with him. "Always liked Reggie Flynn. He was a good one. But are you saying the Flynn daughter—what is her name?"

"Annabelle," Marcus said, her name like a teaspoon of honey across his tongue.

"That this Annabelle wants to marry someone in her brother's new world?" Calliope shook her head as if that wish were utterly foolish.

Marcus shrugged. "Can you blame her? She's spent her life living with the consequences of actions taken by the men in her life. She's being offered the chance at something stable—why wouldn't she take it?"

"If the alternative was you?" she scoffed. "Is she daft?"

Marcus laughed. "No, she's quite brilliant, actually. You would like her if you met her. She's not like anyone I've ever known. And she wants me, but we both know it can't last."

Calliope watched him for a moment. "Why did you come here, Marcus?"

He blinked at the sudden, pointed question. "Am I not welcome?"

"You are welcome every day and twice on Sunday, you know that. I want to see more of you, I miss you." She tilted her head. "But what do you want me to tell you about this girl?"

"Tell me that it's impossible and I should walk away. Tell me to think about the business and not have my head in the clouds."

She took his hand. "Marcus, it's impossible and you should walk away. Get your head out of the clouds and think of the business."

He squeezed his eyes shut. His words, repeated back to him just as she'd asked. But they were like a vice around his heart.

"Now, do you want to know what I *really* think?"

He opened his eyes and found her watching him far too intently. "Calliope…"

"I think if that girl is anything like her father or her brothers, she would be bored to tears by some titled fop who never got into any trouble. I think if she is coming to you, she must see in you her true heart and desires. And I think that if *you* need to talk to someone else about your problems that you must care deeply for her. And you should never walk away from that."

"This does not help me," he said, smiling at her despite her words.

She didn't return the smile. "It isn't what you think you should hear. That's something different."

Her hand still covered one of his and he cupped it with his

free one. "I do adore you, Mama. You know that."

Her face brightened. "I love it when you call me that. And I know, lovie." She pushed to her feet. "Now, will you stay for supper? We can talk more about your girl. Or you can tell me that your man of affairs, Abbot, has been pining for me."

He laughed as he shook his head. Calliope's great joke was that she would one day shed her title of widow and marry Abbot. He had a feeling that scared poor Paul to death.

"Of course I'll stay. Who else will indulge your fantasies? Though if you want to torture Abbot, you should just come to the club more often."

"I may just do that," she laughed, linking her arm with his to lead him from the room.

But even as he joined in her laughter, he couldn't stop his mind from turning to Annabelle. Calliope refused to help him separate himself from her. And now he had a tiny, terrible glimmer of hope that he would have to squash before their next meeting.

CHAPTER FIFTEEN

Annabelle could hardly breathe as she sat at Marcus's desk in his office. Did the man not know that when he leaned over her, it stopped her heart? Or was he actually *trying* to kill her?

"You see here, where your membership fees are collected?" she asked, hoping her voice didn't tremble as much as her hands were. He nodded. "By going through some of your records while you were downstairs dealing with...what was it exactly?"

He shrugged. "A fight over a woman."

Annabelle tensed. "Does that happen here often?"

Marcus shook his head. "Not very often. It is more common for two 'suitors' to decide to share a lady rather than duel over her in these halls."

Annabelle gripped her fist against the desk. Two men, one lady? That sounded incredibly shocking and highly erotic. She wanted to ask him more, perhaps even be shown how such a thing was possible, but instead she bent her head.

"Ah, I see. Well, at any rate, it seems you haven't changed what you change for membership in a very long time."

He pressed one hand to the desk, dangerously close to her own, and leaned in. "Not for ten years, since I inherited the place and made the first changes and updates."

She glanced up. "You inherited the club?"

He continued to stare at the ledger a moment, then slowly looked down at her. Their eyes met and she saw a flicker of pain in the bright green of his stare.

"Yes," he said softly and explained no more. "I suppose you are correct that in ten years enough has changed that perhaps I should reexamine my fees."

"One other thing I noticed was that you have some members who do not fall under a lifetime membership and yet they have not paid you their annual fee in several years."

"They are established members," he murmured, looking over the list she had compiled. "We press them, but do not expel them."

"I think you should reconsider," she said. "I'm certain most, if not all, of these people can more than easily pay your fee. And they cannot bring in so much business that they make up for what they take. They are taking advantage of you."

She folded her arms and Marcus chuckled. "I did not know I had picked up a champion when we agreed you would review my books."

Annabelle reached up and removed her reading spectacles, setting them on his desk before she said, "You have obviously worked hard to make this place the success it has become. I simply hate to see you throw away even a farthing's worth of profit from all you've done."

He was quiet for a few seconds, but then he leaned in even closer, gripping both arms of the chair she sat in before he dragged it away from the desk and turned her to face him. His hands bracketed each chair arm, so she was trapped, caught with only his handsome face to stare into.

And stare she did, her breath hitching as she fell under the spell of his strong jaw, full lips and utterly spectacular eyes.

"Marcus," she whispered, despite herself.

He smiled. "Do you know how often I've thought of you since we last met, Annabelle? How often I've thought of having you alone in this space?"

She swallowed. "I hope it is as often as I have thought of

you."

His eyes went wide at that admission before his normally stern mouth turned up in a grin. "You thought of me, Miss Flynn? And what did you think about?"

"Very inappropriate things," she admitted, feeling the rush of heat to her cheeks.

His smile faltered slightly. "Like what?"

"Like being here alone with you," she began. "Like feeling your hands and your mouth on me, all over me. I'm afraid those thoughts are a sickness now, I cannot do anything to purge them from my mind."

"Then would you like to surrender to them?" he whispered.

She nodded. "Yes. Please, yes."

He said nothing more, but merely grasped her, pulled her out of the chair and into his arms. She couldn't help herself but surrender. It felt like forever since he'd touched her, despite the fact it had only been a few days. She melted against him. His fingers tangled in her hair, tilting her face up and up, but he didn't kiss her. He just *looked* at her.

"Do you know how many women I've had, Annabelle?"

She flinched. She didn't really want to consider that. "Is that an appropriate question to ask your lover?"

He smiled, but it was only a flicker of his earlier grin. "Not at all. There had been many. Not here—*they* are right that you are the first woman I have ever brought to my private rooms, to my business. But I have not been a monk outside of these walls. And yet, despite my experience, when I'm with you…"

He trailed off, and she tensed. "What?"

"It is like the first time I've ever seen a woman. Like nothing else ever mattered before."

She blinked. That was not what she'd expected him to say. And yet, trapped as she was, she couldn't turn away from the intimate admission. She could only look into his eyes and see that he meant every word. But that couldn't really be true.

Those things he said were too precious and too close to feelings she would not, *could* not allow herself to feel.

"Marcus," she whispered, shaking her head.

The light in his eyes faded at her indication of the negative, but he didn't pull away. Instead he moved closer, and suddenly his mouth was on hers, hard and insistent. His hand slid down her back, caressing her spine before he cupped her backside and lifted her against him, grinding the hard ridge of his cock against her thigh.

She shivered at the feel, knowing he was ready and randy for *her*. She couldn't deny she was the same for him. The moment he had entered the room almost an hour ago, her body had grown wet and she hadn't stopped tingling. And now he would touch her and he would make those desires fade, at least for a short while.

He maneuvered her through the office, kissing her and fondling her the entire way, until they reached his chamber door. He fumbled to open it, and they nearly fell inside when he finally managed it. Still, he didn't stop kissing her, but guided her to his bed where he finally stopped and drew away.

"If I could rip that dress off of you, I would," he drawled, letting his fingertips travel along the bodice of her gown. She shuddered as he crested over her breast, the pad of his thumb stroking her nipple through the fabric.

"Then I'd be naked and trapped here," she whispered.

He smiled. "Perfect. I'd keep you that way until you'd given me everything."

He started to unbutton her gown, and she stared at him. "But we can't share everything," she reminded him gently. "As much as I would like that."

He didn't hesitate in his unfastening and he didn't look up. "Trust me, Annabelle, I couldn't forget your rules even if I tried."

She frowned. There was a strain to his voice when he said that which she didn't understand. He couldn't possibly care what she did when she wasn't here with him. She was a diversion, an attraction he wanted to rid himself of feeling just as she *had* to rid herself of these dark desires in her soul.

Marcus Rivers wasn't the kind of man to truly care for anyone, she thought, but most especially not a woman like her. He could have opera singers and mistresses and widows who would know exactly how to please him. She was just…Annabelle Flynn, a woman not of his world, nor of the world she was trying to invade at balls and Society gatherings.

His fingers brushed her chin, and she sucked in a breath when she found him focused entirely on her.

"Why such a sad expression?" he asked, his voice low and hypnotic. She found herself wanting to curl into him, to tell him everything she'd ever feared and loved and lost.

Instead she shook her head. "You should know this is difficult for me as well. I take no pleasure in denying you."

"I-I know that," he said.

His mouth covered hers again and she sighed in both pleasure and relief. Talking to him was so confusing sometimes, it was better to just touch, tease, pleasure. Those things were separate from the things he made her feel and think and fear.

He opened her dress and pushed it and her chemise aside, baring her from the waist up. She found herself arching her back, giving him better access. He smiled as he pulled away and simply stared at her.

"These beautiful breasts haunt my most wicked dreams," he purred as he cupped them, pushing them together gently, thumbing her nipples, this time without fabric to stop her from feeling the touch.

She gasped and let her head dip back over her shoulders. He laughed. "So sensitive." Leaning forward, he licked one hard nipple and she jolted. "Do you feel that all the way in your pussy?"

She jerked her face to look at him. He continued to lick and suck her nipple, but he was watching her.

"Yes," she admitted.

"And are you wet and aching for me?" he asked, again so benign, as if he were asking if she wanted tea.

"Since the moment you came in to the room," she said, this time through clenched teeth. He was teasing her, testing her. But couldn't she do the same? "And what about you, Mr. Rivers?"

He sucked her hard and then said, "What about me?"

"I felt how hard you were for me," she said, blushing at the directness of her words. "Felt your cock press against me. Are you ready to feel my hands stroke you, my mouth suck you?"

He straightened up and tugged the gown off her waist. It fell at her feet. "You are treading in dangerous waters, Annabelle," he said, his voice sharp. "Because I have been hard for you for far longer than the first moment I saw you tonight. I have been aching for you for days and if you are not careful, you will feel how close I am to losing control."

"You, lose control?" she taunted, even though his ardor was frightening as much as thrilling. "I wouldn't believe it until I saw it."

"Minx," he spat, then dragged her against him. "If you keep teasing, then you shall see it."

She met his gaze evenly. The part of her that strove for propriety told her to stop this game with him. To back away. But the darker part of her, the larger part, urged her on. And in that moment, she folded Society Annabelle away and unleashed her true self.

Slowly she eased her hand between their tightly pressed bodies, wiggling between them until she found the ridge of his cock. She stroked him through his trousers, watching as his jaw tensed, his eyes fluttered shut, his breath exhaled gently.

"Annabelle," he said, but this time his voice was pleading.

"Take off your clothes and let us begin," she ordered, pushing from his embrace and stepping back to watch him.

He did not deny her, but took his time removing each item. His gaze never left her as he removed his jacket, tugged his shirt from his waistband, slowly unfastened it. Finally he tossed it away and she was the one who lost her breath.

"How are you so well formed?" she murmured, stepping closer to touch him. She flattened her palm against his flesh, reveling in the warmth of his skin against hers, the way his muscles flexed.

"Because I'm not a worthless fop," he growled.

She winced. He was addressing her desire to *marry* one of those worthless fops. Although right now she couldn't recall why that had ever seemed like a good idea. Especially when she could have *this* standing in front of her. This specimen of male perfection. This man who, if she told him she would allow it, would claim her and please her until she was weak.

And that would destroy all her dreams.

She blinked and stepped away. She couldn't allow her dark desires to be her only guide. She had to keep her reason alive in the midst of these pleasures.

He moved his hands to his trousers, his gaze almost challenging as he stripped them open and shrugged out of the fabric.

She caught her breath. He was magnificent. Even better than she had remembered. Every part of him was hard and muscled, from his thighs and backside to the thrusting ridge of his cock which curled against his stomach proudly.

She wanted him. So desperately.

Without thinking, she reached for him, wrapping her hand around him in a tight fist and stroking over him once, then twice.

He growled low in his throat, and without warning he pounced on her. He grasped her waist, tossing her on the bed and then braced himself over her, his breath on her neck, stirring her tangled locks.

She arched beneath him, rubbing her body against his in a desperate bid for control, but he shook his head. "You are mine right now, Annabelle. Don't forget that."

His mouth crushed hers before she could respond, but he

didn't stay like that for long. He nipped her bottom lip with his teeth lightly and then dragged his mouth down her naked body. He suckled back and forth between her breasts and then slid to her stomach, tonguing her navel.

Her body was on fire with sensation, but he never settled in any one spot on her body, leaving her discombobulated and moaning with the pleasure he taunted her with. Finally, his mouth glided over her hip and he pushed her legs open, revealing her sex.

She recalled his mouth against her before and blushed, but she also lifted toward him, aching for the relief he could bring with his wicked mouth.

He chuckled. "So eager. But I think we should try something different."

He stroked his fingers over her sex, opening her lips gently. She couldn't help but cry out as he touched her, playing her like a virtuoso with an instrument. He leaned in, still stroking his fingers against her gently. She waited for the brush of his tongue against her, but it didn't come.

"Marcus?" she whispered.

He smiled up at her. "You want my mouth?"

She nodded, not caring how desperate she appeared.

"Not today." He rose up, positioning himself between her legs. She watched, awestruck, as he lowered his cock toward her.

"No, we said—" she began, a weak protest when his body inside of hers was exactly what she wanted.

He shook his head. "I will not breach you."

She had no response for that. If he didn't intend to fill her, she didn't know what else he could do. Until he nestled his cock within her outer folds and stroked along just the outside of her sex.

"My God, Annabelle," he groaned, stroking along her again. "You are so wet."

She gasped at the slide of him along her sex. He was so hard against her softness, and the head of his cock pressed her clitoris perfectly. He gently increased his rhythm, taking his time, being careful not to let his member dip into her sex and break the promise he had made.

She felt her orgasm growing as his speed increased. It blossomed from where their bodies ground against each other, tingles spreading through her legs, her stomach, her arms, until in a starburst explosion of light and pleasure, it erupted.

She cried out, flexing against him, but also reaching for more. She shook and he stroked on until she finally collapsed, weak on his pillows.

She expected him to pull away, perhaps to ask her to pleasure him with her mouth, but instead, he glided his fingers along her opening once more and then began to stroke his cock, lubricated with her juices.

She sat up on her elbows, unable to look away as he jerked his hand over his hard flesh. His eyes fluttered shut, his neck strained and with a massive shout, his seed spurted free.

CHAPTER SIXTEEN

Marcus panted, struggling to recover his breath and opened his eyes. He found Annabelle still splayed across his bed, watching him, her eyes wide and filled with renewed desire. He wrinkled his brow in confusion.

"Why look at me that way?"

She smiled. "I liked watching you lose control," she explained. "Almost as much as I like when you take mine."

He shook his head. She had no idea how powerful her desires were. How her words moved him body and soul.

"And yet you see what we do here as dark and twisted, don't you?" he asked.

She frowned. "When we are together, there is nothing dark or twisted about how I feel. But a lady isn't supposed—"

He rolled onto his back with a huff of breath, cutting her off. "I'm sorry, but what you are about to say is pure foolishness. A lady isn't supposed… You have been downstairs, Annabelle, you've seen ladies, powerful ladies, doing exactly what you crave and even far more!"

She worried her lip. "I know. I know that they are here and that they are engaging in such activities. But tell me something—not everyone in your club wears a mask, do they?"

Marcus turned his face to look at her. "No. It is not mandatory, but encouraged. Most do."

"And those who do not, are any of them women? *Ladies*?"

He hesitated, not wanting to give the answer she sought as proof that what she felt was wrong. Worse, that what they shared was wrong.

"No," he finally admitted. "I've only ever seen the gentlemen forgo their masks."

She nodded. "And if someone were to storm into this place and uncover those engaged in certain activities…ones like those we observed from the peepholes in the hall, for instance…who do you think would be more damaged?"

"It would depend upon rank, who managed to push past my guards, what they were looking for," he said.

She shook her head. "The men or the women."

"Annabelle."

"You and I both know that the stories of the men might hurt them, yes, but you're right that it would depend upon the circumstance. Most of them would walk away embarrassed, perhaps, but not materially damaged. I can tell you, even after a short time in the *ton*, the women would be destroyed. Hell, even in the far less stringent company I kept before, the discovery that a lady was engaging in activities in a sex club would have meant social death."

"There are widows who flaunt their behavior more openly," he offered, but the tone was not convincing. How could it be when he knew she was right?

"Widows," she repeated. "And usually those with money and some power thanks to the ranks or reputations of their husbands. Women who have no need to ever marry again and don't care about Society. I am not married. If I do not marry, I wouldn't be thrown into the street, of course, but I would have no chance at a respectable life."

He flopped on his side. "You keep saying a respectable life, but how in the world can you say you are not respectable? You are a lady in every sense of the world and those around you know it."

She reached up to gently cup his face, and Marcus almost purred into the warmth of her hands, despite the frustrating nature of this relationship. "I am naked in the bed of a man who owns a popular but incredibly notorious club. How could anyone call me a lady if they knew that I had done this? That I craved it?"

"That you craved *me*, you mean?" he pressed, a sting working through him at the words.

She was rejecting him, as much as her family's reputation or the life she feared she would lose if she gave in to her true nature. Her true nature wasn't good enough.

And neither was he.

"*You* are why this is so difficult," she said with a shake of her head. "You are...incredible."

"But beneath you." He began to push out of the bed. "And not just because you will not let me take you."

She grasped his arm. "Not in my estimation. Marcus—"

Whatever she might have said was interrupted by a sudden pounding on the door to his office. Marcus shot a glare through the adjoining room.

"Marcus, let's finish this," she said, sitting up and wrapping the sheet around her.

"I can't ignore it," he snapped, grabbing his trousers and shoving them on as he walked through the office to the door. He yanked it open. "What?" he shouted at whoever had interrupted him.

He was surprised to find Abbot standing on the other side of the barrier. And judging from the way his friend's gaze flitted over Marcus's half-dressed frame, the surprise was mutual.

"I'm sorry to interrupt your..." Abbot shook his head. "...your work, Rivers, but we have a situation. With Crispin Flynn."

Marcus squeezed his eyes shut and waited for Annabelle's reaction. Just as he had suspected, she let out a pained cry and rushed from his bedroom with only a sheet wrapped around her lithe body.

"My brother?" she burst out as she skidded to a halt beside

him.

Abbot shifted, moving his stare to a fixed point far behind Annabelle. "Er, yes, Miss Flynn. He is making huge bets, Rivers."

"How huge?" Marcus asked.

"Ten thousand pounds."

Annabelle lifted a hand to her lips. "My God, he'll be bankrupt if he continues this way."

"See if you can distract him. I'll come down straight away, I need to dress."

Abbot nodded and left the room with an expression no one couldn't read as relief. He clearly didn't want to be standing in the room with Marcus and his apparent lover. Marcus was not looking forward to what would surely be a pointed conversation with Abbot later.

"Marcus," Annabelle breathed as he closed the door behind his friend. She clutched his arm and her sheet slipped slightly, revealing a tantalizing curve of her breast.

He pushed aside his wicked thoughts. "I'll go down, Annabelle."

"I'm coming with you," she insisted.

He shook his head. "No, you aren't. I can handle—"

"I'm coming with you!" she repeated, this time shouting.

He stared at her. In this moment, she was as wild as either of her brothers had ever been. And determined. If he argued with her, it would only mean more time lost.

"Fine. Get dressed and make sure you wear your mask," he snapped as he moved toward the bedroom with her at his heels. "And you will listen to everything I say, Annabelle."

She nodded, but as they entered his chamber to dress, he had a sneaking suspicion that she was lying. And there was very little he could do about it.

For the first time since she came to the club, as she followed Marcus through the crowd, Annabelle wasn't looking at the couples engaging in erotic play. Her mind was too occupied with thoughts of her brother.

Marcus walked with purpose and it was difficult to keep up with him as he maneuvered with ease through the people. His mouth was set in a grim line, though he still acknowledged patrons at the tables and nodded to those who said his name.

He was at home here.

He made a sharp turn, and she found herself in the same hallway where they had spied before. She blushed as Marcus led her into the dark corridor.

"Marcus," she began. "I don't want to—"

"Your brother is in the gambling room here," he said, sliding open the barrier to look inside. "We've been ensuring he was in a room where we could watch him."

Her lips parted. "You have been keeping an eye on him?"

Marcus nodded. "I told you and Rafe that I would. I keep my word, despite what you may believe."

She reached out to take his hand. "I believe you to be honorable."

He said nothing, but continued to look into the peephole. He blocked her view, so she stood, not exactly patient, but waiting as he observed whatever was going on inside.

Suddenly there was a crash from inside the chamber where Marcus observed her brother. He jolted and shook her hand away. "Wait here," he barked as he began to race back down the corridor. "Don't you dare move!"

Her breath coming short, Annabelle hurtled herself into position so she could see inside the chamber. Her brother had flipped the gambling table. Money and cards were scattered around the room. And now Crispin staggered, taking wild swings at the very large, very serious-looking man he had been playing against.

And the man did not look happy or forgiving.

"Cheat!" Crispin roared, just barely staggering out of the

way of the man's meaty fist.

Before he could swing again, the door flew open and Marcus and several of his staff ran in. Three of them restrained Crispin's gambling partner even as Marcus moved toward her brother.

"Cris," he said, his soothing tone unlike anything she had ever heard. It actually reminded her of Rafe talking to Crispin. Marcus even used his long-abandoned shortening of his name. "Cris, listen to me."

"You let a bunch of fucking cheats into your club, Rivers," Crispin slurred.

Annabelle tensed at the ugly language, but leaned closer to watch Marcus's reaction. He could have become angry, but instead he laughed. "Whoever pays, you know."

Crispin's gambling partner reared. "I'm no damn cheat, Rivers."

Marcus glared at him. "Do calm down, Porter. Take him out, get him a drink, men."

The servants complied, half-escorting, half-dragging Crispin's partner away. That left Crispin, Marcus and Abbot in the room together.

"What is the cause of all this, Crispin?" Marcus asked softly.

"She's gone, my brother is gone," Crispin slurred.

Annabelle blinked. *She*?

"I don't know who *she* is," Marcus said softly. "But your brother is perfectly fine. I had supper with him not three days ago."

Her brother snorted. "You had supper with the fucking duke."

Annabelle turned her head as pain slashed through her. Crispin had never accepted Rafe's inheritance of their cousin's title. It seemed to break him to know Rafe had to change to fit his new future. Even though Crispin had actually *helped* their brother when his life with Serafina wasn't certain.

"The duke and your brother are the same," Marcus

reassured him.

"No, they are not. Rafe cannot be who he once was."

"He seems much the same to me," Marcus said.

"*You* are not his brother."

"No," Marcus agreed. "I do not have that privilege, you are correct. But I have known you two a very long time. I owe you both a great deal. And I want to help you."

Crispin looked at him, and Annabelle could see his misery. "How can you help me?" he grunted.

"Let me get you sober and we can talk about it," Marcus offered. "You and me, no one else. You *know* I am on your side."

Annabelle held her breath as she waited for her brother's response. She watched Crispin's face, and for a heartbeat she thought he might accept Marcus's offer. And then he pulled away from the man who was apparently a much closer friend than she had imagined and barked, "Just get me a drink, Rivers. That's how you can help me."

Marcus sighed, his shoulders rolling forward. "I'm afraid I can't do that."

"I pay you to do that," Crispin said, his voice low and angry.

Annabelle covered her mouth at his dismissive tone. But Marcus didn't even flinch.

"You *pay* for the privilege of gaming and whoring in these halls," he corrected softly. "A privilege I can remove at any time, my friend, although I hope you don't push me so far."

Annabelle knew what her brother would do even before he moved. She saw his posture stiffen, his fist form at his side, his face twist in animal, out of control emotion that had nothing to do with Marcus. He was going to swing.

"Crispin!" she screamed out as he did so.

Her brother jolted at her voice and his punch went wild. Marcus was easily able to step out of the way of it and Crispin staggered to the ground.

"What the hell?" he barked, looking around, looking

directly toward the peephole where she stood. Worse, Marcus looked toward her too, his face a mask of horror.

She stepped back into the darkened hall, flattening against the wall opposite the peephole. What had she done?

Her brother stared in the direction of the hall for a moment more and then glared at Marcus. "Spies, *friend*?"

"You know these rooms," Marcus said, his voice mild, though she could see the strain in his muscles.

"Go to hell," Crispin snapped, then marched out of the room.

Annabelle ran down the darkened hallway and into the main room. She saw her brother weaving through the crowd, barely avoiding smashing into others. She took a step to follow him, but was stopped as Marcus stepped from the gambling room and caught her arm.

"Don't," he whispered, drawing her back. "He's drawn enough attention to himself as it is, don't drag yourself down with him."

She spun on him. "I can't let him go! Not in this state!"

Marcus said nothing, but motioned with his head to Abbot and began hauling her across the room, away from Crispin's departing back.

"No!" she said, pulling against his grip, but to no avail. "Marcus!"

He ignored her and dragged her up the stairs to his office. Abbot followed and wordlessly closed the door behind them as Marcus released her.

"Marcus!" she repeated, pled, begged.

He nodded. "I know. I know you are upset, and you have every right to be. But Annabelle, what were you thinking saying his name, attempting to follow him when I specifically told you not to move?"

"He is my brother!" she shouted, slamming her hand on Marcus's desk, as if she could make him understand if she brought the room down.

"And he is my friend," he snapped back.

She stood for a moment, panting and staring at him. Then she nodded. "Yes. Yes, I saw that."

"You have wanted Rafe to offer Crispin help. You've believed in your heart that if the offer was made, Crispin would take it," Marcus continued, his voice softer now, filled with tenderness—not for Crispin, but for her. "But I offered him the same and he refused, Annabelle. Violently."

Abbot cleared his throat. "Should I place Mr. Flynn on the banned list for the club?"

Annabelle spun on him. Crispin banned? She knew he deserved nothing less. After all, he had attempted an assault on the owner, flipped over a table and caused a disruption that those downstairs were likely screeching about, rather than whispering. He'd worn no mask during it all.

Her heart sank.

"No," Marcus said.

Abbot shook his head. "No?"

"No," he repeated, his eyebrows lifting as if to challenge Abbot to question him. "If Crispin doesn't come here, he will have nowhere to go where he'll be looked after. However, it's obvious we need to control this situation more. When he gambles, be certain it is with one of our men. They won't let the situation get out of hand and can return any 'winnings' at the end of the night." He began to pace, and Annabelle could see his mind turning. "When he drinks, be certain it is watered down. And if you can steer him toward a woman, by God, do it. He'll be less trouble."

Abbot wrote down the notes carefully. "You intend to coddle him."

Annabelle glared. Marcus's man wasn't wrong, but she hated him for pointing that out, regardless. He had influence, and he might change Marcus's mind about taking care of Crispin.

"I intend to do everything I can for a friend who saved my life," Marcus growled.

Abbot hesitated only a moment before he nodded. "Then it

shall be done. I will go down and begin making arrangements and try to soothe the ruffled feathers. Unless there is anything else?"

"No," Marcus said, leaning his hands on the desk, his head bent.

Abbot left the room and for a long time after he had left them alone, all Annabelle could do was stare at Marcus. This man, her lover, her brother's champion, this unexpected man…he held such sway over her. And yet she could do nothing with her feelings.

"Marcus," she whispered.

He lifted his head, but didn't look at her. "Please don't ask me how your brothers saved my life. Not tonight."

She flinched. He would not share that story with her. It was too personal; perhaps she had not earned it. And yet she wanted to know.

"When, then?" she asked.

He finally turned toward her. "Next time. When our emotions are less heightened. I will tell you, Annabelle. I'll tell you everything."

She nodded before she moved toward him, sliding her hand against his cheek. "Thank you Marcus."

She lifted to her tiptoes and pressed a kiss to his mouth. He groaned at the touch, opening his mouth to grant her access. She took it, tasting his tongue, teasing him as he had teased her so very many times.

Then she stepped back. "And I'm so sorry," she added before she adjusted the mask on her face and left the room. Left him.

And left herself more confused and in turmoil than she had ever been in before.

CHAPTER SEVENTEEN

Marcus was sitting as his desk an hour later, looking at the swirling patterns of Annabelle's handwriting, when there was a light knock. He tensed. After tonight, there was no one he wanted to see. No one he felt prepared to talk to.

And yet he had a club to run and he couldn't ignore his duties.

"Yes," he croaked out, his voice barely carrying.

The door opened slowly and Abbot stepped inside, leaning on the doorjamb as he examined Marcus at length. Marcus forced his gaze to the paperwork before him.

"Is there something going on downstairs that I need to know about?" he asked softly. Abbot didn't respond long enough that Marcus looked up at him. "Well?"

"No, nothing downstairs."

"If you have no club business to discuss, then I'd like to be left alone for a while," Marcus ground out.

"I have club business," his friend said, pushing off the door, shutting it behind him and settling into a chair across from Marcus.

"God, Abbot," Marcus groaned.

"Are you lovers, then?"

Marcus glared at him. "It's none of your damn business."

"Perhaps not. Are you?"

Marcus leaned back in his chair, watching Abbot closely.

He had known Paul Abbot for almost as long as he had run this club. They were of an age, and he trusted the man across from him with his money, his business…and he would even go so far as to say his life.

Despite all that, telling him something so personal was difficult. Marcus had been trained long ago by bitter circumstance not to give others too much of himself and had few confidantes.

"I'm not asking as your man of affairs," Abbot said softly. "I don't care about impact on the business, though later I may point out to you, yet again, that your actions could very well have one. But tonight, in this moment, I am asking you as a friend. Because I think you could use one. If you agree, then let me ask again. Are you lovers with Annabelle Flynn?"

Marcus rubbed a hand over his face, and then he shrugged. "It is more complicated than that."

"How so?"

He met Abbot's stare. "She requires she remain virginal for her nameless, faceless future husband who I will no doubt be unworthy to even shine his rotting shoe."

Abbot leaned away. "She said that? She seems many things, but not cruel."

"No, she never says it," Marcus whispered. "But I know it, don't I? We both know what I am."

"A successful self-made man who was a friend to her late father, as well as both her brothers? A man who chooses to protect one of her brothers even to his detriment?"

Marcus pursed his lips. "She wants respectability. The kind that comes with a title. The kind I could never provide thanks to this club and my personal history."

"Hmmm." The noise Abbot made was noncommittal. "So no sex. But obviously a great deal else, judging from the scene I encountered earlier in the evening."

"Yes," Marcus admitted, his tone rough as he thought of the slick sweetness of Annabelle's body, the aching drive he'd had to violate their agreement and claim her as his. The massive self-control it had taken not to do so.

"Does anyone else know?" Abbot asked.

"My mother."

Abbot's eyes went almost impossibly wide. "You told Calliope?"

Marcus shrugged. "I needed to talk to someone who would tell me exactly what I needed to hear. Who wouldn't whitewash the truth."

"Well, Calliope is certainly that. And what did she say?"

"Nothing to help," Marcus said with a long sigh. "Though she did ask after you, of course."

"That's my girl," Abbot said, his tone filled with teasing.

"You two are of a mind, at least."

"That's because your mother is an incredibly smart woman and we both care about you." Abbot's face was entirely sincere. "Though when I asked you if anyone else knew, I meant more from Annabelle's part."

Marcus scrubbed a hand over his face. "I don't know. I suppose she might have told someone, but considering her drive to protect her reputation, I doubt my name crosses her lips except when I force it here in this office."

"And so this is why she comes here? For an almost-affair with you?"

"No. The situation between us arose because we both found ourselves drawn together, physically. I suggested we not fight it and this is as far as she will allow. So I take what I can get." Marcus pushed from the desk. "But she comes here because she truly believes she can save Crispin. That if she can observe her brother at his worst, she can help bring back his best."

"Do you agree?"

He stared out at the writhing bodies below. The night was coming to an end and most of those left in the club had given up on cards and were now focusing on far more pleasing activities. He hated them all for it, for taking something he couldn't have.

"I don't know. Annabelle is stubborn enough that perhaps she can force his hand." He sighed. "But after tonight, after seeing Flynn so lost, I doubt she can fix him. He'll have to want to do that all on his own, whatever demon haunts his every step. I fear it will hurt her deeply."

"You care for her," Abbot breathed.

Marcus stiffened. "Nonsense."

"No, it isn't. I can hear it in your words, I can see it in the way you watch her, the way you tense when you talk about her. The fact that you sought council from your mother reinforces my theory even more."

Marcus glanced at his friend over his shoulder. "I know she isn't for me, Abbot, you needn't worry about that. Whatever we share is temporary at best. According to her eldest brother, the duke, her Season is going very well. I will likely be a unpleasant memory soon enough."

He frowned at the thought. He hoped Annabelle wouldn't come to regret him over time. But perhaps if she found a husband she loved and respected, she would wish she hadn't surrendered so much to Marcus.

"Rivers," Abbot said, his tone suddenly different. "Who wrote in your books?"

Marcus turned to find Abbot had stood and moved to his desk. He was leaning over the ledgers, both eyebrows raised. Marcus cleared his throat. "Annabelle is very clever with figures. And she has some good ideas for managing some of our affairs. Perhaps we can discuss them another day."

Abbot looked up at him. There was no anger on his face, just pure, unadulterated surprise. "Be careful, my friend," he said softly. "Not because I don't trust your judgment, not because I dislike this woman, not because I don't understand why you're drawn to her…"

"Then why?" Marcus glared at him.

Abbot shifted in discomfort. "I've known you almost a decade, Rivers. You don't normally allow yourself to feel for anyone, no matter the circumstances. You may not know the power it has when you care so deeply."

Marcus gritted his teeth. He could tell Abbot again that he didn't care about Annabelle. He could deny it to the sky and the moon and the sun until the world ended. But in his heart, he knew it wasn't true. And he had a suspicion saying it out loud would only prove Abbot's point all the more.

Instead, what he had to do was purge those feelings from his mind. Separate the desire he felt for Annabelle for any silly feelings he'd ever associated with her starting that long ago day when he first met her.

That was the only way to protect himself. The only way to save them both.

"I'm so glad we could have tea together, just the two of us today."

Annabelle was pulled from her reverie by Serafina's voice. She glanced over to find her brother's wife watching her, a bright smile on her beautiful face but a strange look in her eyes. Annabelle pushed away thoughts of Crispin and Marcus, as she had been for nearly two days, and instead forced a smile for Serafina.

"I am as well," she said, and did not have to lie. "I so enjoy our times together."

"Yes." Serafina refreshed her tea, her gaze flitting to Annabelle as she did so. "But I fear you are distracted much of late."

Annabelle swallowed hard. "Am—am I?"

"I think you know you are, my dear. Would you like to talk to me about why?"

Annabelle searched Serafina's face, trying to determine how much she knew. From her tone, it seemed she meant more than she said, but her face revealed nothing. But then, her sister-in-law had her reasons for developing such a skill, though she no longer had need to use it.

"I suppose anyone would be distracted by a foray into Society," Annabelle said, dropping her gaze. Unlike Serafina, it was hard for her to hide her emotions and she feared they would be clear upon her face.

"I feel it is more than that." Serafina reached forward and took both Annabelle's hands. She squeezed gently, forcing Annabelle to look at her. "Are you certain there is nothing you need to tell me? Perhaps something that would be difficult for you to explain to Rafe or your mother? Because what is the use of having a sister if not to confess our deepest secrets and obtain advice, perspective and even aid?"

Annabelle sucked in a breath. She adored her brother's wife. As Serafina had just said, she was the sister Annabelle had never had, and in the months she and Rafe had been married, the two had grown closer than ever. Which meant she wanted so desperately to tell her everything.

But telling Serafina anything meant telling Rafe the same. And she could not imagine her brother would not be enraged if he knew her desperate plans. If he knew how far she had gone with Marcus and how much further she longed to go.

Rafe would tell her to forget Crispin, to abandon him until he was ready to reach out to his family once more. After seeing her brother lose control two nights before, she couldn't do that. Even if she knew it was sound advice somewhere in her heart.

And yet her lips parted, they trembled with the words she so desperately wanted to say out loud. Serafina leaned forward, anticipating the truth, blue eyes wide with readiness to comfort and council.

"I-I am only worried about my future in Society," Annabelle finally said, turning her face so she wouldn't see Serafina's recognition of that bitter lie. "And worried about Crispin. He seems bent on destroying himself."

Serafina sighed. "I can imagine your brother's condition at present much troubles you. I never had a brother of my own, but I have come to care about you all so much since my marriage to Rafe that I also think of Crispin often and fear for his safety."

Annabelle shot her a look. "Is there no way you can convince Rafe to reach out to him? To offer him assistance?"

Serafina tilted her head. "Do you not think he has? Over the past few months, when Crispin has sunk to his lowest, Rafe has offered him help multiple times, only to be rebuffed soundly and often rather cruelly. I assure you, it breaks his heart to let Crispin go, knowing he is in deep pain and that Rafe can do nothing to help him."

Annabelle drew a breath at the tears that leapt into Serafina's eyes at her words. She had been making the assumption that Rafe was simply choosing to be cold toward their brother, but she could see now his deep emotions, reflected in Serafina's empathetic pain for him.

"I have been too hard on Rafe, I can see that," she whispered. "And after what I've seen, perhaps he is right."

Serafina jerked her face toward her. "What you've seen? What do you mean?"

Annabelle bit her tongue. What an idiotic confession, dropped in a moment of unguarded weakness and revealing too much. "I only mean knowing that Crispin has separated himself from us all," she hastened to lie. "After my discoveries when I snuck into Mr. Rivers' carriage that night a few weeks ago."

Serafina's eyebrow arched. "Yes, Mr. Rivers. He is a very interesting fellow, isn't he?"

"What do you mean?" Annabelle asked, hearing her own voice crack and trying desperately to keep it from happening again.

"At supper, he was very witty and engaging. You seemed to like him a great deal, actually."

Annabelle turned her face. "How could you not? As you said, he is unexpected."

"Hmmm."

Annabelle's eyes went wide. "What does *hmmm* mean?"

Serafina got to her feet, a slow process thanks to the

increasingly rounded belly that held her child. She walked across the room before she turned to look at Annabelle. "I cannot be with you as you make your way in Society. For that I am truly sorry, because I might have been able to ease your transition."

Annabelle blinked, uncertain of this sudden shift in subject from Marcus to her debut. But not sorry for it, Marcus was an infinitely more dangerous topic. "I understand," she said slowly.

Serafina continued, "But I *have* been able to observe you during your weeks out in the world of the Upper Ten Thousand, and I see that you are garnering interest from Lord Claybrook."

Serafina swallowed. *Claybrook.* She had not thought of the man in days, actually. The moment he left any room they shared, it was as if he no longer existed. Not a good beginning, she knew, but she had no intention of admitting that to Serafina.

"Yes, I'm very pleased about that fact," she said, hoping her voice sounded brighter than she felt. "If we were to make a match, I think it would be a good one. For me, especially, considering that he is so well regarded. And I'm certain my dowry will not hurt his coffers."

Serafina's lips pinched together. "I hate to hear you speak so cavalierly about the rest of your life. To put your future in terms of advantage and wealth when I know better than anyone how much those things can damage if they are all one shares with one's intended. What about friendship and attraction? What about *love*, Annabelle?"

"Not all of us can be so lucky as you and my brother have been," Annabelle whispered.

"Yes, we are lucky that we were brought together by circumstance and yet found such a connection that will keep us in each other's arms and hearts for all time."

"And yet Rafe is also an undeniably good match," Annabelle pointed out gently.

Serafina shook her head. "I would love your brother if he had not a farthing for bread. If he had no property and no title." She met Annabelle's eyes. "If he were no more than a notorious club owner."

Now it was Annabelle who leapt to her feet. She walked away from Serafina, her hands shaking at her sides and her eyes unseeing as she stood at the sideboard, staring at her brother's bottles of whiskey.

"Well, I have no one I love so deeply," she said, her voice trembling.

Serafina was quiet for a very long time, and Annabelle had to force herself not to look at her sister-in-law. Finally, Serafina sighed. "The best laid plans are often not as good as we believe they will be. And maybe what you think you want is not what you actually need."

Annabelle spun toward her. Serafina's face, so kind and open, still told her nothing about what she knew. Or *thought* she knew.

"I wish it were so easy as want and need," Annabelle said. "And that I had choices as to how I would be seen by the world at large. But right now is my only chance to have the life I have wanted, Serafina. I must take it, mustn't I?"

Her sister-in-law blinked and her smile faltered. "Only you can decide that, Annabelle. Only you can know what you are willing to lose to get what you think you want."

Annabelle bent her head, her mind spinning on Marcus. Marcus's mouth, his touch, his soft and gentle words that brushed over her skin and settled beneath it.

"Now are you *certain* you have nothing to reveal?" Serafina asked. "Nothing that I could help you with at all?"

Annabelle swallowed hard. "No. I'm afraid I must determine my future on my own. There is nothing else to say in the end."

She saw Serafina's disappointment at her answer, but the flash of emotion was gone from her face as quickly as it had come. She smiled again and retook her seat.

"Would you like more tea?" she asked, as if the deeper, darker conversation they had shared had never happened.

Annabelle nodded as she too sat down again. But she couldn't help feeling that she had missed an opportunity here. And she hoped she wouldn't regret it later.

CHAPTER EIGHTEEN

Marcus watched as Annabelle scribbled notes from her place at his desk. Her mask had been replaced by her spectacles once again and she was focused on the task at hand, just as she had been since she arrived half an hour ago.

But he knew in his heart that something had changed between them. There was a skittishness to how she held herself and her glances toward him had been furtive rather than natural.

"Annabelle, what is wrong?" he finally asked, coming around to sit on the other side of his desk, forcing her to look directly at him.

She shook her head far too quickly. "Nothing. Of course nothing."

He leaned back and folded his arms. "Annabelle…"

She caught her breath, stared at his ledgers for a long, silent moment and then whispered, "Do you think my brother will return here tonight?"

Marcus pursed his lips. "It is his regular night to come, yes. But he is late. It could be that after his recent outburst, he may stay away for a while."

Her cheeks flamed, and he saw both embarrassment and pain in the pinkening of her face. "I-I am sorry, again, for the way he behaved."

"Why do you apologize?" he asked with a shrug. "You

didn't cause him to lose control."

"Why do you think he is so unhappy?" Her voice cracked as she asked the question.

He stared at her hand, clenched on the desktop. He so desperately wanted to touch it, to comfort her physically. But that was most definitely not his place.

He leaned forward anyway, and did exactly that. He covered her hand briefly, letting his fingers stroke over hers.

"I wouldn't know," he said, voice rough as he pulled away. "You know him better, don't you?"

To his surprise, she bent her head and a tear slid down her cheek. "If you had asked me a year ago, two years ago, I would have said I knew him better than anyone except for perhaps Rafe. I would have told you I thought of him not just as my sometimes destructive brother, but as my friend."

Marcus drew back. He had never heard a lady call her brother a friend. But then, Annabelle was entirely singular. Which was why he liked her so damned much that it physically hurt.

"But not now?"

She shook her head. "Since Rafe's marriage, I have watched Crispin spiral out of control, but I have no idea on earth why. When he was going to hit you, I knew what he would do; that is why I cried out. But when he looked around, trying to find the voice that said his name, it wasn't my brother I saw in his face. That man was a stranger."

"He said something about *she*," Marcus offered, thinking back to that night. "Was there a woman?"

"There is always a woman with Crispin," she said with a sigh. "But I've never known one to make him weak or to hurt him."

Marcus stared at her. He would have said the same thing about himself before he met Annabelle, or perhaps it was more correct to say before she staggered into his club and forced him to do more than stalk her mother's drive, watching for a glimpse.

"Perhaps he met the right girl," he said, his voice low as he searched her face.

"She would have to be the wrong girl if she has hurt him so much," she growled, her protectiveness of her brother bright on her face.

Marcus shook his head. "Sometimes people don't mean to hurt those they care about. It just happens."

She jerked her gaze toward him. "I-I suppose that's true. I'm sure I have hurt people in my past without meaning to do so. And though I hope I won't, I fear I will repeat that in the future."

Marcus turned his face. He wasn't certain she was talking about him, about their arrangement, but that was where his mind took him regardless. He could clearly picture the moment when she would walk away from him. And soon after that, she would certainly forget him, even while he was haunted with images of how close he'd been to perfection, to happiness.

To love.

He pushed out of his chair and paced away from her so she wouldn't see his ridiculous thoughts on his face. So that he wouldn't have to look at her while they infected his mind.

He cleared his throat. "I think your brother is lucky indeed to have you as a friend."

She sighed. "It seems he is lucky to have one in you as well. You could have had him banned from your club and you didn't. You could have hit him back and you didn't."

Marcus shifted, not looking at her. "I would never do that."

"Because you feel you owe him and Rafe?"

He nodded. "Yes."

"You told me the last time you saw me that you would explain to me how it is you came to know them, why you feel you owe them so much." She moved toward him. "Will you tell me now?"

He slowly faced her. She was so beautiful, so desirable, so everything he had ever wanted and more than he would ever have. Perhaps telling her the story of why he owed her family would be a reminder to him of why he couldn't want the things he wanted now.

He motioned to the fire and the two chairs before it. She moved there slowly, tucking her feet up beneath her and watching him as he sat beside her.

He took a long breath, wishing it would calm him. "I met your father and your brothers when I was fourteen years old," he said with a shake of his head as memories flooded him. "There was a club that your father used to frequent."

"Like this one?" Annabelle interrupted, bringing him back, temporarily, to this place and time.

He shook his head. "No, not quite. The Donville Masquerade is a high quality establishment, I pride myself in its cleanliness, its safety and its reputation. But the club where I met them wasn't any of those things. It was a gaming house, and there was always a fight happening. It was owned by a bastard named Jack Quill. He was a drunk and a skinflint and he took whatever opportunity he could to steal from the clientele."

"And my father went there?" Annabelle said, her voice filed with incredulity.

Marcus shrugged. "You know how your father was. He liked to game and Quill paid odds well. Probably because he knew his patrons would rarely win; they were so sauced they were all practically crossed-eyed."

"And where did you fit in?" she asked.

He hesitated a long moment. Here was the difficult part. "I worked for Quill."

She tilted her head, and he could see she didn't fully understand. Of course she wouldn't. At fourteen, she was still in the schoolhouse, reading her books and sewing and playing pianoforte. She had no concept of the desperation of the street.

"So that was how you met my father, at the gaming club."

"And your brothers," he said. "Your father brought them along, despite their tender years."

He expected Annabelle to be shocked by that fact, perhaps even horrified, but instead she merely shook her head. "Oh, Papa. So predictable. And were they the youngest gamblers in the place?"

He smiled. "Indeed, they were. Though your father didn't let them game often. I believe Quill's establishment was a bit of a lesson for them in how far a man could fall if he let drink and cards and bad company mix."

Annabelle pursed her lips. "For all the good those lessons have done Crispin."

"Only recently," he said softly.

She nodded, but the pain lingered in her dark eyes. "So there they all were, in your father's club…"

"He wasn't my father," Marcus snapped, stiffening.

She leaned away from the sudden sharpness of his tone. "I'm sorry."

"Quill essentially owned me," he said, bitterness in his voice that he couldn't contain even after all these long years. "And he never let me forget it. He forced me to slave for him, steal for him, do his bidding, and when I didn't do it right, or when he'd had a bad day or when he felt like it because it was Tuesday or Friday or Sunday…he beat me. Sometimes with his fist, sometimes with a stick, sometimes with a hot iron if he was truly angry."

Annabelle gasped, and in that sound he felt, again, the disparity of their childhoods. Annabelle who had been raised with such love, he who had been nearly drowned like an unwanted kitten once, who had been beaten until he couldn't move, who had been reminded daily or even hourly that he was trash.

"Marcus," she whispered, and now it was her hand that reached for him, covered his, squeezed with such small, but meaningful comfort. "I'm so sorry."

"One night Quill was enraged. He had asked me to empty a barrel in the back. It was filled with…" He flinched. "You don't want to know what it was filled with. But it was so heavy and I was hardly more than a child. I couldn't lift it, I tried dragging it, but it wouldn't budge. Quill came in and he started screaming at me. Just screaming and screaming. And then the screaming stopped and the hitting, punching and kicking began."

Annabelle made a pained sound in her throat and her hand tightened on his. It was odd, for the pressure of her fingers seemed to help him as he fought through the layers of memories, the nightmare of pain that always accompanied thoughts of that night.

He swallowed. "It all becomes foggy after a while. But Quill flipped the barrel's disgusting contents onto me while he beat me. He told me that was what I deserved. And then he told me that if I was so worthless, he wasn't about to keep me around. He said he was going to kill me and toss me into the river with the other boys who couldn't do their jobs."

Next to him, Annabelle covered her mouth with the hand that wasn't clenching his.

"I don't know if he would have done it or if he had done what he claimed before. But he was kicking me over and over and I was certain I would die. I almost welcomed it, just to get away from him. From his boot, from his hand, from the life that wasn't a life at all."

"But something stopped him," she whispered. "Because you are here."

Marcus swallowed hard, fighting the emotion that mobbed him for a moment. "I remember the kicking stopped and I looked up and there was a man, lit up like an angel and he was pulling Quill away, tossing him aside like he was nothing. And even though he was a gentleman, that much was clear in his dress and his smell, he picked me up, covered in shit and piss and God knows what else, and he carried me away."

"Who?" she breathed. He met her eyes, held steady, and watched as they widened. "My father."

He nodded. "Crispin had snuck out of the hall and saw what was happening to me. He told Rafe and together they rushed to your father. He never hesitated a moment to come to my aid, despite not knowing me."

"You were of an age with his beloved sons and no one deserves what you went through." She shook her head with a soft smile. "Of course he would do so. Flawed but wonderful, my father."

"Indeed."

"And *that* is why you feel you owe my family."

He nodded. "That night and what happened after. I woke in a clean bed three days later, my wounds tended to, including the one that gave me that scar you examined so closely the first night we were together."

She flinched. "My God."

"There was a woman there, sitting by my bed. Calliope Rivers. She and her husband, Oliver, ran this place. Your father had taken me here. I suppose he knew what they would do."

"Wasn't Quill enraged? He believed he owned you, you said."

Marcus laughed. "He didn't give a damn. After all, your father bought and paid for me. Paid him handsomely, I learned later. Far more than I was worth."

Annabelle lunged for him, covering his cheeks with her soft hands, drawing him closer. "Never say that again, Marcus Rivers. Never, ever claim you are not worthy. My father made a good bargain, whatever the price, and I'm sure he would tell you the same if you could ask him."

He covered her hands, lost for a moment in the fervent passion of her expression. She was shaking with indignation at both the circumstances of his childhood and the way he dismissed himself. He ached for how much she seemed to care, for the feelings that true connection stoked in him. He knew their names and how foolish they were under the circumstances.

He could not love Annabelle Flynn.

"What happened with Mr. and Mrs. Rivers?" she asked, drawing back as if she read his mind and knew distance was required as he did.

"They took me in, healed me. The first chance I had, I tried to run away."

She gasped. "Wh-why?"

"Because I'd spent my life like an animal in a cage. I acted as such," he explained. "I ran ten times in that first year. I also shouted at them. And I stole from them twice."

Her lips parted. "What did they do?"

"Quietly and kindly broke me, like the skittish colt that I was." He smiled. "They brought me home and spoke to me compassionately. They could have sent me to the workhouses or even had me transported, I suppose. I was old enough for either. But they didn't. And after a year, I began to calm. They offered me their name and I took it. They offered me education and I drank it in. But mostly, they offered me love. And I soaked in it."

"They sound like amazing people," she whispered, blinking at the tears that shone in her eyes.

"Calliope is remarkable. Funny and free. Oliver was the most decent man I ever knew. He died ten years ago and left me the club. I doubled its profits in a year and tripled it in two. I wish he could have seen that."

Annabelle smiled. "I'm sure he does, Marcus. I'm sure he sees it and they are both proud of you. You should be proud of yourself."

"But now you see why I owe your family so much. Without the intervention of your brothers, intervention on behalf of a boy they shouldn't have given a damn about, without your father taking matters into his own hands, I would likely be dead."

She gazed up into his face, understanding on her features. "I'm so glad they were the men they were and saved you so you could become the man you are."

He blinked, once again caught up in her beauty. Then he shook his head. "He came by to see me often, you know. Your father. First man to sign up for lifetime membership to the club. Your brothers soon followed suit, and with them came more and more." He shrugged. "They were my patrons, I suppose."

"I think they would say friends," she whispered.

"And I have repaid them by seducing their sister, his daughter," he said.

She cocked her head. "Is that what you are doing? Seducing me?"

"Didn't I?" he asked.

She got up slowly and moved to his chair. As she lowered herself into his lap, she shook her head. "You and I *both* knew exactly what we were doing when we started this affair, Marcus Rivers. I'm no shy wallflower, that is certain, and I do what I desire. That much of me, at least, is a Flynn."

"Annabelle," he whispered.

She gently covered his mouth with two fingers. "Please don't tell me why I should walk away, Marcus. Or what I should do or don't do. Right now I don't want to hear it. Right now I simply want to be in your arms. I want to feel your body against mine. I want *you*."

He shivered as she pulled her hand away and replaced it with her mouth, driving her tongue against his, demanding what she believed he would withhold.

Except he hadn't been about to deny her. Instead, she had interrupted him in a far greater folly. He had been about to tell her that he loved her.

Because that was the truth that burned in his heart, his blood, his soul. And only her desire had saved them both from its destructive power.

CHAPTER NINETEEN

Annabelle trembled as her hands found Marcus's jacket. She slipped them inside and she reveled in his warmth. It was proof he was alive, he was here with her. Knowing that he very nearly hadn't been, that he had likely only been saved because of her family…it struck a fear in her that was far more than mere empathy for an abused child. The very concept of Marcus not existing was…

Horrifying.

She pushed the jacket from his shoulders slowly, allowing herself to feel every inch of his shoulders, his arms, as she did so. He stared up at her, his green eyes dark and filled with desire and…and something else. Something deeper and richer, utterly terrifying.

She blinked and returned her focus to tugging his jacket out from the chair behind him. She tossed it aside before she moved on to his shirt. But she continued to feel his stare as she worked on every button. Continued to be surrounded by warmth that had to do with far more than body heat.

She had to get her head out of the clouds. Marcus Rivers couldn't *care* for her. Want her, certainly, but anything deeper had to be a mistake. It had to be a case of her overlaying her own strange feelings onto him. She simply had to forget those feelings, pretend they didn't exist. It was the only way.

Her fingers moved faster over his shirt, pulling it open,

nearly popping the buttons free as she struggled to strip him down and find the passion between them rather than the emotions she didn't want to face.

He didn't move as she did so, he didn't stop staring at her face, and finally she made herself look at him.

"Annabelle," he whispered, lifting his hands to cover hers. "There should be no desperation here."

She caught her breath, watching how their fingers intertwined. His hand was bigger than hers by far and yet it looked so right closing around her flesh. As if they fit in ways she didn't want to comprehend.

She shook her head. "There will always be desperation, Marcus, in something so temporary."

She'd said the words as much for herself as for him, but she saw them hit the mark. His bright eyes dulled a fraction and his mouth tightened. He slowly released her hands and pushed to his feet, making her stand with him so she wasn't deposited on her backside on the floor.

"Yes, a good point," he said, his voice as strained as his face.

He caught her elbow, and suddenly she was being rushed out of his office, through his chamber door. Only then did he spin her around and strip the buttons along the back of her gown open with no effort. He tugged her dress off and kicked it aside, then followed suit with her chemise.

He turned her to face him and looked her up and down. She felt no shame in his frank appraisal, only desire for him. Desire for his touch.

"Lay down on the bed," he ordered.

She cocked her head. "Will you not remove your clothing?"

For a moment his lips pursed, as if he were considering not doing so. But then he pointed to the bed. "Lay down and I will."

She did as she had been told, settling onto his pillows as she watched him finish taking off the shirt she had unbuttoned.

He sat down on one of the chairs in his bedroom to remove his boots, and his trousers followed after that. She sucked in a breath.

It was amazing to see this man naked. Every time it took her breath away. She stared at every curve of muscle, every stretched inch of skin from his chest to his stomach to his hard cock. Then she reached for him. He obliged her silent order by coming to stand beside her.

She dragged her fingers over his stomach, his hip and around his back. There she found the scar. When she first saw it, she'd been surprised and curious. Now she touched the ridge of hard skin and flinched at what had almost been lost.

"Don't worry, love," he whispered as he leaned over, covering her, pinning her to the bed with his weight. "It doesn't hurt now."

She closed her eyes as his mouth slanted over hers. She wrapped her arms around him, clinging to his as he kissed her until time melted away and everything in her world was reduced to his tongue touching hers. She lifted into his kiss, reaching for more. And he gave it, his hands gliding down her body until he cupped her breasts and began to gently glide his thumbs over her distended nipples.

She gasped at the electric zing of pleasure that rocked to her sex. It clenched at emptiness, waiting for him to fill her.

But he wouldn't. That was their bargain, at any rate. She would never feel him flexing inside of her. At the moment, that fact was as painful as if he had taken her breath.

But she ignored the loss and instead focused on the pleasure. She slid her nails against his back, eliciting a chuckle from his lips that was lost as he began to glide along her body with his mouth. She tensed as his tongue replaced his fingers on her nipple and his hand moved lower until he covered her sex with thick fingers.

He spread her open, smoothing his index finger at her entrance. Then, slowly, gently, he pressed inside. She jolted and he looked up from her breasts.

"If I am gentle, I won't breach your barrier," he explained as he began to pump his fingers in and out in a smooth rhythm.

She found herself lifting into his hands, turning her head at the stretching of her body for him. But it still felt so empty. She wanted what she'd seen in books over the years. She wanted his cock filling her. His cock driving into her even though it seemed impossible that he could fit inside.

She grunted her dissatisfaction and he stopped moving. Slowly he withdrew his fingers, licked them clean and then rolled to his side next to her.

"Am I hurting you?" he asked.

She shook her head.

"Then why the unhappy face, Annabelle?"

She pressed her lips together. She had been the one to set the boundary for him that he would not penetrate her. It would be unfair if she were to change the rules now. So she lied.

"I only want to touch you too, Marcus," she said.

He licked his lips. "Do you remember what we saw when we looked through the peephole to the lovers one of the first nights you were here?"

She nodded and understood completely. "You want to do what they did?"

"Pleasure each other at the same time." He nodded and lay back. "Will you straddle me as that lady did her lover?"

Annabelle blushed as she turned to face the foot of the bed and then draped her leg over Marcus. His cock was just below her, and she took him in hand, focusing on him instead of her own slight embarrassment.

She stroked over him, brushing the head of him against her face. She felt Marcus stiffen beneath her, his breath sucking in, and smiled. It was always a pleasure to make him shudder. With gusto, she took him into her mouth and began to plunge him deep within her throat.

She smiled around him as his hips lifted toward her. But the smile faded as he buried his tongue deep into her sex behind her without warning or preamble. She gasped as he stroked her, driving her toward orgasm with relentless tasting, teasing, sucking that had her grinding her body against him.

She dove into her own work to center herself, and they fell into a similar rhythm as they pleasured each other. Their strokes began to match, as if they were truly joined in the most intimate way. Annabelle shuddered as her orgasm built, built, and finally as Marcus sucked hard on her clitoris, she exploded. She cried out, his cock falling from her lips, riding him hard as he brought her through the wild tremblings of her release, forcing more and more pleasure on her until she begged him to stop, begged him to continue.

She fell forward as the tremors began to fade, panting.

"God, I want to be inside of you," he murmured.

His words made her open her eyes. She stared down at his still-hard cock and once again her fantasies took her to places where she could not go. But it seemed Marcus could read her mind, for he shifted suddenly, sliding from beneath her and curling his body around her from behind. She felt his cock against the slippery entrance to her body, and it took all her self-control not to simply back up against him. She was so wet, she had no doubt he would slide in without trouble. And then she would be his in every sense of the word.

He slid along her entrance without breaching her. "I want to feel your body milk mine with your orgasm, Annabelle. I want to stroke inside of you until you scream out."

She shut her eyes. He was seducing her with those words, with those images. She couldn't do it. Why? She was having a hard time remembering why.

Respectability. Yes, that was it.

"I can't," she all but sobbed.

He stopped rubbing against her, and for a moment it felt like the world had stopped spinning. The room was perfectly silent.

Finally, he said, "You can't with *me*. You won't."

She looked at him over her shoulder. His face was a hard mask. She couldn't read his emotions in his expression. But she heard pain in his tone. Faint, but there.

"I can't," she repeated. "I want—"

He turned his face. "I know what you want, Annabelle. I understand the concept of your respectability. Please don't reiterate it."

She rolled over and got to her knees to face him. "It's not…" She shook her head. "It's not easy for me either, Marcus."

"It must be easier for you," he growled. "You don't feel—"

She dove toward him and cut him off by kissing him. She didn't want to hear how he felt in this charged moment when it might sway her to change her mind about promises made and actions determined long ago.

She felt his hesitation, but then he crushed her to him, holding her so still and steady that she had no chance for escape.

"Fine," he snapped as he pulled away. "You won't allow me this. What will you give? Because I want to be inside of you, Annabelle. I want to claim you, I *need* to claim you."

She swallowed. "My mouth, my hands, are they not enough? What would be enough?"

He stared at her, holding her gaze even as he wrapped an arm around her waist. He massaged her hip, not gently, but purposefully. Then he cupped her backside, and she shivered with the intimate touch. But just as she had begun to relax, he slipped his fingers between the globes of her buttocks and pressed against the entrance there. A forbidden, dark thrill of pleasure pulsed from where he touched and she stared at him, unable to blink or think or move.

"Here," he growled.

Her lips parted. "Can you…can you do that?"

He nodded. "Yes."

"Will it hurt?" she whispered.

His hesitation spoke the answer before he said, "At first, but I will make sure you receive more pleasure than pain,

Annabelle. And in the end, this will be better. Your proper husband—" he spat those words, "—will never think to take you here. So this will always be only mine. Only *ours*."

She stared at him. What he was suggesting was terrifying not only in the act, but also in the emotion he implied. If she allowed him to take her...*there* it would be a secret that hung between them even long after he had exited her life. He would take a part of her with him. She would keep a part of him.

And it would hang within her marriage. She knew it. And she didn't give a damn.

"Yes," she whispered, as desperate to offer him a claim as he was to stake one. "Yes."

He groaned with desire and yanked her against his hard chest. He delved his tongue deep into her mouth before he turned her so she was once again facing the foot of the bed. She moved to her hands and knees out of instinct and held her breath as she waited for what would come.

But he didn't merely jam himself inside of her. To her surprise, she felt his fingers against the rosebud of her bottom once more. He pressed them to her. They were wet and slick with more than just her juices. She peeked over her shoulder to find he had retrieved some kind of oil from a drawer in the small table beside his bed and was using it to lubricate her. The pressure of his fingers was gentle as he opened her and then slipped one digit inside.

She gasped at the shock of being entered so, and he froze, letting her become accustomed to the breach.

"Is it painful?" he asked.

She shook her head as she looked at him. He was straining as he hovered behind her, his cock rock hard and his hands actually shaking.

"No, just...odd," she promised.

"I'm going to move, Annabelle," he warned her. His finger thrust, withdrawing and then pressing in again, this time further.

There was a twinge of pain to the act, but also a

blossoming pleasure that was very unlike when he touched her clitoris or licked her sex. After a moment, the strangeness of it began to fade and she found herself arching into it, into his fingers as moans left her lips.

"My God," he muttered as he slipped another finger inside and continued to stretch her. "You are like heaven."

"Please," she gasped as she lifted her backside shamelessly. "Please."

He stopped moving his fingers and stared down at her. Their eyes met over her shoulder and he jerked out a nod. "I'll go slowly, Annabelle. So slowly."

She watched as he wetted her bottom again with the oil. She caught her breath, clinging to the coverlet as her body began to tingle, throb, lose control. What was he doing to her?

"Marcus," she moaned.

He stroked a hand over his cock now, wetting it as well, and then he rubbed himself over her. First over her sex, and she hissed out pleasure. Then he moved the hot head of his member against her bottom.

"Slow," he promised again, though she wasn't certain if that was directed toward her or to himself.

He pushed and her body opened to accept him, stretching to accommodate his length and girth. She gritted her teeth at the mix of pleasure-pain at this invasion. Inch by inch, he took her until she felt his hips come flush with her backside.

"There," he groaned, the strain obvious in his voice. "Are you well?"

She nodded. "It's full, it's...there is pain, but more pleasure. Is this like it is elsewhere?"

He leaned over her, cupping her breasts. "No, different. But I promise I'll make it good for you."

He thrust slowly, gently, and Annabelle let her eyes flutter shut. The wickedness she always tried to fight, to ignore, to change in herself, swelled high, taking over. She found herself grinding back against him, demanding more without words. And he slowly, gently gave it. He thrust into her, allowing her body to stretch before he began to increase the tempo of his hips.

She met him at every stroke, her breath coming shorter as the dark pleasure built higher and higher until it was an inferno she feared would burn her alive. But just as she feared she wouldn't survive, he reached between her legs and pressed against her clitoris.

Explosions, volcanoes, fireworks all burst before her eyes, and Annabelle screamed as pleasure mobbed her and washed over her. It was the most intense sensation she'd ever experienced and she clung to the bed as she rode it out.

Behind her, she was vaguely aware of Marcus's grunting thrusts, and then she felt him tense and there was a burst of hot seed inside of her.

They collapsed across his bed together, their bodies still joined. His arms came around her, and he cradled her as her wild mind calmed.

She didn't know how long they lay together. It could have been a moment, it could have been an hour, it could have been a lifetime, but finally she pulled away, separating them, and rolled to face him.

He was watching her closely as she stroked her hand over his cheek. "That was wonderful," she whispered.

She expected him to smile, but he didn't. "I should not have done it."

"Why?" She tilted her head. "Because I was inexperienced? This was our bargain, Marcus. And I...words cannot describe how much this moved me."

"I should not have done any of it," he said.

She blinked at the harshness of his tone. "Marcus."

He pulled from her arms and got out of the bed. He stared down at her, but it was as if he had never seen her before. "You wanted darkness, Annabelle—well, you've had your fill of it. Now go home and play in the light. You are no longer welcome here," he growled.

She sat up, his words hitting her in the heart as if he had

aimed an arrow straight at her. "Why? Why?"

"Must I say it?" he asked, raising his hands. "Will my utter demise be all that pleases you?"

"I don't underst—"

"I love you, Annabelle," he growled. "As much as I hate myself for such a weakness, as much as I despise you for making me feel it."

"No," she whispered as she stared at him. She had to be losing her hearing…or her mind. "That can't be."

"Because I'm so beneath you and an animal such as myself couldn't dare feel such a thing for you?" he sneered. "If only that were true. But once I'm rid of you, perhaps it will be again."

"Marcus!" she said, her eyes wide and filling rapidly with tears she couldn't control in the face of his coldness, his hardness and the words that he said that tore her into pieces. He loved and hated her. That was what she had done to him. What her rejection had done.

"Please," she whispered.

He stepped into his trousers, the lines of his jaw taut with tension, with anger, with pain. He might have said something to her but before he could, he was interrupted by a banging on the door from the stairs.

"Marcus, ignore it," she pleaded, lifting the sheet up around herself.

Instead, he ignored *her* and stormed through the room. "What?" he shouted.

There was no expected answer from the hall. No sound of Abbot's voice or another servant. Instead, Annabelle heard the door fly open, bounce off the wall behind it, and then her heart stopped. Her mind stopped. Her everything stopped.

"What the hell is going on here, Rivers?" a voice asked. A very familiar voice. Her brother Rafe's voice. "And just where is my sister?"

CHAPTER TWENTY

Marcus stared into the very angry face of the Duke of Hartholm, but as Rafe pushed into the room past him, his eyes went wider. Rafe was not alone. Behind him were two women wearing masks, but it was clear who they were. Rafe's wife, Serafina, and his mother, Mrs. Flynn. The older woman was very pale and Marcus jerked his gaze toward Rafe.

"You brought your *mother* here?" he snapped as he peeked into the stair to make sure none of them had been followed. Not that a great deal of damage hadn't, in theory, already been done.

Rafe spun on him. "You have *no* quarter to talk to me about propriety when my sister is here and you are half-dressed."

The duke's gaze moved through the room, and at the open door to Marcus's bedchamber, he hesitated.

"Bastard!" he burst out as he strode toward and then through the door with the women and Marcus right behind him.

"Annabelle!" Rafe barked as he entered the room and found his sister beside Marcus's bed.

Annabelle had obviously made an effort to dress, but she was in nothing more than her chemise, her stockings and one slipper. As her brother entered the room, she grasped the sheet and tugged it around herself. She straightened up and held her gaze on her family, despite her cheeks, which burned with humiliation.

In spite of the circumstances, Marcus melted at the sight of her. Everything he had told her a moment ago was true. Well, everything but one thing.

He loved her. Oh, how he loved her. There was no denying that to himself. He hated himself for being so foolish. She had told him from the beginning that she would not, could not, lower herself to his level. He even understood why, based on her past.

But he'd told her he despised her, and that was the lie. He could never. And yet he had to pretend so that she would go away and end this torture.

Something that would be much easier to ensure now that her brother stood in his bedchamber with half-naked Annabelle.

To his surprise, it was Serafina who spoke next. She looked at Annabelle, then toward Marcus and said, "Well done, Annabelle."

Rafe turned on her, a look of horror on his face. "Serafina!"

She shrugged one shoulder delicately and shot a look toward Mrs. Flynn. The older woman's lips were parted and her cheeks were flushed, but there was no anger on her face.

"Rafe, we will discuss this," Serafina said, holding up a hand when her husband began to talk. "*Yes*, we will. But why don't we give Mr. Rivers and Annabelle a moment to compose themselves and to dress?"

She caught her husband's arm and began to drag him from the room. He shook her off. "Are you actually suggesting we leave them alone together?"

"I think whatever damage there is to be done has been done," Serafina said softly. "Rafe. Look at me."

Rafe did as his wife said. She held his gaze a moment and a wealth of unspoken communication went between them. Marcus couldn't help but stare in the sight of it. It said so much about their love for each other. Their respect and care.

He found himself looking toward Annabelle, but her head was bent, her breath short, her eyes swollen with tears. She would not look at him. And that was for the best, really.

"Fine," Rafe said through clenched teeth. "Dress yourselves. But if you are not out here in five minutes, I will break down the damn door. And one of the three of us may not come out alive."

He glared at Marcus as he said it, but pushed past him and back into the office. Marcus sighed, entered the bedchamber and shut the door. He was alone with Annabelle again.

And yet he didn't feel their normal connection. She still refused to look up at him, but stared at her discarded clothing.

"How did they know I would be here?" she whispered.

He shrugged as he caught his shirt and tugged it over his head before he started fiddling with his buttons. "I'm certain we will find out the answer to that question in a moment."

She finally looked at him, her dark eyes hollow and empty. "I'm sorry."

He stopped dressing and forced himself to meet her eyes. There was so much of him that wanted to take her in his arms, to comfort her, to tell her that he would fix this for her in any way he could. That they would face the consequences together.

But that wasn't what she wanted. It certainly wasn't what she deserved. She wanted a man with a title. Stealing that from her was cruel to them both. It would lead only to resentment and regret in the end.

"Get dressed," he said, putting his back to her with great difficulty. "I'm in no mood to be shot in my alleyway tonight."

He heard her sharp intake of breath but ignored it as he focused on finding and then putting on his boots. Behind him, he could hear her struggling with her gown. "Will you help me?"

He turned to find her wrinkled and half-buttoned, but the gown she wore fastened in the back and she didn't seem to be able to reach any further. He hesitated. Touching her was always a danger, a temptation. And now that he had been inside of her, he wanted to do more.

What had he been thinking?

"Marcus?" Her face drained of color as she waited. "You won't make me go out like this, will you?"

"Of course not," he said, his tone as formal as it had been the first night she came to his club. He turned her and fastened her buttons swiftly, working hard not to touch her as he did so. "There. We are as presentable as we can be. Shall we face them?"

She looked at him, straining to find some connection between them. The connection he refused to share when he knew this was all coming to a screeching halt.

"Marcus—"

He cut her off by walking to the door and opening it. He motioned for her to leave, and she took a long breath before she did so. Before she walked with her head held high past him and into his office where her family waited.

Where the end would come.

Annabelle could scarcely breathe as she entered the room. It was funny—she was about to face her angry, likely very disappointed family, but it was the man behind her whose dismissal hurt her most.

Marcus hated her for rejecting him tonight. For making it clear that he was not worthy of her virginity, and more importantly her future. Even though she didn't believe either of those things. He was more than worthy.

Only she couldn't say it. Because a life with him was a life with her father and brothers all over again. She would be dogged with whispers, looks, broken relationships...

And she was too much of a coward to face that after a lifetime of the same. Wasn't she?

She found that Serafina and her mother had taken seats by

Marcus's fire, but Rafe continued to stand at the fireplace, his hand fisting and unfisting as he watched her leave Marcus's chamber.

She had never seen him so angry.

"Annabelle," he snapped as she bent her head. "What the hell were you thinking?"

She pursed her lips. "I have done far less than you or my brother have over the years, I would wager."

Rafe shook his head. "Don't be glib. It is different and you know it. What are you doing? Why are you here? What is this about?"

Annabelle looked toward Marcus, hoping she would find an ally in him. But he stared straight ahead as if she weren't even in the room. She was alone. And she felt it keenly.

"It's about Crispin," she whispered.

Her brother jolted, jerking his stare toward her, his eyes narrowing. "Crispin," he spat out.

She nodded, but before she could say more there was even further pounding on the door. Annabelle turned away. "God, what else?" she moaned.

Marcus muttered something beneath his breath and yanked the door open. And there stood Crispin, with Abbot on his heels. Her brother was disheveled, yes, but as he entered the room she could see he was not drunk. At least not yet.

"What is going on?" he barked as he looked around the room. "I saw Rafe pass through the hall with people with him, but I couldn't believe…what are you doing here, Mama, Serafina?" He turned his gaze toward her. "Annabelle?"

Rafe glared. "An interesting question, brother. It seems Annabelle has been coming here for your benefit, and I would wager our 'friend' Mr. Rivers has been taking advantage of her desire to help you."

Annabelle lunged forward. "That is a lie! Marcus never took advantage of me."

"You were in his bed," Rafe hissed.

Abbot stepped in and slammed the door behind him,

exchanging a look with Marcus that spoke volumes. If Crispin had recognized his entire family traipsing across the hall, did that mean others had too? Had every sacrifice she'd made been for nothing?

Crispin spun on her, and his wild eyes erased her thoughts. "In his bed?" he repeated in horror.

Annabelle stared from one of her family members to another, then to Marcus with his cold glare. She shook her head. "I would appreciate it if every one of you would shut up," she snapped, folding her arms. "Before you start making accusations and threats and screaming down this club, I *will* be heard."

Both her brothers snapped their mouths shut, she supposed out of surprise at her outburst, but she thought she saw her mother and Serafina exchange a very brief smile.

"First, you all obviously came here tonight looking for me. How did you know I would be here?"

Serafina got up. "That would be my fault, Annabelle."

Annabelle turned her gaze on her sister-in-law, her *friend* in surprise. "You?"

"Our maids are sisters. Deirdre talked to Bridget about what you were doing. She was concerned for you. And Bridget talked to me. I tried to speak to you about it earlier, but when you denied you had anything to share, I was put in a difficult spot."

Rafe shook his head. "She told us tonight."

Heat flooded Annabelle's cheeks. "Why didn't you address this with me directly, Serafina?"

"I tried. I did. I even thought I could wait and broach the subject with you again, but Bridget and Deirdre were so worried and I..." Serafina sighed. "I felt I had to tell your brother. We do not keep secrets."

Annabelle stared up at the ceiling as the horror of what was happening hit her. "Deirdre...damn it."

Rafe snorted out a laugh. "I'll give the girl a fucking...I'm sorry, Mama...a damn commendation for telling the truth."

Crispin nodded. "She never should have been in the position to keep such a secret in the first place."

Annabelle folded her arms. "You have no place to talk about secrets, Crispin Flynn."

Slowly, their mother rose. "All of you, hush now. I want to hear from Annabelle exactly what is happening here."

Annabelle flushed. Her poor mother, having to walk through that wicked hall below. With a cry, she rushed to her, grasping both her hands.

"Mama, I'm so sorry. So sorry you were exposed to the wickedness below because of me and my choices."

Her mother arched a brow. "You think I've not seen such things? I was married to your father." Annabelle snapped her mouth shut and her mother touched her cheek. "I'm not angry, love. I'm just confused. You said you wanted to marry in Society. To have propriety after so many years of being punished for the behavior of your brothers."

Both Rafe and Crispin shifted at that assessment, and Annabelle shot them a glare. Then she shook her head. "Very well, Mama. Let me start at the beginning."

She grasped her mother's hand and then began to tell the story. She left out her bargain with Marcus to explore desire, of course, but told them all the rest. About how she wanted to help Crispin and since Rafe wouldn't she had followed him here and all the rest.

When she was finished, Crispin paced away to lean on Marcus's desk, his back to her.

"Marcus helped me," she explained, looking at him. He didn't meet her stare. "He protected me, in fact."

"Protected you into being compromised," Rafe said, his fists shoved at his sides.

She waited for Marcus to explain, to deny what her brother said, but he still said nothing. He stood stoically, as if he were merely waiting for this to all be over.

Perhaps he was.

She swallowed. "The position you found us in tonight did

not look well, I know. But...but Marcus did not compromise me. I am still untouched."

That wasn't exactly true, but in the sense that a future husband would know, it was.

"Bollocks," Rafe growled.

"Do not make me explain myself to you," Annabelle snapped. "Give me the respect of simply believing me."

"So you didn't come here because you didn't truly want a Society marriage?" her mother asked.

Annabelle drew back. Was that disappointment in her mother's voice?

"N-no." She glanced at Marcus again. "My plans have not changed."

"You did this for me," Crispin muttered, the first time he'd spoken in a full ten minutes. "*Because* of me."

Annabelle stepped toward him. "I love you, Crispin. I wanted to protect you, but I made my own choices."

Crispin glared at Marcus. "*He* should have stopped you. *He* should have sent you home."

Rafe nodded. "Yes, he should have. Rivers, how could you? How could you after everything we have been through, everything we've done?"

Annabelle turned her face at the admonishment. Now that she understood what Marcus had endured, she also knew how much her brothers meant to him. And yet he still remained stoic in the fact of their anger.

"I very much appreciate what you and your father did for me," he said, his voice quiet. "And you're right that I shouldn't have allowed Annabelle to come here. It was...a weakness."

She flinched. A weakness. *His* weakness. And knowing him, one he could overcome once she disappeared from his life. All they had shared would be forgotten, by him because he had to. By her because she chose a different path.

It was all so bloody awful.

Rafe's brow wrinkled and he stared at Marcus closer, as if seeing something in him that he hadn't ever noticed before.

Annabelle stepped between them, hoping to diffuse the situation even though she knew she couldn't.

"Vent your anger on me, not him," she said softly. "He is and has ever been your friend. If anything, I took advantage of his kindness, nothing more."

Rafe's gaze flitted to her and he shook his head. "Come, we should go home. Enough damage has been done here to last you two lifetimes."

Abbot, who had been silent since his entry into the room, stepped forward now. "I can show you all to a private exit so you do not have to walk through the hall and draw attention to yourselves."

Annabelle's mother nodded. "Thank you, that would be very appreciated."

Abbot motioned to the door and her family began to filter out, but Annabelle stayed put, unable to stop looking at Marcus. He held her stare for the first time since he left her in his bed, but she could read no emotion in him. It was as if a light had been blown out, and she ached for it to return.

"Come, Annabelle," Rafe said, his voice sharp.

"I want a moment," she said.

Her brother moved toward her, but it was her mother who stopped him. "Leave her alone, Raphael," she said softly. "It will take a moment for the carriage to be brought to the back at any rate. Leave her be."

Rafe made an angry sound deep in his throat, but he said nothing more and left the room. Once the rest of them were gone, Annabelle stepped forward.

"Marcus," she whispered. "What happened?"

"I don't know what you mean, Miss Flynn," he said, his voice stiff and formal.

"We shared something beautiful, Marcus. Please don't pretend it was ugly."

His lips pressed together and he shook his head. "It was never ugly. It was just a mistake. For both of us, Annabelle."

She recoiled from those words. "Please don't say that."

He turned away. "Go home, Miss Flynn. And it would be best if you did not return."

She lifted her hand to cover her mouth, stunned by his dismissal. Stunned further by how deeply it cut her to hear it. It was as if he had cut open her chest and removed her very heart with callous precision.

Stepping backward, she reached for the door handle. But before she turned it, she said, "I am so very sorry, Marcus. For everything I've done that has hurt you. I promise you it was not my intention. Good…goodbye."

Then she turned and blindly fled the room.

Marcus leaned against the window, watching the thinning crowd below. How long had it been since Annabelle walked out of his life for good? A moment? An hour? It already seemed like forever because he knew it would be.

He had guaranteed that.

"And better for her," he said, needing to hear those words out loud. Perhaps that would help him believe them.

The door behind him opened, and he turned just in case Rafe or Crispin had returned, spoiling for the duel he so richly deserved. But it was only Abbot who came in. His friend looked tired.

"You knew this was a bad idea from the start," Marcus murmured as he returned his attention to the glass. "You may rub my nose in it if you like."

Abbot said nothing, but he walked past Marcus and went to the sidebar where he poured two tall glasses of whiskey. He handed one over to Marcus and sighed.

"I hope you know me well enough to know I would not celebrate your pain, friend. Nor the horror that transpired in this room tonight."

Marcus downed the drink in one swig and set the glass

down on the desk behind him. "Did *they* leave?"

Abbot nodded. "Yes. *They* were almost entirely silent, except for the younger Mr. Flynn."

Marcus winced. "He caused problems?"

"He would not stop talking and he refused to depart with the rest of his family. The Duke of Hartholm was quite angry, but left with the women without incident. And shortly thereafter Mr. Flynn called for his horse and rode off into the night. Should I have stopped him?"

"No. I'm afraid I am in no position to offer my help or friendship to him now. I have lost that right with my actions." He cleared his throat. "How was…how was Annabelle?"

"Pale," Abbot said, much quieter. "But not tearful."

"Good." Marcus sat down and pretended to stare at the paperwork before him. "Perhaps that means she recognizes the end of our affiliation is for the best."

"Is it?"

Marcus looked up at his friend's incredulous tone. "Surely you know it is. Look at the trouble is has caused for you, for me, for *her*…"

"I don't know," Abbot mused. "It seemed you two always looked happy when you were together." When Marcus glared at him, he shrugged. "But what do I know? I've only been at your side for almost ten years."

"Then you should know exactly why the idea of being with her…loving her…is so foolish," he snapped. "You know where she comes from and what I am. She made it clear, numerous times, that she could not offer me everything."

"With her words or her actions?" Abbot pressed.

Marcus slammed a hand on his desk. Why was his friend encouraging ridiculous thoughts that would only hurt him in the end?

"Both," he snapped. "Words until tonight, but actions in the last few hours. She made her decision clear."

Abbot was quiet for what seemed like an eternity. Then he finished his drink. "Then you are right to let her go."

"I know that," Marcus said through clenched teeth.

"I'm certain the loss hurts, though. Is there anything I can do?"

He looked up as his friend and found Abbot looked entirely serious. He appreciated the offer, but he shook his head. "Let me work. And don't mourn for me, Abbot. I haven't lost anything. I never had it to begin with."

CHAPTER TWENTY-ONE

Annabelle poured herself a cup of tea and settled onto her favorite chair. She took a long breath and enjoyed the sound of silence around her in the parlor. Certainly it had been three days since she had experienced such a thing.

Ever since her removal from Marcus's club...ever since he had told her never to return, she had been surrounded. Her mother clucked and implied, but never asked questions. Rafe checked in on her like he thought she would run away the moment everyone's back was turned. And Serafina merely apologized and kept trying to do things that would "help."

But no one could help. In the end, Annabelle had made her decision. Living with it was simply proving far more difficult than she'd ever expected it to be. Especially when thoughts of Marcus haunted her mind and kept her from sleep.

Today, though, her family had all seemed to recognize that she was safe to leave alone. Her mother had gone to call on a sick friend, Rafe had left town on estate business and there had been no hint of Serafina as of yet.

So Annabelle was alone with her thoughts and the memories that continued to haunt her.

"It's only been a few days," she told herself.

But that was a lie. The loss was so keen because she knew it was permanent. She would never see Marcus again, never touch him again, never hear his laugh or be able to talk to him about her life or his. What they had shared was resoundingly and permanently over.

And that truth was like a knife to the gut. A painful, slow death that made her want to weep whenever she pondered it for more than a moment.

The door to the parlor opened and her mother's butler, Sanders, stepped in. She forced a smile for the man, for it wasn't his fault that her world had been destroyed.

"What is it?"

"You have a visitor, Miss Flynn."

"Not the duchess?"

He shook his head. "No, Miss."

She breathed a sigh of relief, which was quickly followed by confusion. "I'm not certain I am up for visitors, Sanders. Who is it?"

"It is Lord Claybrook," he explained.

Annabelle froze. She had turned down two invitations since her final encounter with Marcus, so she had not seen Claybrook in days. Her heart actually sank at the thought of having to sit with him, pretend with him.

But that was what she had chosen, wasn't it? And perhaps this was her punishment.

"Please send him in."

The servant left and Annabelle rose to her feet, smoothing her gown and checking her hair in the mirror above the fireplace. It was important to be perfect, after all. It was important to be right.

And a tiny voice inside of her screamed, *It was never this hard with Marcus!*

She ignored the voice as the door behind her opened and instead turned to greet Claybrook with a wide smile.

"My lord," she said even as she nodded to Sanders to indicate he could depart.

"Miss Flynn," Claybrook responded with a smile as the servant did just that, leaving the door at a very proper open position.

"Come join me, won't you?" Annabelle asked motioning to the two chairs before the fire where she had just been exploring her reverie. Torturing herself.

Lord Claybrook nodded, and once she had seated herself, he did the same, careful to adjust his jacket so it wouldn't be wrinkled. She observed him for a brief second before they began to speak. He was handsome enough, of course. Always polite. Never anything but kind.

But that little voice persisted. Not Marcus. Not Marcus. Not Marcus.

"And how is your family?" Claybrook asked.

Annabelle jolted, brought back to reality with his words. She smiled, trying not to think of the encounter at Donville Masquerade. About Crispin's leaving them once again, guilt over her joining whatever other pain he felt.

"They are well," she lied, her voice cracking a little.

He didn't seem to notice. "Excellent, I'm happy to hear it. And is your mother in residence today? Or perhaps your brother will be here at some point?"

She blinked at his odd line of questioning. "I...no, actually. My brother has business to attend to today in the country. As far as I know, he will not be home for two days. But his wife is in residence at their home if you need to reach him."

"Oh, no, it is nothing like that." Claybrook wrinkled his brow. "Two days, eh? That is unlucky, but it isn't the end of the world."

Annabelle shook her head. He seemed to be muttering to himself rather than talking to her. "My lord?"

"And your mother?" he pressed.

She hesitated. "Mama is out calling on a sick friend. She will be back before supper."

She certainly hoped he wouldn't wait around that long. A few hours to herself were exactly what she needed now. And it was becoming increasingly clear that she didn't feel like spending those few hours with this man.

That tiny voice screamed again and she wished she could gag it, for it was only confusing the issue.

Claybrook frowned, disappointment clear on his face. "Hmmm. Well, you and I can speak first, can't we? It isn't improper with the door open as it is."

She fought the urge to scowl. "Why don't you simply explain to me what you want to say, my lord? I find myself very confused at present."

And annoyed, but she didn't add that.

He cleared his throat. "You and I have spent some time together in the weeks since you came out in good Society. And I have enjoyed it."

Annabelle blinked. She knew how she was expected to respond to this compliment, but in this moment the words felt very hard to say.

"Miss Flynn?" he said when she simply stared at him.

"I'm sorry. Yes, I have also enjoyed our time together." She didn't know why it felt so false to say that sentence. It wasn't entirely untrue. She hadn't *not* enjoyed their time together and it was almost the same thing.

"Good," he said with a thin smile. "Miss Flynn...*Annabelle*..."

She stiffened. He had never said her given name before. It sounded very odd coming from his proper lips. In that moment, she tried to imagine him moaning it, whispering it, as Marcus had done so many times. She found it was impossible to do so.

Claybrook continued, utterly unaware of her inappropriate thoughts. "I know you have a desire to elevate yourself. And your dowry is very tempting. Since we get along so smashingly, I have come here this morning to ask for your hand in marriage."

Annabelle sucked in a breath. Since she was a girl, she had pictured how she would be asked for her hand. When she was younger, the proposals were always very romantic, but as she realized that her name might affect her prospects, they had become less so.

But none had been so pragmatic as this. Claybrook stared at her, the same thin smile on his face as had been when he asked after the health of her mother. He didn't seem nervous or excited or even especially *happy* to ask for this match.

"I—what?" she managed to squeak out, if only to buy herself time to formulate some kind of response.

His smile faded slightly. "I am asking you to marry me, Miss Flynn. Obviously, asking your mother and brother first would be proper, but in a way this is better."

"Better?" she repeated, his words still rolling in her head. *Elevating herself, tempting dowry...*

He nodded. "Because I wish to talk to you about a small issue that will be of concern in our marriage."

She stared. He was talking about their marriage before she had even agreed to a wedding. He was that certain in her answer. And why wouldn't he be? He was a good catch, and no other man had expressed as much interest. She would be a fool not to capitulate.

She cleared her throat. "And that issue is?"

"Your brother," he said solemnly.

"Rafe?"

He shook his head. "No, the *other*."

He said the word with such disdain that she turned her face away from it like it was a physical blow.

"Crispin," she managed to whisper. "His name is Crispin."

Claybrook didn't seem to care, for he continued on without acknowledging her correction. "I have heard some troubling things of late, Miss Flynn, about your brother."

"Crispin," she repeated.

And again, he ignored her. "I have heard he had an altercation of some kind with a club owner in the hells." He wrinkled his nose in disgust. "I do not frequent such places, of course, but many with influence choose to spend their nights with such riffraff."

Annabelle pressed her lips together. Now this man wasn't only dismissing Crispin, but Marcus. "I believe a great many do, my lord. I've heard whispers that such establishments are quite successful."

He recoiled slightly, as if just her knowing something so basic were a disgusting fact.

"I have no doubt some men make their fortunes in such revolting ways, but that does not mean they are acceptable. Nor is the behavior that your brother has exhibited in front of a great many people. And not just with this incident. There are other rumors that have circulated, which I shall not repeat. Needless to say, I'm troubled by it."

"Why?" She shook her head and tried to meter her tone. It was difficult when she was beginning to feel angry. "I don't see why it has anything at all to do with you."

"How can it not when I have just asked you such a question, Miss Flynn? Your family and whatever...*difficulties* they cause will directly impact me and the future of our heirs."

He wasn't wrong—she knew that better than most. Hell, it was why so many men refused to even consider her. But having him so directly broach the subject was still trying.

"And what would you have me do?" she asked, folding her hands in her lap, letting the nails dig into her skin to keep her from shouting.

He sighed. "If you are to accept my proposal, I must insist that you do not see your brother again. In order to protect both our reputations."

Annabelle shot to her feet in surprise. He watched her, a mild expression on his always neutral face, but said nothing as she paced away from him. At the sidebar, she stopped and began to fiddle with the bottles of alcohol lined up there.

"You would ask me to abandon my family," she finally said when she had found enough composure to speak.

She heard him stand. "Not your family. Your brother."

She spun around to face him and couldn't control her tone when she barked, "You do not think that is the same thing?"

"One of the rumors circulating is that your brother has already cut himself off from the rest of you. This cannot be much of a loss, Miss Flynn, especially when you consider the great advantages you would gain from our union."

Nothing he said was wrong. This was exactly the mindset Annabelle had shared when she decided to use Rafe's new position to enter upper Society. To pursue a marriage with a man of standing. And yet hearing Claybrook say it, hearing his terms, it was offensive to her.

"I love my brother," she whispered. "I love Crispin."

He cocked his head as if he didn't fully understand the point she was making. "I think one would be very foolish to let love determine whether one made a match or not."

Annabelle shook her head. She thought of her parents' match, which had brimmed with love until the day her father died, and even beyond his grave. And she thought of Serafina and Rafe, who had nearly thrown away a love that burned so brightly between them that it made it hard to look at them sometimes. They were a partnership in every sense of the word.

And in that moment, Annabelle realized she wanted nothing less than what her family had already found. She also realized that the only man in the world who could give her that was Marcus Rivers. A man who understood and accepted her for all that she was.

A man who she loved with all her heart.

"You are smiling," Claybrook said, stepping toward her. "Does that mean you have come to a decision?"

Annabelle blinked. Poor Claybrook. He was not going to like what she would say.

"I have, my lord," she said, meeting his gaze because he deserved it. "I am afraid I will have to respectfully decline your offer."

Claybrook froze in his crossing of the room, and his face finally reflected more powerful emotion—he looked utterly confused. "I beg your pardon?"

She shifted. This was not enjoyable, by far. "I'm so sorry, Lord Claybrook. I do very much appreciate your offer and I recognize how fortunate I am to have received it. But I must decline. I cannot marry you."

Claybrook flexed his hands at his sides. "Miss Flynn, you cannot be serious, especially if you recognize how fortunate you are indeed to receive this offer. Perhaps we should set it aside and wait until you have your mother or brother here to guide you."

Annabelle almost laughed at the idea that anyone in her family would force her to accept. Her brother didn't give a damn about Society and her mother had never seemed to fully approve of her plans.

"I do not need a chaperone to advise me," she insisted. "I fear my answer would remain the same, my lord, if we had an audience of ten or none and if we waited a few hours or a few years to discuss it again. I do not think we are a suitable match after all, and I could not in good conscience accept a proposal that I fear would ultimately bring us both pain."

His face twisted with anger. "Do you think you shall have a better offer, Miss Flynn? Has your experience since you entered Society not shown you that no man will have you? I was *lowering* myself to you. It is only your dowry that could ever tempt a man to link himself to your scandalous family name."

Annabelle stiffened. "You have apparently been separated from your manners by the shock of this answer, and I think you should leave, Lord Claybrook."

His posture became rigid and his expression returned to one of serene control. "I do apologize, Miss Flynn. You are correct that my response has been less than gentlemanly. Do forgive me."

He bowed formally and exited the parlor. She followed him into the foyer and watched as Sanders handed over his hat. As Claybrook placed it on his head, he nodded to Annabelle.

"Good afternoon, Miss Flynn," he said with another of those bows.

She nodded, but as he exited the home, she sighed. "No, I believe it is goodbye."

She watched as he mounted his horse and rose away as if the hounds of hell themselves were on his heels.

"I shall need the carriage," she said to Sanders, smoothing her gown as if to wipe away the unpleasantness of what had just transpired. "I want to go visit Serafina right away."

"Yes, Miss. I will arrange it at once."

She smiled at him and then walked to the stairs. She had made a decision thanks to Claybrook's unexpected proposal. A momentous decision, indeed. But she would not be able to enact it alone. She could only hope that Serafina would help her.

CHAPTER TWENTY-TWO

Serafina smiled as Bridget and Deirdre left the parlor together, their arms interlocked and their heads close together.

"It is nice to see their bond," she said.

Annabelle smiled as well. "I tend to agree, though that bond did rather put me out, didn't it?"

Serafina's expression fell. "You are not angry at Deirdre, are you?"

She sighed. "No, I suppose not. She told her sister a secret. They are so close that it should have been expected. And since I am here to do the same, I cannot judge her."

"A secret?" Serafina tilted her head.

"Yes." Annabelle swallowed past the lump in her throat. "To a person I very much consider my sister and not just because she married my brother."

"Oh Annabelle, I think of you as the same in every way. Does that mean you don't hate me for telling Rafe and your mother about where you were?"

Annabelle moved to sit beside Serafina on the settee. "Hate you? How could I ever hate you? You were put in an untenable position. And in the end...well, perhaps it was best that the truth came out. It highlighted some facts I was hesitant to face."

Serafina was watching her closely now, her blue eyes reading everything. Annabelle allowed it, *wanting* her to see.

"Lord Claybrook paid a call on me today," she whispered. "He asked for my hand in marriage."

Serafina's lips parted and for a moment there was a flash of hesitation, disappointment on her face. Then she smiled and it was gone.

"Congratulations!" She moved to hug Annabelle, but Annabelle shook her head.

"I refused him," she said softly.

Serafina gasped. "But—but isn't that what you wanted? Wasn't that the purpose of coming into Society? Claybrook is titled, he has some fortune and he has no blemish on his character."

"And I thought all that would be enough. But it turned out that it wasn't." Annabelle sighed. "I tried to care about him. I tried to just like him, but there was nothing warm or affectionate to our courtship. I don't even know if he desired me. It seemed to be only a match of good circumstance to him. And he..." She trailed off with a wince as she recalled his words.

"What?" Serafina said, leaning forward.

"He would require me never to see Crispin again if we were to wed," she whispered.

Serafina collapsed back on the settee and her hands came to cover the swell of her belly. "I see."

"Yes. I could not picture denying my family for a 'good match,' Serafina."

Serafina's lips had thinned with upset. "Of course you couldn't."

Annabelle shook her head. "I also realized he wanted something more without him saying it. He wanted me to deny *myself*. And the worst part is that I led him by example. I told him with my actions that I was willing to do just that."

"What do you mean?" Serafina asked.

Annabelle smiled, and for the first time in a long time her smile felt right. It felt like her own.

"I am a Flynn, like my father, like my brothers. I have a

wild heart that I have tried to ignore or deny for years, but most especially since I began to look for a staid and respectable husband. But I was never happy doing it."

Serafina nodded. "Your brother said as much."

"Rafe did?" Her lips parted. "Why didn't he say anything to dissuade me from the path I was on?"

"Because he knew his actions, *their* actions, had caused you to lose so much already. He refused to stop you from pursuing whatever your heart desired. But he worried to me, more than once, that you would lose yourself in the quest to be respectable."

Annabelle shook her head. "He will crow when he finds out I have determined he is correct."

"I think not." Serafina covered her hand. "I think he will be pleased, but not triumphant."

Annabelle cleared her throat. "And what will he think if I pursue love, instead? Even if it is not appropriate?"

Serafina drew back. "Love is always appropriate."

"What will he think if I say I am in love with Marcus Rivers? What will he think if I say I want to marry him?"

"You are not asking what Rafe thinks, you are asking what *I* think," Serafina said softly. "And I will tell you exactly that."

Annabelle held her breath. Serafina had been raised as a lady of the highest order. Marcus's world had to seem terrible to her.

But to her surprise, her sister-in-law grinned. "I am not shocked to hear you are in love with him. I saw it on your face that awful night a few days ago. Who can blame you? He *is* devilishly handsome."

Annabelle nearly choked on her laughter. "He is that, though I'm surprised you would say as much."

Serafina waved her hand. "I am married, not dead. Any woman would say as much if she were honest. He's no Rafe, of course, but when I said well done in Rivers' office, I meant it."

"I'm beginning to realize I vastly underestimated you," Annabelle mused.

Her sister-in-law smiled, but it faded a fraction as she said, "If you love this man, I hope you will marry him. Because I know how desperate that feeling of love can be if you feel it cannot turn out well."

"I know you do." Annabelle leaned in. "Which is why I am asking you for help now."

Serafina hesitated, but then she nodded. "I don't know what help I can offer, but I will try any way I can."

"Even if my brother won't approve?"

"If you end up happy, I swear to you, he will approve." Serafina tilted her head. "You know rank means nothing to him and despite his present anger with Rivers, Rafe likes him a great deal. He'll accept any decision you make. And if he doesn't right away, then I will persuade him."

"Excellent, I hoped you would say so. But I'm afraid I'll need more than your help with Rafe. I need your help with my plan for Marcus."

"Isn't your plan for Marcus simply to tell you love him?" Serafina asked. "After all, as clear as it was that you care for him, it was equally clear he cares for you."

"Was it?" Annabelle shook her head. "All I felt from him that night was his disdain even if he did confess, rather reluctantly, that he cared for me. Or once cared." She sighed. "I don't even know anymore."

"Great God, I probably sounded just like you last year, didn't I?"

Annabelle smiled. "My brother was worse, I assure you."

"And look how well it turned out."

"Yes, I have hopes I might be just as happy in a year as you are now. But only if I can convince Marcus to see that I care for him. You see, that night you all came barging in, I-I denied him something he wanted. And I made him feel as though he wasn't worthy of me. I hurt him. I knew it that night and I know it now." She shook her head. "If I go to him, I fear he'll refuse to see me. And even if I somehow obtain an audience, he'll likely reject any overtures I make. He won't believe me. His pride and his heart won't let him."

"You have a lot to make up." Serafina nodded slowly.

"I do," Annabelle admitted.

Serafina sighed. "Very well, tell me your plan. You have a partner in me!"

Annabelle clapped her hands together with relief and joy. "I'm so glad. Now for my plan. It is quite shocking, so prepare yourself. And it may require the help of Mr. Abbot."

Marcus paced the halls of the club, making his usual once-a-month notes about upkeep and changes to be made to the look and feel of the place. Normally, he enjoyed the exercise, but this afternoon it was nothing more than another wretched chore that didn't take his mind off of persistent thoughts of Annabelle.

He had not seen her in four awful days. And he had hoped that time would prove to be a friend in their parting, but instead it was becoming his worst enemy. He wanted her all the time, he missed her all the time, he dreamed of her both day and night.

"You are an idiot of massive proportions," he admonished himself as he checked off another room on his list.

"Rivers?"

He turned to find Abbot behind him. Obviously the man had heard Marcus talking to himself, but he said nothing about it.

"What is it?" Marcus asked, straightening up.

Abbot shifted, almost uncomfortably. "Have you made your way to the east wing yet?"

Marcus glared at him. "Since you are fully aware of my usual route of inspection, you know I have not."

"I would suggest perhaps you'd like to change your habit and go there now," Abbot said. "There is a problem in room three."

Marcus looked at his sheet. He had several other rooms to inspect before he changed wings, and the east wing wasn't even the next on his schedule.

"Great God, man, you are meant to manage things here, can't it be managed?"

Abbot shook his head. "I'm afraid this must be dealt with entirely by you."

Marcus closed his eyes and counted to a slow ten in his head. He had snapped at poor Abbot at least five times in the last few days. Taking out his frustration on his friend wasn't the best route, and he knew it. But damn if the man didn't make it difficult.

"Fine," he ground out when he had calmed himself enough to do so. "I will go to room three in the east wing. Right now. Instead of completing my list."

Abbot held out a hand. "If you give me the list, I'll start the staff on any changes you've already noted and I will return this to you when you have dealt with the situation."

Marcus shook his head, but handed over the list before he exited the parlor and headed down the hall. "Now it is a situation? What in the world could be so dashed important?"

"I could not even begin to explain it, Rivers," Abbot said, that put-upon tone to his voice that Marcus knew so well. "It must be seen to be believed."

Marcus ground his teeth together once more and said nothing else as he cross the empty main room and entered the east wing hall. He paused at the door to room three, which was for some reason closed, and stared at Abbot.

"I swear to you, if this is some foolishness…"

Abbot shook his head. "It is not. Please." He motioned for Marcus to enter, and he did so.

The shades were always drawn in the private rooms, but normally lamps and a fire had been lit on days when Marcus did his inspections. Today, neither had yet been done and he entered into pitch blackness.

"What the hell—" he began.

"Now," Abbot interrupted him mildly.

Marcus was hit on three sides by heavy bodies, his hands and legs caught by unseen, yet entirely strong arms.

"Bloody fuck!" he bellowed, fighting against the concealed as they hauled him across the room. He was pressed into the bed there, and his arms and legs pulled wide. He felt ties go round his ankles and wrists, no matter how he struggled, no matter how he tugged.

And then the attackers were gone. He could see them leave the room, only shadows outlined in the light from the hall.

"What the hell, Abbot?" he shouted, still tugging against the ties.

His friend said nothing, but entered the room. Marcus tensed as he sensed the other man moving around the room. When he heard the sound of flint, he was met with a lit lamp. Abbot moved to the next and the next, slowing bringing the chamber up to full light. He moved to the fireplace and lit it as well before he stepped to the foot of the bed.

"I insisted on darkness so that you would not later fire those who tied you up," he explained.

"Unlike you," Marcus roared, pulling against the binds that were seemingly impossible to break.

"You won't fire me," Abbot said with a small smile. "Or if you do, you'll change your mind soon enough."

"And why would I?" Marcus asked, glaring a hole in his friend.

"Because I make this place run as much as you do." He turned to leave. "And because your mother likes me."

"What the hell is this about?" Marcus snapped, but Abbot was already tugging the door behind him.

"You'll see," his friend called out before he shut the barrier, leaving Marcus bound to the bed and utterly at the mercy of…whatever was going on.

He thrashed a few more times, but unless he broke the

bed, it was evident he wasn't going anywhere. "Damn it!" he shouted.

The door to the chamber opened in that moment, and he caught his breath as Annabelle stepped inside.

She was not wearing a mask, though it likely didn't matter in the middle of the day, with only his turncoat staff in residence. She wore a dark green gown, stitched with black flowers all along the skirt. Her hair was bound loosely so that little tendrils fell along her cheeks and her neck. She was utterly, perfectly, gloriously beautiful, and he turned his face so he wouldn't be swayed by that fact.

"What is going on, Miss Flynn?"

She shut the door and quietly turned the lock. Then she moved to the wall and slid down the privacy screen that blocked the peephole hidden there. As she latched it, she said, "You are going to hurt yourself flailing around like that, Marcus."

"Untie me," he growled.

She turned to face him. "No, I think not."

He strained against the binds. "Annabelle."

She sighed. "I won't release you, Marcus, so stop acting a fool and be still."

He shook his head at her retort, but relaxed against the bed. "Explain yourself."

She nodded. "I will."

He watched her as she calmly strode to a small table by the fire. She reached into the drawer there and drew out a very sharp pair of scissors. As she approached him, she smiled.

"No need to worry, I have no intention of hurting you." She set the scissors aside and began to unlace his boots. As she removed them, she said, "I only want to make you more comfortable and ready."

"Ready for what?"

She glanced up his body as she drew one boot away. She caressed his foot gently, sending shock waves of reaction through his body.

"You mustn't be angry at Mr. Abbot," she said, ignoring his question. "He didn't ignore your order to refuse me in every way. It was a letter from my sister-in-law that drew him to me. And once I explained myself...and begged a little...he was convinced I was in the right. He is only doing this because he cares about you."

"Cares enough to have me trussed up by my own staff?" Marcus barked, though he watched unblinking as she removed his second boot. She tossed it away and slid her soft fingers beneath his trousers, caressing his legs as far as she could reach.

"Again, my plan, not his."

"Why?" he growled.

She snatched up her scissors and quickly cut a long line up his trouser leg. He jerked away, and she stopped. "I am sorry, and I assure you I will pay for a new suit for you, of course."

"What the hell are you doing?" he asked, but didn't flinch when she cut the other leg of his pants.

"I'm undressing you. Obviously, I would normally simply have you stand and do this in a more conventional way, but since you would likely make your escape or turn the tables on me, I can't risk that. So cutting away your clothes must do." She smiled up at him, utterly wicked. "I must admit, I'm rather enjoying it. Are you?"

"You shouldn't be here," he panted.

She snipped a few more times and then tugged. His trousers fell away around him, leaving him naked from the waist down. She smiled at his half-hard cock.

"You don't really think that," she insisted. "But I knew you would say it, and that is why I have resorted to this kind of plan."

"What plan?" he asked, tracking her as she moved to his shirt. Thank God he had left his jacket in the office upstairs, for she didn't hesitate before she began snipping away a second time, shredding the fabric of his fine shirt like it was nothing.

"I made a terrible mistake," she said, setting the scissors

aside and rending the shirt open with her bare hands.

Now he was naked, and he stared up at her. "I'm guessing this moment is not that mistake."

"No." She reached up and cupped his cheek. It took everything in him not to lean into the touch, not to turn his face to kiss her palm. "My mistake, my love, was in running from all the beauty and passion and love I found in you. My mistake was believing I needed something different than the perfection right here before me."

He shook his head. "You don't know what you're saying—"

"I do." She leaned in closer, close enough that he felt her breath on his face. "I love you, Marcus Rivers. I love you with all that I am."

CHAPTER TWENTY-THREE

For a brief, unguarded moment, Annabelle saw Marcus's true reaction to her confession. He lit up, joy and relief on his face, but then he covered it. His expression went hard and heartless.

"I don't give a damn," he ground out.

She nodded. "I deserve that, I think. But I don't accept it. I did however, expect it, which is why you are currently tied naked to a bed."

"What are you talking about?"

"I knew you would deny me, partly out of your pride and partly because you think you must protect me from what I want. So I thought of that first night when I came here. When you had my brother tied to a bed so he could sober up. And I thought, what a marvelous idea. So I arranged it. And now we have all day to talk together. With the door locked and the peephole latched, even if your evening's festivities begin, no one will interrupt us. So you are mine. In body, at least. And I hope, very soon, in soul and spirit."

She smiled at him. How could she not? He was trying so hard to remain detached but his body betrayed him. His cock was hardening with her every word, her every touch. He wanted her.

And if she was forced to do so, she would use that against him.

"You want a respectable life, Annabelle," he spat. "You will not find that with me. So leave."

"Yes." She sighed. "My respectable life. I did say that, I did reach for it. And when I obtained that one thing I thought I wanted more than anything, I found it to be very, very empty."

He glared at her. "What do you mean?"

"I received a proposal from an earl," she confessed. "Yesterday."

His jaw set. "Then I don't understand why you aren't gleefully announcing your engagement and planning for a life."

"I *am* planning for my life." She shrugged. "A life with you."

"Annabelle—"

"Do shut up, Marcus. I don't want to have to gag you," she said with a shake of her head.

He pressed his lips together, his frustration plain on his face, and she took the rare opportunity of his silence to continue.

"Do you know how utterly bored I was in Society? Do you know how hard I had to work to not only to fit in but to give a damn about those fops? It was *torture*, Marcus. Worse torture was the fact that I would think of you every moment I was pretending to be the kind of woman one of those men would want. I thought of your touch."

She glided her hand across his stomach and enjoyed how his breath hissed out. "I thought of your kiss."

She leaned in and dragged her tongue across his nipple. "I thought of all that passion which bubbled unfulfilled between us."

She stared at his cock and then reached for it, stroking him just once, just enough that he lifted his hips. "But more than that," she confessed, backing away. "I thought of *you*. Of how easy it was to talk to you, to share with you. Of how you offered me kindness without a thought to how that made you look. You respected my mind, you pleasured my body…you gave me everything I ever wanted. You gave me more than I thought I deserved."

He shook his head. "Annabelle, please. Please don't say these things. You told me what you wanted, I would hate myself if you walked away from it. And you would hate me too. Perhaps not today when you've convinced yourself that your second choice is good enough, but some day."

"You think you are my second choice?" she asked, sitting beside him on the bed. His hands flexed, and she knew he wanted to touch her.

"You wanted—"

"I told you, he asked me to marry him. And I found *he* was my second choice. In fact, he wasn't my choice at all. There was only you, Marcus. And I should have realized that a long time ago. I should have known it from the moment you first kissed me. Hell, from the first moment you met me and all I could do was watch you, half intrigued, half terrified of you."

His brow wrinkled.

"Yes, you had that much impact on me. Even all those years ago." She shook her head. "But I was foolish and driven by fears and desires I was certain could make me become someone else. But I-I don't want to be someone else anymore. I want to be Annabelle Flynn. *Your* Annabelle. I want my dark desires and my wild heart to have a safe home with yours."

She stopped talking and watched him, waiting for his response. She could see how much her words moved him. She could see him fighting against his wants, his feelings for her and his desire to protect her, and probably himself, from what she asked for.

And the second won out. His face hardened to steel and he looked at her with a mask of disdain she would have believed entirely if she didn't know him so well already.

"Go away, Annabelle," he spat. "I don't want you. You were a game, a ruse, a toy. And I'm tired of you."

She nodded. "That is why you didn't take my virginity?"

He glared at her. "It wasn't worth anything to me."

She bent her head with a long sigh. "I can see you intend

to be difficult. I hoped that wouldn't be the case, but one cannot always have what one wants. So now I suppose we move on to the second part of my plan."

He rolled his eyes, but she could see interest there where he tried to hide it. "And what is this second part?"

She stood up from the bed and quickly stripped open her gown that she and Serafina had agonized over just for its ease in removal. As she shed out of it, she revealed the rosy pink chemise beneath. The very sheer chemise that left no curve to the imagination.

"I am going to…how would you put it, my darling…I'm going to *fuck* you." She watched his eyes widen and his cock grow hard at her very direct words, and smiled. "It seems your body will betray you even when you say you don't want me."

"Damn it, Annabelle," he growled, pulling against the binds again. "You *know* I want you. But don't do this, you'll regret it."

She ignored him and focused instead on his body. His beautiful body that she had wanted for weeks and only experienced in limited, yet very satisfying, ways. And now he was hers.

All hers.

She got back on the bed next to him and leaned over, kissing his flesh gently, savoring his heat and flavor. She felt him tugging those binds, straining to escape so that she couldn't force him to feel what he felt.

She sucked his nipple gently and the struggling stopped.

"Damn it," he breathed, his eyes shutting.

She smiled against his flesh. She'd won for a while, though she had no belief that he wouldn't fight her further. But for now she swirled her tongue around and around the flat disk of his nipple, sucking and stroking until he groaned, and she moved to the opposite one. She repeated her actions there for a while before she began to inch down the apex of his body.

"I love kissing you," she murmured against his flesh. She stroked her cheek against his stomach. "I could do this all day long."

He groaned, and she smiled up at him.

"I won't. I have far more interesting plans for you."

"Please don't," he whispered again, but there was no heat to the denial. He wanted her, he had only convinced himself that he couldn't feel that way. That he *wouldn't*.

"But I must," she said, meeting his stare. "I must, Marcus. And you know why. In your heart you know why and you want me to give myself to you. It's all right if you're afraid."

He stiffened. "I'm not afraid."

She tilted her head. "Of loving me, I think you are. Of sharing yourself completely with me, not just this way with our bodies, but more, you are. Of taking what you fear I don't understand, you are. But I love you. And even though I'm afraid of the future, too, I'm willing to face it if I have you at my side."

She smiled at him, watching as pure disbelief crossed his face. And then she slid lower down his body, pressing kisses to his muscular hip. He jolted at the contact. At the brush of her hair across his cock.

She turned her face, resting her cheek against his hip and leaning in close to his hard erection. He was ready for her, with his body she had already won. He was trying to protect her, even though he admitted he wanted her.

"You frightened me the first time I saw this," she admitted, reaching out to drag one fingernail across his length. "But I began to crave it. Dream of you sliding me beneath me and slipping deep inside. Today it won't be a dream."

He tensed, but made no further protest as she wrapped a hand around him and stroked over his heat. She shifted, pinning his legs with her body, and darted her tongue out over him. It was a familiar act and her body swelled with increasing desire as she did it. And she was happy for it too. Despite all her careful confidence, she was nervous about seducing him. Nervous at surrendering herself.

And nervous about what would happen once she

eventually loosened his ties and gave him the freedom to reject her.

"I love you, Marcus," she murmured between long licks of his cock.

"No," he moaned, his tone both pleasured and pained.

"Yes, I do. Denying it won't make it change. I love you."

He squeezed his eyes shut and he squeezed his fists as he struggled, this time emotionally, with her words.

She straddled him, positioning herself over him, and his eyes flew open again.

"Wait, wait, you can't be ready," he grunted. "Not when I haven't touched you."

"I want this," she insisted.

"Then come up here. Straddle my mouth and let me ready you so it won't hurt as much when you finally...when we finally do this."

She stared at him. "You would pleasure me despite your misgivings?"

He nodded. "I don't want to hurt you more than I have to, Annabelle. Come here."

His voice changed slightly, and she smiled. He loved her. In that moment, she knew it even though he denied it over and over. He loved her and this was his act of love even though he was angry and hurt and lost.

She slid up until she was able to lower herself over his mouth. She clung to the headboard of the bed as he began to lick her, parting her folds with his tongue, finding her clitoris by feel.

She rocked against him, riding the strokes, reaching for the pleasure that was already sparking between her legs.

"Come," he whispered against her sex. "Come for me."

She arched her back as he sucked her clitoris and followed his order instantly. Pleasure cascaded through her and she trembled in its wake, her hips jerking as he continued to suck and lick her tender flesh.

As she began to come back down from the high, she slid

away from him and looked into his eyes. "You can't tell me you don't love me."

He said nothing but merely watched as she moved back to her original position, poised above him for the claiming of her virginity.

"Go slowly," he finally whispered. "Go bit by bit."

She nodded and opened herself, lowering onto his cock. He pressed into her sex, then began to glide inside until it was an inch and then she flinched as pain rippled through her.

"A little more," he urged, and she did as he asked, taking more of him, more of him until he was fully seated in her, their bodies flush. "Now hold still. Is there much pain?"

She stared into his eyes, in wonder at the fullness in her sex, the stretching from their bodies being joined. "A little," she admitted. "But not as bad as I thought it might be."

"For some women it is terrible, for others not as bad," he explained. "And my God, Annabelle, you are heaven."

She smiled. "I wondered when you would admit it."

"And now you must move. If you don't, I won't be able to control myself and I'll lift you off this bed."

Her eyes went wide. He had a wildness in his stare that told her how much he was struggling for control. She rolled her hips, mimicking the acts she had watched here between couples, the drawings she had observed over the years. She moved and eventually she found the rhythm that came naturally between them. She clung to his shoulders, rocking over him as the pleasure he had created with his mouth began to slowly build again with the movement of her body.

"That's it," he murmured, watching her face. "A little more, angel. Just a little more."

"Oh God," she groaned. "I'm—I'm...yes!"

She came a second time as she stroked over him, digging her nails into his flesh, crying out his name, and as she did, his neck tensed, his body thrust up into hers, and he groaned as his hot seed spurted inside of her.

She collapsed onto his chest, her breath harsh and hard,

her body limp and languid with pleasure and they lay there together.

Marcus looked down at Annabelle, who had curled herself against his side, stroking her hands along his chest. Her skin was flushed with pleasure and her eyes bright with all the love she kept repeating she felt for him.

And he was beginning to believe that she truly did feel that way. Leave it to Annabelle to break into his club, turn his employees against him and then stake her claim on him in such a way.

That wild heart she had always wanted to deny was powerful indeed when she fully unleashed it.

"Annabelle," he murmured.

She looked up at him, her expression one of pure happiness only tinged with concern about what he would say. "Yes?"

"Untie me."

She worried her lip for a moment, then leaned down to unloop the knots around his ankles. He stretched his legs, watching her as she reached for one hand. She hesitated, looking at him. "You aren't going to walk away, are you?"

He shook his head. "No."

She untied one wrist, and as soon as his hand was free, he yanked the other one loose, flipped her on her back and covered her with his body. She yelped now that the tables had been turned and she was trapped rather than him.

"Why do you think you love me?" he demanded.

She blinked up at him. "I don't *think* I love you. I *know* I love you. And the reason is because you have always accepted me for who I am. You have always seen me, in a way no one else in the world does. When I'm with you, I am safe and I am real and I am…I'm free. I can't lose that, Marcus. I know I provide very little value to you—"

He cut her off with a laugh. "Are you in jest? Of course you provide something to me."

She tilted her head. "What do I provide?"

"You challenge me. You drive me mad because you are so damned unpredictable. And you accept *me*. But I don't want you blinded by some fairytale, Annabelle. My life is not like yours, even the life you led growing up, outside of the *ton*."

She nodded. "I'll learn."

"The club runs as it runs. And I will continue to run it. I get lost in my work. I sometimes am forced to deal with very scandalous matters. You will lose more friends for loving me than you ever did for the behavior of either of your brothers."

"But I'll gain you," she whispered, her dark gaze even on his. "And I'll help you in the club. Living here will be an adjustment, but—"

He laughed. "I have a house, Annabelle."

She cocked her head. "You do?"

He nodded. "I have the chamber here for days when I forget to go home, forget to eat, forget to sleep. But I have a feeling that if you were waiting for me at my very nice house on Charles Street, I would make it a priority to race back to you every morning."

"Are you saying you would allow me to wait for you in your very nice house on Charles Street?" she asked.

He shut his eyes. After a life that had consisted of so many ups and downs, so many heartbreaks and successes, Annabelle offered him a dream he wasn't certain she fully understood. And in this moment, he wanted that dream. He wanted it more than anything in the world.

"Yes," he whispered. "If you would marry me, Annabelle Flynn, I would share my life with you."

Her eyes lit up and she lifted her mouth to meet his. He kissed her without hesitation, without anything but all of the love he felt for her. All of the love they shared and would share forever.

"Of course, your brother will likely kill me when I ask for your hand," he laughed as he pulled away.

She shrugged as if this was easily surmountable. "Then do as would be expected of a proper Flynn and whisk me off to Gretna Green tonight, Mr. Rivers. Rafe won't kill my lover if that lover is my very loved and very happy husband."

He smiled down at her, unable to keep the grin from his face. "I think I shall do just that, Annabelle. But later." He pushed her legs open and gently breached her a second time. "Later."

EPILOGUE

"Do you hate me for marrying her?" Marcus asked Rafe as they stood together at the fireplace watching Serafina, Mrs. Flynn and his own mother coo and sigh over Annabelle's tale of their stolen wedding in Scotland and honeymoon by the ocean. The Flynns had, of course, accepted Calliope as easily and swiftly as they did everyone. Not for one moment did he feel she was held apart. Even now, Annabelle had an arm around her new mother-in-law's waist and was laughing.

Rafe looked at him and smiled. "No. Not if she is so happy. And you know, we have always looked on your quite as our own brother. Now it is true. And God, would our father have approved."

Marcus frowned even though his heart swelled at those words. "*We*," he repeated with a shake of his head. "And yet I have heard from Abbot that Crispin has not returned to Donville Masquerade since that night when you all burst in on Annabelle and me."

Rafe sighed. "Yes. He has disappeared from all the places that I watch as well. I think he doesn't want to be found."

"Do you think he is all right?" Marcus asked.

Rafe shrugged. "I hope so. Perhaps you and I can formulate a plan to find him."

"You had best involve Annabelle," Marcus said as she separated from the others to approach him, her smile wide.

"She will not be left out, you know."

"Left out of what?" his bride asked as she slipped her arms around his waist and stared up at him with adoring eyes.

"Left out of anything," he teased. "You are a stubborn wench."

"Are you sorry you married me, Mr. Rivers?" she teased back.

"You'd best not be," Rafe joined in, though Marcus could see that his brother-in-law was not finished with the topic of Crispin. "There is no returning her."

Rafe laughed as he walked away, but Marcus's laughter faded as he looked into the eyes of his wife. His love. His life. His Annabelle.

"I wouldn't return her," he whispered as he dipped his head to kiss her. "She is worth more than gold."

Other Books by Jess Michaels

THE NOTORIOUS FLYNNS
The Other Duke (Book 1)
The Widow Wager (Book 3 – 2015)

THE LADIES BOOK OF PLEASURES
A Matter of Sin
A Moment of Passion
A Measure of Deceit

THE PLEASURE WARS SERIES
Taken By the Duke
Pleasuring The Lady
Beauty and the Earl
Beautiful Distraction

MISTRESS MATCHMAKER SERIES
An Introduction to Pleasure
For Desire Alone
Her Perfect Match

ALBRIGHT SISTERS SERIES
Everything Forbidden
Something Reckless
Taboo
Nothing Denied

Jess Michaels raffles a FREE Kindle or Amazon gift certificate EVERY month to members of her newsletter, so sign up on her website:
http://www.authorjessmichaels.com/join-the-jess-michaels-newsletter/

**Take a Sneak Peek at *The Widow Wager*
Book 3 of the Notorious Flynns:**

CHAPTER ONE

July 1814

Crispin Flynn came awake in throbbing, painful inches. His head burned like it was on fire and his stomach churned with bile and whatever God-awful spirits that remained there from the previous night's reverie.

Or had it been reverie? In truth, he couldn't remember much after the moment where he got on his horse and rode out from his home, hell bent on drink and women and gambling and… well, utter self-destruction. None of that sounded as fun as reverie, especially not in the cold light of morning, which he could feel burning against his still-shut eyelids.

He hesitated to open those eyes, firstly so that he could avoid that light a little longer, but secondly because he was never certain anymore where he would find himself after a night out. He had awoken in gutters, in his carriage, and once in the bed of an obliging duchess whose husband he had only just avoided a duel with.

And the third reason he avoided opening his eyes was that once he was awake all the troubles of his world came rushing back, crushing him and drowning him in their wake.

Yet he could not pretend he was dead forever, so he gingerly opened one bleary eye. He flinched at the burning light of the sun that pounded down on him from the window he faced.

He was not in a bed, but on his own settee. He recognized the brocade fabric that his mother had chosen for the chaise what seemed like a lifetime ago. He let out a sigh of relief. At least if he had managed to stumble home, he could not have done too much damage.

He opened his other eye and swallowed back the rush of vomit that greeted him. His body would punish him for what he had done to it, but it was worth it to turn off his mind for a few blissful hours.

Slowly, he moved, inching his way onto his back. Every muscle in his body hurt, which meant he had probably danced on a table, fallen off a horse or gotten into a fistfight last night. On a bad night, it could be all three. Certainly he would hear about it, though, if he had truly done any damage. He always did and he always paid the tab without argument or question and with whatever semblance of an apology he could muster for the sins he committed when he was out of his right mind.

He rolled a little further and froze. He could see his bed about ten feet away from the settee. And it was not unoccupied. A lump was under his covers. A woman-sized and shaped lump.

He groaned. Now he was going to have to kick some light skirt out of his house. Always entirely awkward.

At the sound of his groan, the lump spun around to face him and Crispin froze. The lady-shaped lump had the most beautiful face he had seen in years. She had bright grey eyes filled with intelligence and a heart shaped face with full, pink lips. Her hair was red, too. Damn, but it would be. He'd never been able to resist a red-headed woman who offered to perch herself on his knee.

He sat up.

"Morning, love," he drawled, happy he didn't cast up his accounts or pass out thanks to the wildly spinning room when he moved so quickly.

She said nothing, but also sat bolt upright to reveal she was fully clothed in a wrinkled green gown. Slowly, she pushed herself across the bed, as far away from him as she could get.

Crispin covered his forehead with one hand and tried to maintain some of his dignity at least. He attempted a smile.

"If I owe you blunt, you can collect it from the butler on your way out," he said.

Her eyes went wide at first, then narrowed to angry slits that barely revealed the sparking grey beneath.

"I am not a light skirt, Mr. Flynn," she snapped.

Crispin was distracted for a moment by the musical quality of her voice, which even when angry was probably the prettiest thing he'd heard in an age. But then he realized what she'd said in that beautiful voice and he stiffened.

"Aren't you?" he asked.

She folded her arms. "Certainly not."

He cleared his throat and managed to get to his feet without toppling over sideways. It seemed he had succeeded in getting himself in quite a pickle, indeed, last night. This one might be harder to extract himself from than the usual paying for a broken vase or returning a stolen phaeton.

"Damn. See here, miss, I was deep in my cups last night and I may have said or done things I don't recall."

She was watching him with those grey eyes still, wary and seemingly ready to run. "You must think me very stupid," she all but growled.

He shook his head. "Honestly, miss, I do not remember a damn thing." He looked at her a little closer. "I wish I did, actually."

Her brow wrinkled and a fetching pink color filled her cheeks at the compliment. Then she tilted her head. "Are you being truthful, then? Do you really not remember last night?"

A sinking feeling worked its way through Crispin. A feeling that screamed he had really done it this time.

"No," he said softly.

She held his gaze for a moment, as if she were reading him. As if she were determining his honesty with just a sweep of her stare. He shifted beneath the intimate quality of the exercise and then watched as she rose to her feet. She had as pretty a figure as she did a face, with a lovely bosom and the hint of a flare of her hips as her wrinkled gown fluttered around her.

"Then I suppose I should start by saying good morning, Mr. Flynn," she said, but did not extend her hand. "My name is Gemma. I'm your wife."

Crispin's stomach churned higher and he slumped back onto the settee with a moan. "No." He shook his head. "No, that cannot be true."

She pursed her lips. "I'm afraid it is very much true. We married in the middle of the night last night. Despite my protests."

Crispin jerked his stare back to her. Protests? Had he forced this woman? She was dressed now, but that didn't mean he hadn't. Great God, he would never forgive himself.

"You are my wife," he said slowly.

She nodded, her jaw set with strength even as tears sparkled faintly in her eyes. "Yes," she said on a gasp.

He swallowed hard. "Gemma. Is that what you said your name was?"

"Yes," she whispered a second time.

He nodded. It was a pretty name to go with her pretty face. A pretty face that seemed to entirely hate him, which gave him even more pause about what he'd done in his stupor.

"Gemma, I need you to tell me exactly what happened last night." He shook his head. "I need to remember."

ABOUT THE AUTHOR

Jess Michaels writes erotic historical romance from her home in Tucson, AZ. She has three assistants: One cat that blocks the screen, one that is very judgmental and her husband that does all the heavy lifting. She has written nearly 50 books, enjoys long walks in the desert and once wrestled a bear over a piece of pie. One of these things is a lie.

Jess loves to hear from fans! So please feel free to contact her in any of the following ways (or carrier pigeon):
www.AuthorJessMichaels.com
PO Box 814, Cortaro, AZ 85652-0814

Email: Jess@AuthorJessMichaels.com
Twitter www.twitter.com/JessMichaelsbks
Facebook: www.facebook.com/JessMichaelsBks

Jess Michaels raffles a FREE Kindle or Amazon gift certificate EVERY month to members of her newsletter, so sign up on her website:
http://www.authorjessmichaels.com/join-the-jess-michaels-newsletter/

Printed in Great Britain
by Amazon.co.uk, Ltd.,
Marston Gate.